New Adult Romance on Earth and Beyond

LOVE IN A NEW WORLD

JESSICA E. SUBJECT

ISBN: 978-1-988428-06-2

CONTENTS

LETTER TO THE READER

Dear reader,

This month I am celebrating six years published. It has been a roller coaster ride of ups and downs. I've learned a lot and am still learning. I thank you for taking a chance by purchasing and reading my books, and everyone else who has helped and supported me along the way.

My publishing journey has been much the same as my journey through life, the most extreme roller coaster ride happening in my late teens and into my twenties. Those were the years I left home to live on my own then with my boyfriend. I was trying to figure out what I wanted to do with my life. I fell in love, started a family, and so much more. This is the reason why many of the characters in my books are in this age group. It is how I "write what I know."

The heroes and heroines in the stories in this collection are trying to figure out who they are, a fact that may have been hidden from them their entire life. They are learning to live on their own while some of their parents struggle to let go. And they are falling in love for the first time.
I hope you enjoy this collection, and check out my other stories of falling in love across the universe.

Wishing you much love and books!
Jessica

Abandoned by her parents...

Born on Earth, Nixie was left on the planet Schedar when her parents returned home. Growing up on the pleasure planet, she follows in the footsteps of the woman who raised her, and learns the art of erotic massage. But Nixie yearns for a different life, one where she receives as much pleasure as she gives.

A runaway prince...

In an attempt to escape his arranged marriage, Prince Mekai flees to Schedar. For, he could never love his betrothed when he already loves another, a fantasy woman who invades his dreams every night. When the woman he seeks carnal pleasure from turns out to be the same one in his fantasies, he believes fate brought them together.

Fated lovers or forever enemies?

Just when Nixie and Mekai believe they have a chance at happiness with each other, they find out why their races are at war, and why they can never be together.

BEYOND REACH
CHAPTER ONE

Benignus eyed him, as if confident he would change his mind. "Mekai, are you certain you want to go through with this?"

Grinning at his fair-haired friend, Mekai had no doubt. He'd made his decision long ago. "Yes, go in there and enjoy the woman you have craved for more than two star cycles. I have no use for her."

"And when the king comes in?" Benignus scanned the tapestry-rich corridors of the castle's west wing. "I know he's going to send me to Tenebrae."

"He's not going to send you to the prison colony." No one had been sent there from Carbae, ever. The planet was simply used as an idle threat to misbehaving children. Mekai placed his hands on his friend's shoulders. "I give you permission to deflower my betrothed. She will be yours, as it should have always been. Just be sure she is on top when we come into the room."

He slid open the door to his grand suite, a place he would not return to any time soon, not before experiencing what the universe had to offer. "She waits for you. Now, go in there and take her."

His friend and gentleman of the bedchamber patted him on the back. "Thank you, Mekai, and star's speed."

After shoving Benignus through the door, Mekai waited in the hollow silence—usual for this part of the castle—for some indication his plan had worked before leaving to search for his father. Through the darkness engulfing his room, he couldn't see a thing, but the sounds of wet lips in action caught his attention.

His cock stirred. *Almost there.*

Rubbing his hands down his arms, he tried to escape the chill common to the kingdom. The sun didn't shine underground and fires only burned in the kitchen and the north wing, where his parents slept.

"Oh, Mekai, I'm so glad you decided to deflower me before our wedding night. Take me this instant."

Don't fail me now, Ben.

"No, Madelia. It's me, Ben. Don't worry. No one will know."

"Oh, even better. Will Mekai be joining us?"

A threesome? Oh, gods. Could he get any harder? He and Ben often discussed sex, what their first time would be like, and whom they wanted to lose their virginity to. He'd had plenty of offers from fair maidens, those he could never have any affection for. Not with the strange woman invading his dreams every night. A woman he cherished and had made love to in the fantasia world for as long as he knew the definition of sex. Though, he had yet to meet her, and never would if he didn't leave Carbae.

Ben, though, had always been fond of Madelia. She had never shown any interest in him before tonight, but Mekai, betrothed or not, refused to betray his best friend.

He'd plotted this night ever since his wedding date had been set, for no matter how hard he tried, he could never care for Madelia. Watching his parents pretend to love each other over the years had been enough for him. No way in Tenebrae did he want the same kind of relationship for himself. And then, he'd heard rumors from the bajulus who brought supplies to the kingdom about a planet in the Wopavian system where visitors paid to receive sexual pleasure from the revered Suavitas. That was where he planned to travel. He wanted to experience every sensation before he settled down with anyone. And maybe, if he proved lucky, he could forget about the fantasy woman. Once his marriage was called off, he planned to sneak away from Carbae and get busy living.

A whimper broke the silence. "Oh, Benignus, how you fill me so."

His cock jumped, demanding attention. He'd love no more than to watch them fuck, stroking himself while thinking of the woman of his dreams. But then he'd never get a chance to leave.

Rushing down the corridor, he ignored the lavish silks of purple and gold hanging on the walls, for the extravagance did not suit him. He wanted to rule his father's kingdom on Carbae, the moon of Ubetron, no more than he wanted Madelia as his queen. Not until he was ready to settle down. The excessiveness of this lifestyle had never held any appeal to him anyway. Even as a child, he'd preferred to explore the caves of Carbae with the common children, or stow away on a supply ship to visit other planets, only to be dragged back home by his guard.

Reaching his father's study, he burst through the door. The warmth hit him like a brick wall. He drew in a quick breath. "Father, I need your help. Benignus is very ill. He's been in the lavatory with the sickness. I believe he ate some tainted food."

The king peered up, examining him. "No one else has shown any signs of the sickness. Seriously, at twenty-one star cycles, I would expect the two of you to have outgrown your antics. What kind of trouble have you gotten into this time?"

"No trouble at all, sir. Please help him. I have him resting in my bed now, but he is too ill to move to his own quarters."

"Thornton!"

The stout man—and the only Terran friendly with his father—entered the room as soon as the king beckoned. "Yes, Your Majesty?"

"Fetch the doctor and bring him up to the prince's quarters." The king stood up, his purple robe billowing behind him. "Let's go."

Mekai hurried to follow his father, hoping Benignus had stuck to the plan and would last long enough to get caught.

"Were you in those caves again? You know the black magic there causes the sickness."

He sighed. The humid caves were filled with bacteria, occasionally causing visitors to become sick if they didn't wash after returning from them. His father, though, preferred to live in his own fantasy world. "No, Father, we went directly to my quarters after dinner."

"Honestly, you two cause more trouble than any common child."

His father reached his suite first. The lights flashed on and in an instant, they were treated to a view of Madelia, who sat on top of Benignus, speared by his cock.

"What is the meaning of this?" The king's face turned from its usual shade of blue to bright red, heat radiating from his body even in the cooler part of the castle.

Benignus scrambled out from under Madelia. He held his stomach. "I was there lying on the bed and she climbed on top of me. I was too weak to push her off."

Smirking behind his father, Mekai winked at his friend.

Madelia chose that moment to turn around and glare at him.

"And you, woman?" the king asked.

She cowered under his father's glare. "I thought he was…. Oh, fuck. I was set up."

"No one talks like that to me or anyone while on my land."

Everyone cringed. His father hadn't been born into a kingdom, but had given himself the title after settling on Carbae. He'd been the president of Ubetron, and when he and his followers left for the moon, he'd changed his title to king, and declared the state a monarchy. Though Mekai had never understood why his father left in the first place. Every picture he'd seen of his birth planet, the luscious forests and open sky, had left him with an ache to flee from Carbae.

But oh gods, his childhood had been hell, growing up in the cold-climate underworld. He'd been a toddler when his father moved him there. He grew up speaking in the "proper manner," yet his schoolmates spoke in the old world way. He'd learned the rough dialect and every curse word, yet he took care to revert back to the royal tongue when at home in the castle. He couldn't wait to leave.

"Mekai." His father pulled him forward. "Since she is your betrothed, you must decide her fate."

Just as he'd hoped.

He stuck out his chest, attempting to appear noble while his insides jumped for joy. "Since Madelia deflowered herself with my gentleman of the bedchamber, she shall be bound to him for the rest of her life."

"Then let it be so," the king proclaimed.

Benignus grinned. He finally had the woman he'd always wanted. Mekai yearned to find an ounce of his friend's happiness.

"Gentleman of the bedchamber, my ass. More like jack-off partner," Madelia muttered. "At least he knows how to fuck," she said, tossing her comment in Mekai's direction.

Thornton and the doctor appeared at the door, panting like Terran dogs. "Is everything all right, Your Majesty?"

Time to go. Mekai refused to stick around for Ben's betrothal ceremony, for surely they would have another woman for him by then, too.

"Prince Mekai, where are you going?"

Shit! He refused to turn around and acknowledge his father's question, for the king would never chase after him. And the two men who would still had to catch their breath.

Mekai rushed to the south wing and down a flight of stairs, toward his waiting Personal Space Transport Vehicle. He'd already packed clothing appropriate for Schedar's warmer climate and enough nourishment to last his entire journey inside the PSTV.

He climbed in. After starting the engines, Mekai steered the ship up the narrow rock tunnel and out into space. The fold that would take him to the Wopavian system lay straight ahead.

So long, Carbae. I'm off to live my life.

BEYOND REACH
CHAPTER TWO

Nixie trailed her hand up then down the Elikashe's scaly thigh.

Sound asleep. Time to leave.

She slid off the bed. Clients had to pay extra to have her stay until morning, and even then, she tried to avoid falling asleep with them. Grabbing her tubes and bottles of massage oils and creams, she packed them away in her bag. After a long night, she yearned to go home, get as much sleep as possible before her next appointment.

Leaving her client's suite, Nixie headed down to the main floor of the guest quarters. She passed through the office to drop off her bag.

"Done already, Nixie?"

Spinning on her heels, she faced Garesh, the muscular Schedarn man—a level Four Suavito—who had trained her and several other level Ones in the art of erotic massage. If he hadn't been like a father figure to her, she'd swoon over him like the rest of her classmates had. During their lessons, he'd worn only loose-fitting pants made of filmy palan, which exposed his golden, god-like body to his students. Sometimes, to illustrate his lessons of a male's erogenous zones, he'd strip down to nothing. On those days, she'd tried to listen more than look. Creaming her panties over her instructor was not all right. What would Cyresse have said?

Nixie knew there was something going on between the two of them. He spent a lot of time at the house of her guardian and mentor. But she'd never seen them touch each other intimately, and he stayed away when Cyresse entertained clients. If only she could figure out their relationship.

"Yeah, he's asleep and my arms are sore. I'm going to need a full day off to recover." Her last client had extremely knotted muscles under his scale-covered body. A feat for any masseur, whether they included a happy ending or not.

"No can do. I've already booked you a client. He's from Ubetron, so you won't have to dig so deep." Garesh winked at her. "Wanted an experienced Suavita, but wasn't willing to pay for Cyresse. Plus, she's already booked."

Nixie groaned. Clients who weren't willing to pay the high price usually expected more than they paid for. And one from Ubetron might not even want her anyway. "Um, Terrans and Ubetrons are enemies. Did you forget that?"

"Not at all." He eyed the appointment book. "Says here he prefers a Terran."

"Huh?" Did he plan to torture her?

"Some like to taste the forbidden fruit. It's a very common fantasy here." He shooed her away. "Now go home and rest. He wants you for the entire night."

Something else to look forward to. She slumped out of the office, leaving the tall deversorium where she worked.

She weaved through the streets, passing natives and tourists, some guiding big, black uidisses to carry their abundant purchases. Never would she have any use for the large creatures, as she could walk faster, and only purchased items in small quantities. A gust of wind blew her hair into her face. She brushed the strands aside and looked up to see the large red feet of a taravis coming at her. Another form of transportation she never understood. She ducked out of the way—the creatures were blind, and their riders didn't always steer with accuracy—and continued past the vendors selling creams, oils, clothing, and jewelry made from ipsum, a legal stimulant grown all over the planet.

Finally reaching the outskirts of Sturban, she turned down the laneway to her house. *Sleep*. She entered the domus, planning to snooze as long as she could.

"Good afternoon, Nixie." Cyresse set a pitcher filled with her ipsum cold tea on the table in front of two Gregacian men. "You remember Dodume and Donad."

She nodded. How could she ever forget the two pale-faced men who'd tried to get her services for free the last time they'd visited? Regulars of Cyresse, they visited often and sometimes asked her to join them after they'd have their fill of her mother. But without the ipsum in her blood stream they often used, she'd had time to leave the domus before they followed through on their threats to tie her up and rape her.

"It's good to see you again." Dodume grinned at her, revealing his rows of pointed white teeth.

"Yes, very good." Donad raised his bushy eyebrows. "I do hope you can stay this time."

"I...I just came by to grab some supplies. I have another appointment shortly." She rarely had day-time appointments, but Cyresse didn't seem to notice. Nixie had always come and gone as she'd wanted.

"That's too bad." Dodume sat back and took a sip of the tea. "Perhaps another day then, since we're here all week. Maybe longer if we can arrange it." He winked at her.

Nixie rushed to her room then packed scarves and robes for the next few days. Living at home would not be possible until Dodume and Donad left. Then she'd return and help Cyresse recover. They'd drain her of all her energy and leave without remorse. Cyresse was helpless to stop them, the ipsum taking away her inhibitions.

Before she left, Nixie glanced at Cyresse. Should she really leave her there all alone with those monsters?

I'll be fine, Nixie. I can take care of myself better than you think. I understand why you want to leave though. Don't worry about me.

Only through Cyresse's thoughts did she find the woman she once knew, the woman who'd rescued her as a child, not on a constant high from the ipsum the clients preferred. Nixie couldn't telepath back though, and only received the thoughts Cyresse was willing to share.

Taking a deep breath, she left the house then headed back into the city.

Where would she go? The office. She didn't have any friends who would put her up for a few days. Before she'd started training, her friends had all been jealous, knowing she would one day be a trained Suavita. They'd come over and dressed in Cyresse's scarves and gowns, pretending to service their clients. But as they grew up, Nixie lost contact with them, most of her friends moving out of the city or off-planet to raise their families. She only had Cyresse and Garesh to rely on.

Walking into the silky rear-end of an uidiss, she came to an abrupt halt. The creature had been walking at a steady pace and then stopped. She'd failed to notice in time. Wiping fluff off her face, she turned around and walked into another hard body. "I'm so sorry."

Hands clamped down on her arms. "Are you all right?"

She stared up into deep brown eyes. Chewing her bottom lip, she nodded. If this man hadn't been holding on to her, she would have fallen to the ground. The word swoon held no meaning for her until now.

Am I only like this because of the ipsum I inhaled back home? Or was there something more she found heart-racing about the blue-skinned, well-muscled hunk of an Ubetron who held her up?

No, she couldn't feel anything for him. Their races had been sworn enemies for years. Everyone across the galaxy knew that. Yet here she was, standing face to face, gazing intently at him, with no will to move.

He smiled at her, drawing her attention from his eyes to his lips. How would they taste? She'd never kissed anyone intimately before.

"You look familiar. What's your name?"

Name? Gods, what was her name? "Ni…Nixie." Had she told him, or only thought the word?

He released her arms to brush his fingers along her jaw line. How she remained standing, she had no idea.

"Nixie. A beautiful name belonging to a beautiful woman. Have we met before?"

Moisture pooled between her thighs. Her cheeks warmed. "Thank you, but no." She'd definitely remember meeting him.

As he trailed a hand down her arm, she sighed. Her entire body tingled from his gentle touch.

"Okay, weird. You must remind me of someone else. Now tell me, why were you in such a rush that you walked into the rear end of that slow-moving beast? We're supposed to be on vacation, enjoying all this planet has to offer."

Laughing at his description of the uidiss, she leaned against his arm. Never before had she enjoyed a man's attention like this. "I'm not visiting. I live here. Have my whole life."

He raised his eyebrows. "Really? So, what was it like growing up on the pleasure planet?"

"I…I don't know. Normal?" She couldn't think clearly around him. Her tongue felt numb in her mouth.

His smile traveled all the way up to his eyes. He leaned closer and rested his hand on her hip. "Then perhaps you could be my personal tour guide," he whispered in her ear.

"I can't. I have other plans."

He drew back and frowned, but she could still see the glimmer in his eyes.

"I'm jealous of whoever you're going to be spending your time with."

She giggled at him. "I'm just going to sleep. It's been a long day, and I'm afraid I wouldn't be good company." There was no way she would tell him she had to spend a few hours that night with another man.

His smile returned. "Tomorrow then? I'd really like to see you again."

See her? Like an actual date rather than as a client? The idea made her feel like the most desirable woman on the planet. "Sure, I'd like that, too."

"Great. Now, before you go, could you point me in the direction of the Sturban deversorium? I have an appointment with a Suavita, and I can't seem to find my way back."

Her heart lurched. He'd flirted with her, made her desire him, and then thrown his appointment in her face. Would her life always be like this on Schedar, men seeking only sexual release and nothing more? In that case, she'd need to harden her heart, or end up lacerated by rejection. "Find it yourself."

Spinning away from him, she ran. She didn't need the hurt and rejection. Only sleep if she wanted to be ready for her evening appointment.

"Nixie, wait." He tried to grab her, his blue fingers skimming across the back of her hand, but she ducked away.

She took back alleys and private paths to get to the hotel; she had to escape. But would he follow her? When she reached the office, she hid under the desk Garesh occupied.

"As much as I like you, I am not in need of your services."

She slapped his thigh. "I'm not offering my services. I'm hiding."

"From whom?"

"No one important. Listen, the client I have tonight, are you sure you can't find someone else to take him?" She would refuse to service him if he turned out to be the man she'd seen on the street. Sure, he'd made her heart flutter, but she couldn't remain in control of her feelings if she had to pleasure him.

"No. Everyone else is booked with regular clients, or have other specialties that have been requested."

Taking hold of his ringed nipple, she pulled. "Please, Garesh."

"Ouch!" He took her hand and squeezed until she let go. "No, not unless you'd like to service two men at the same time."

She shook the pain from her hand. "Fine. Then can you at least tell me the name of my client."

"I can do that." He eyed the appointment log. "It's Mekai. That's all I've got."

Shit. She hadn't found out the name of the guy she'd bumped into. Dropping her bag to the floor, she peered around, hoping to locate some place to sleep.

"What are you doing here anyway? I thought you were going home."

"I don't want to talk about it." She spotted an empty room, not much bigger than a closet to her left, and picked up her bag. "Can I rest in there?"

"Sure." He tossed her a pillow and a blanket from the shelving behind the check-in desk. "I'll make sure you're up in time for your appointment."

"Thanks." Her mind spun out of control as she walked away. In a short period of time, she'd run into two men who'd haunted her nightmares and one who stirred unfamiliar desires in her. If she continued training as a Suavita, would her life be filled with never-ending heartache? Perhaps that's why the Suavitas took the ipsum, to avoid these emotions. How would she ever get to sleep now? She lay on the cushion, pulled the uidiss-skin blanket over her, and closed her eyes.

BEYOND REACH
CHAPTER THREE

Mekai sighed heavily, waiting on the bed. He couldn't get the young Terran woman he'd met on the street out of his mind. *Nixie.* Not only was she absolutely stunning, she also reminded him of the woman he'd dreamed about for years.

But she shouldn't be in his thoughts; Terrans and Ubetrons did not mingle. They didn't even speak from distances. Their planets were positioned far from each other, across the universe. Bad blood had been spilled many star cycles ago, causing a rift between the two societies. And yet, he would bridge the gap, if given the opportunity, just to experience Nixie.

He closed his eyes, envisioning her beautiful face, her long, raven-colored hair flowing down her back, her almond-shaped, violet eyes. Oh, he craved her, a feeling he'd only felt for an imaginary woman until now.

A knock on the door startled him from his thoughts.

Shit! His Suavita had arrived. He'd been lucky to get an appointment so soon after his quarantine period. The bronze-skinned Schedarn man at the desk wanted him to take tomorrow night, but a few gems he'd managed to collect from the caves of Carbae had persuaded the man to rearrange the schedule. How would the woman sent to him feel if he turned her away? He'd never get his money back, but could he enjoy the pleasures the Suavitas were known for if he had another woman on his mind? Perhaps that would further heighten the experience. And how would he find the Terran woman anyway? He knew nothing but her name and the sight of her shapely body.

Might as well enjoy the planet while I'm here. "Come in."

The door to his suite slid open and the woman slipped into his darkened room. "Sir, I'll be your Suavita for the evening. Would you like me to turn the lights up?"

"No, leave the room dim." He planned to picture Nixie bringing him pleasure instead.

The woman gasped. He opened his eyes to get a better look, but couldn't see her facial expressions. Somehow, though, he could sense something familiar about her.

"Mekai. Your name is Mekai?"

Yes, he knew that voice, had heard it earlier in the day. "Nixie? You're my Suavita?" Could he get any luckier? His heart hammered in his chest. He didn't have to imagine anything. The woman he'd planned to fantasize about, had always fantasized about, stood in front of him.

"Yes, I am." She kept her tone curt, distanced. "Now, if you don't mind, I'd like to get started. Please get up on the table, sir."

Her accentuated last word stung. What had he done to piss her off?

"I haven't stopped thinking about you since I saw you this afternoon." Gods, could he sound any more immature?

But his words seemed to soften Nixie's glare, and she tilted her head to the side. "I'm surprised, considering you couldn't wait to get here and have fun with your Suavita."

What in Tenebrae? "Yes, Terran, but *you* are my Suavita."

If her eyes held lasers, he'd be ashes on the floor.

"I can easily find a replacement if I'm not to your liking."

Quite the opposite. He slid off the bed. Stepping forward, he brushed a hand down her tanned arm. She belonged with him on Carbae, not here to provide pleasure for others. Where had that thought come from?

She wouldn't be accepted in his kingdom. She was Terran. Right now, he didn't care. "I don't want anyone else. I want you." And he'd give her as much pleasure as she gave him, more even.

She didn't shy away, but calmed down against him. Cupping her cheek in his hand, he ran his thumb along her full pink lips. He couldn't wait to taste them, have them around his cock. Gods, she drove him wild.

He leaned forward to savor her luscious lips, but she pulled away with a whimper. "I can't do this."

"But you're a Suavita. This is what you're paid to do." He wanted the experience to be more than an obligation. Having the night end before it began didn't work for him.

She gazed down at her feet. "This is my first overnight appointment. I…I'm not used to kissing and all that. Only a massage followed by your pleasure."

A beautiful woman like her had never been kissed before, and on Schedar of all places? How was that possible? "You can take the lead then. But join me on the bed."

She stiffened, as if becoming distant. "We'll start on the massage table for the standard rubdown, sir. We'll move to the bed later in the night."

Oh yes they would, and there he'd turn the tides, take control of the night and escort her into the land of oblivion. He need only wait for her to let her guard down.

At the table, he dropped his robe to the ground, ensuring she had a full-frontal view.

What would she think of him? Was she disgusted by his Ubetron form?

His abnormal self-consciousness helped to calm his

raging hard-on, but his mind kept returning to Nixie. He needed to touch her again, taste her, be in her. Finally, he'd found a woman he hungered for. But was the feeling mutual? Could he make love to her the way he did in his fantasies? He lay down, cringing in the process. This was going to be a long night.

"Are you ready, sir?"

Sir, again? "Yes, miss, I'm ready."

She unzipped her appointment bag. "You may call me Suavita."

"And you may call me Mekai." *I plan to have you screaming my name by the end of the night.*

"I prefer *sir*. Please lie still and relax."

He sighed. One way or another, he would break down her walls.

Oil sloshed onto his back, the strong scent of ipsum encapsulating the room. As Nixie's hands met his bare skin, he tensed then melted into a puddle. Her hands worked to loosen every muscle throughout his back, down his legs, and along his arms. No touch had ever made him so rested, yet raring to go at the same time. She'd learned well, digging deep into his body. He couldn't wait to turn over and experience her knowledge of his other erogenous zones.

Trailing a finger down his spine, she whispered, "It's time to move to the bed, sir. Please lie on your back."

With his legs flimsy like rubber, he wobbled over to the bed, his mind set on how to seduce her, make her want him the way he wanted her.

BEYOND REACH
CHAPTER FOUR

From the moment she'd heard his deep, husky voice, her body raced with anticipation. She'd recognized him, remembered the intense, sensual dreams she'd experienced while trying to rest during the afternoon. And she'd only just met him. How would she feel after this appointment ended? Would every client make her experience the same rush of emotions, or only Mekai, the Ubetron man who must remain a sworn enemy?

Sighing, she sauntered toward the bed. She couldn't think about the problems of her race—they'd abandoned her. No one had ever come to find her.

And she had a client to pleasure. That's all he could be. Nothing more.

She crawled up onto the bed, positioning herself between Mekai's spread legs. His ample arousal jutted high into the air, ready to take pleasure in her mouth. But she'd follow procedure, spending time on other parts of his body first. With the ipsum in her system reducing her inhibitions and heightening her body's responses every time she touched his bare skin, if she broke the routine she'd come to memorize, she'd wind up putty in his hands. Not ideal with any client. She had to remain in control.

After she'd poured more oil onto his chiseled blue chest, she leaned forward to massage it in. She pressed firmly into his hard muscles, not having to push through scales and layers of other physiological coverings like some of her previous clients. Mekai's body presented everything out front to her, including his damn enticing cock. Never before had she wanted a male appendage in her mouth so much. She tried to ignore the tip pressing against her stomach, dancing against her skin with every stroke of her hands across his chest. But she couldn't. Cream built up in her molten core, urging her to take the massage into foreign territory. She longed to be filled by a man. By Mekai.

No! She leaned back, skipping the massage of his temples, his scalp, and his underarms, for she was required to lean over him rather than move around to his head, and that would take her core dangerously close to his hard shaft. She couldn't allow him to bring her any pleasure, heighten her emotional connection to him, and leave her susceptible to heartbreak. *Mekai is your client.*

Cyresse and Garesh both swore her heart would recognize the difference between a client and a lover, but she preferred to keep her heart guarded from them all.

Working Mekai's inner thighs, Nixie returned to a safer zone. Yet his engorged flesh now stood tall and in her face, tempting her again to take him into her mouth. His alluring, musky scent radiated into her nasal passages, overpowering the ipsum. Her resolve wavered, but she couldn't give in, refused to give up control. His pleasure and subsequent release remained her goal for the night, not her own.

Mekai thrust his hips into the air. "I'm ready for you to massage my dick with your sweet mouth."

She rolled her eyes. What had she seen in him? He was just there to satisfy his own needs. He'd only be a one-time client, and never call on her again.

In her dreams, though, he'd forsaken his own pleasure for hers, made sure he left her satisfied, complete. She'd never felt that way before, not even by her own devices.

With a deep breath, she sank her lips over his shaft. She couldn't think of what her mind had created, only of what she'd been trained to do. Up and down she traveled, teasing the tip of his cock, giving it a lick or a nip with every pass. She could do this and remain detached.

He moaned and his entire body tensed. "Oh yeah, a tantalizing tongue, just as I imagined. No one has ever made me feel this way."

Her stomach clenched. He'd been with multiple women? How many? Sure, she'd pleasured other men, too, but her job required it. Wait, why did she care? With every word he said, he made it easier to keep her distance from him.

She toured his shaft with her tongue, her mouth, exploring his most sensitive areas, remembering the way his testicles puckered just before he came in her dream.

It wasn't real. He won't want you after tonight.

The faster she made him come, the sooner she'd be rid of him and the conflicting emotions battling in her heart.

The muscles in his legs tightened, and as instructed, she pressed her thumb against his perineum. If she made his orgasm as intense as possible, he could possibly be asleep within minutes, and she'd be free for the rest of the night. She shoved thoughts of something more with Mekai to the recesses of her mind. One day she would be a level Four Suavita and train other Suavitas. That was her future.

"Gods, Nixie, I'm going to come." He thrust into her at the same time he released.

She kept pumping his cock, swallowing all of his cum and priming him to go again.

Sitting straight up, he grabbed her head. He pulled her off his shaft, clutched her wrists, and flipped her onto her back. Positioned between her breasts, he released a second time. "Frolicking farzles, woman, you're good at your job."

He slid down her stomach to settle over her pubic bone and leaned down to capture her mouth. Oh-so-gentle lips tugged at her soul.

She pulled away, gasping for air. "I can't do this, Mekai." He would destroy her self-control. She refused to open her heart to any client, to consider another life.

"I don't plan on letting you leave without hearing you scream in ecstasy." He trailed kisses across her chin and down her neck. "You deserve pleasure, too. You deserve so much more."

As he laid claim to her lips all over again, she melted under his weight and fierce tongue. Perhaps she did want her dreams to become reality. The morning, and the end of the appointment, seemed so far away.

BEYOND REACH
CHAPTER FIVE

Mekai didn't think it possible for his cock to still be rock-hard, but the sensations brought by Nixie's slender body under his proved otherwise. Yet his heart seemed to have swelled inside his chest. He knew he would have to leave her soon, but he never wanted to be with another, couldn't bear the thought of her being with anyone else, either. For the first time, he considered settling down with a woman. With Nixie. For he had already loved her for years.

When she relaxed beneath him, he released her wrists, dragging his fingers down her arms and sides. Never had he met another like her. She'd left him sated and implanted herself in his heart.

I'm not sure how, but it's my turn to leave a lasting impression.

With bittersweet fervor, he fed from the sweetness of her mouth. She dug her fingertips into his back, grinding her pelvis against him.

So tempting to just take her now. He could easily take pleasure from her feminine folds, but how would that make her feel special? Guys from all over the universe received gratification from her. But he wanted her time with him to be memorable, possibly life-changing. This had to be all about her, for her.

Sliding down her body, he sucked on one of her nipples while he ravaged the other breast with his hand. He couldn't get enough.

She writhed beneath him, combing her fingers through his hair. But she still held back, reluctant to let go, to just enjoy as he tried to satisfy her.

"Nixie, relax," he growled. "Or I'll have to make a complaint. How would it look if your client was dissatisfied with your services?"

"You wouldn't." Her nostrils flared as she glared at him. "This isn't part of my training, anyway."

He kissed the tip of her nose. "I don't want to be part of your training. I want you to be mine, my first."

She gasped. "But you're so…. You never?"

He shook his head. "I was taught to wait until I found the right woman."

Her stare weakened and her bottom lip quivered. "I'm not her."

Desperate to leave his mark on her soul, he kissed her, tasted her lips, her chin, and down her slender neck. He wanted more, but only if she agreed. "I think you are, and I'm willing to find out right now."

Pressing her pelvis against him, she moaned. "Oh gods, I don't know."

He saw her resolve weakening, and waited. She had to give up all control. *And I won't give up until she does.*

Running his tongue down her silky nakedness, toward her tender flesh, he spread open her legs and breathed in the evidence of her arousal. Nothing could ever be as tempting.

He drew his finger across the dampness between her legs. *Perfect. So ready.* Leaning down, he licked her swollen nub, his fingers traveling to the deeper heat within.

She bucked beneath him, thrusting her hips into the air.

"Mekai, o...okay. I want more."

As his name rolled off her tongue, followed by her desperate plea, he shivered. No way would he deny her request.

Increasing his tempo, he ground his digits as deep as possible, while sucking her pulsating clit. She moaned. Her slippery core tightened around his fingers. Her cries grew louder. With a deep shudder, she convulsed around him. Her voice rang out, his name echoing throughout the room. But he wasn't done.

Returning to her beautiful, swollen lips, his tongue found hers. Their kiss was the most intimate he'd ever experienced. And she claimed she never kissed clients? Not once did she pull away, tell him to stop. She wrapped her arms around him, holding him tight against her body. He held her and made love to her mouth. Positioned between her tender folds, a thin wall blocked him from sinking in. With a little more pressure, he broke through, taking her virginity, and his. *How had she remained intact as a Suavita?*

Closing her eyes, she whimpered, then bit her bottom lip.

She'd accepted him, but he couldn't continue if she felt any pain. Yet, he never wanted to break their connection. "Look at me, Nixie. If this hurts too much, tell me."

Taking a deep breath, she opened her eyes. "I'm all right."

Ever so slowly, he eased himself into her. *Tight, unbelievably tight.*

"Good." He brushed his thumb across her cheek. "Because I don't want this to end. This feels so right, like I'm meant to be here, with you." *In you.* Just like in his fantasies.

She looked up at him and smiled.

At that moment, he didn't care about her heritage or chosen vocation. He knew he could never leave her. She was the one.

Rocking underneath him, she looked up at him with an intense gaze. The pressure built inside his body, but he held back, hoping to take her over at the same time.

In an instant, she tightened around his cock, her hands squeezing his arms. He couldn't hold his release any longer and groaned in satisfaction. Nixie convulsed around him, milking him with her own climax and calling out his name. With slow strokes, he continued to drive into her, until she relaxed her grip on him.

He flopped down beside her. "You are an amazing woman." He struggled to catch his breath, but couldn't let go of her.

She turned onto her side, coming face to face with him, her breathing still ragged. "Was I…all right?"

He nodded. "More than all right. It was everything I'd dreamed, everything I'd hoped it would be, and yet…." Brushing a hand over her hair, he smiled. "I really care for you, Nixie. I want to spend more time with you."

Returning to her back, she sighed. "You can't have feelings for me. I'm Terran, and a Suavita. I don't get to fall in love, leave for a different life. That time has long passed."

He took her hand in his. "No, you are still young. And I have dreamed about you. *You*, Nixie, for as long as I can remember. Now, I've finally met you in person. We are meant to be together."

"No, this can't be. You're crazy." Her voice quavered.

He gulped. How could she deny everything he felt? Didn't she feel it, too? "I'm not, but I think I'm in love."

She pulled her hand away. "And what's going to happen when you leave in the morning? I refuse to allow my heart to be crushed for one night of pleasure."

"So you admit you felt something?"

"Sexual bliss is hardly the connection you describe."

He rolled onto his hands and knees above her. She needed to know the truth. "Listen, I've been with women before, never all the way, but close enough. But I've never felt any connection with them. I didn't feel anything for my betrothed either, and left before we could marry."

Her eyes grew wide. "You were going to marry someone else, and yet you're here?"

"No. It wasn't by choice. They wanted me to marry her, but I didn't want to. I couldn't love her. I objected to my father over and over, didn't want the same unloving marriage as my parents. He refused to change his mind. So, I formulated a plan. Now she's set to wed my best friend, and I'm here, with you."

A tear slid down her cheek. "I don't understand what you want from me."

He brushed the wetness away. "I want you, Nixie. Only you. By my side and in my bed."

Wanting to remind her of all they'd shared, he kissed her with as much passion as he could muster.

She pulled away, gasping. "I can't. I have clients. I'm a Suavita."

"Then spend your free time with me. I'll pay whatever I have to, to keep you in my bed. You can practice on me. And maybe…." If she didn't agree, he had a feeling he'd never see her again.

"What?"

"Nothing. Just say you'll be my Suavita for the rest of my stay."

She sighed. "Fine."

He lay on the bed, and she cuddled into the crook of his arm. He had a chance, and he planned to use their time together to win her completely.

BEYOND REACH
CHAPTER SIX

Nixie whipped her eyes open. She'd fallen asleep, snuggled against her client. Taking in his now familiar musky scent, she sighed. *Mekai.* He'd asked her to stay, stirring hopes and desires she'd wanted to suppress.

But could she remain distanced from him, serve only as his Suavita, or would she fall hopelessly in love with him, only to have her heart crushed when he left? She sat up, unable to think with a clear mind while lying beside him.

Do I really want to be a Suavita? Nixie had been given a protocol of injections that controlled her reproductive cycle, preventing her impregnation from clients or anyone else she might decide to partake in sexual activities with. Although, she hadn't had any use for the protection until last night. Once she reached level Three, though, she'd go through a process of sterilization. She'd lose the ability to bear children of her own.

Her only chance of another life would be to leave the planet. And how would she do that? Return with Mekai to Ubetron? Yeah, right. She'd probably be shot as soon as she stepped off the transport ship.

She had no other choice but to continue her training on Schedar. The planet was a cultural melting pot, attracting tourists and new residents from many galaxies. Because of her skin color, everyone recognized her as Terran, and once she had her full Suavita designation, they would respect her as a Mistress of the sensual arts. Only on Schedar, could she earn her place.

Sliding off the bed, she gathered her supplies. She needed some space from Mekai, to clear her head of the ipsum and rebuild the wall around her heart. For if she continued servicing him, she had to remain unattached, use him as he had used the other women in his past.

Glancing over her shoulder, she observed the content smile across Mekai's lips as he slept. Her stomach turned as she swept the door open. *Should I have agreed to see him again? Maybe going home would have been a better idea.*

No, Cyresse had clients of her own. Nixie would rather stay here than join in sexual activities with her mother-figure and the two beasts from Gregacia.

She'd return to Mekai. She simply had to deny the connection she felt.

Hurrying down the stairs, she made a mental list of all of the things she needed to do before going back to him. *Take a shower, grab a change of clothes, protect her heart….* In her rush, she'd left her appointment bag by the door. Didn't matter. She'd need her supplies again anyway. Or maybe she'd share a shower with the man who'd left her body humming. Why not both, have some fun for once?

Her excitement flittered away as she traipsed into the office. "Garesh, what are you doing here?"

"I came to check on you." He raised an eyebrow, his stare intense. "You fell asleep with a client, didn't you?"

She nodded. "It was by choice. I…I had a good time."

The Schedarn man studied her from head to toe. "I'm glad your appointment went so well. I admit I was worried at first."

And her, even more so.

"I guess we can go ahead and schedule another overnight appointment then?"

Clasping her hands together, she stared at the floor. "About that. I, um, already have an appointment tonight."

Garesh rushed to the hotel log lying on the desk. His finger brushed across the screen. "It seems you do. Your first repeat client." He returned to her side, placing his hands on her shoulders. "I'm so happy for you. Cyresse and I believed if you had the right client, you would experience so much more pleasure as a Suavita, you would find fulfillment like…."

She stared up into his eyes. "What?"

Glancing away, he sighed. "Oh, nothing. You'll figure it out eventually." He faced her again, grinning. "So, how'd it go?"

Her body tingled at the thought of her night. "Everything went well, but there's something—" Should she even mention it?

"Go ahead." He motioned for her to sit down, then positioned himself on the floor. "You know I'm always here for you."

She took a deep breath, easing back on the cushion in front of the desk. How much should she tell him? "I…I'm beginning to wonder if this is really what I want to do."

"You worry about growing attached to your clients, about wanting more with them."

"Yes, but not only that…." Her clammy hands shook in her lap. "What if one day I want to leave Schedar?"

Garesh gulped. "Cyresse and I knew this day would come."

Really? "What do you mean?"

"I know you don't like to discuss the circumstances of how you came to be in Cyresse's care." He brushed a hand through his hair. "But we figured you would one day want to go to Earth to find your parents and demand answers. And with you now a level Two—"

"No!" She stood up. Her heart raced. "I could care less about why my good-for-nothing parents abandoned me on a foreign planet while they fucked around. They can rot on Tenebrae for all I care."

Perhaps leaving would never be a good idea. What if she ran into her parents? For star cycles, she'd dreaded their return. Now, she believed she'd never run into the people whose image was ingrained into her mind if she remained on this planet. Besides, where else would she go? What would she do?

No, she would stay. She knew what to expect on Schedar.

"Why would you mention leaving, then?"

She returned her focus to Garesh. "I'm not. I was only considering it, but…. Just forget I said anything."

He arrived at her side. "Your client, the one you slept with. Is he the reason you brought this up?"

Gods, how did he know? "Maybe. Well, I thought about leaving before him, wondered what it would be like to do something different. To be something other than a Suavita."

"Good."

"Good? What's that supposed to mean?"

Garesh wrapped his arms around her and kissed the top of her head. She leaned into him, finding comfort as her mind struggled with making a decision. This man and Cyresse had been the only family she had. How could she leave them? How could she leave this life when for so long she'd wanted nothing else?

"If you're having any doubts about becoming a level Three or Four Suavita, now is the time to explore your options, find out what you want in life. You can always come back to Schedar and practice as a Suavita, but once you are sterilized and have the ipsum injection, it is harder to leave this life. Not everyone is cut out for it." He stroked her hair. "Life is all about choices. So if you choose to be a level Four Suavita, I want you to have considered all of your options, and make the decision without any doubts or regrets."

"But what about Cyresse? I can't leave her alone."

"She'll be fine." He pulled away and smiled down at her. "I know on good authority she will never be alone."

Joy radiated within at having Garesh's understanding, his blessing to make her own decisions.

"But—" He returned to the desk again and scanned the log. "I want you to take other clients before you make any decisions. It would be unwise to come to any conclusions based on one experience."

"But I'll have some time before that's scheduled, right?"

He nodded. "Yes, but in a week, I am going to need you. We are already booked for several days after the next ship arrives."

She sighed with relief. "All right." She would have the next six days to spend with Mekai. She only hoped he stuck around that long.

After grabbing her clothing still in the office closet, she rushed back up to Mekai's suite. She couldn't wait to tell him the good news.

BEYOND REACH
CHAPTER SEVEN

Nixie stepped out of the shower, refreshed after a long night of pleasure and passion with Mekai, and then sleeping half the day away snuggled against him. She sighed, rubbing a towel across her sex-swollen mound. The past week had been better than she ever could have imagined. Mekai had paid for her services every night, and she massaged away every tense muscle before he used his own past experiences to take her to new heights in bed. Complete bliss.

But she had a problem. She'd fallen in love. Her heart longed for Mekai. Even now, she yearned to feel his touch, hear his whispered words as his breath brushed across her neck. She'd tried to remain unattached, see him as only a client, but sleeping with him after each session and sharing her hopes and dreams, had kept his pending departure away from her thoughts.

What am I going to do when he leaves? How can I be with anyone else after him? A broken heart waited in her future, but until then, she'd spend every spare minute with the young man who'd captured her very soul.

With an extra day of no appointments on her timetable, she waltzed from the bathroom, naked, with the hopes of an unscheduled rendezvous. She entered the bedroom, only to find it empty.

Her stomach clenched. Why hadn't he said goodbye? A tear trickled down her cheek, followed by another. Pain ebbed from her heart, throughout her body. She crashed onto the bed in a fit of sobs. Something jabbed into her side, and she rolled over.

A note lay beside her. She wiped her tears to read the words.

Nixie,
Please don't think I've left you. Well, I did, but only for a short period of time.
I had some shopping to do.
Meet me at the park we went to on the third day of my stay. I will be there.
All my love,
Mekai.

She sighed, needing to get there immediately.

Reaching for her clothes, she paused. *Maybe this isn't such a good idea.*

She'd already broken down when she'd thought he'd left. What would happen when he finally did? Perhaps she should end this now, before his time on Schedar was over, and she needed to take other clients. Yes, she'd meet him and conclude their love affair.

But what could he be shopping for?

With new determination, she dressed and bounded down the stairs.

"Nixie, you're still here?"

She spun around to face Garesh, who stood beside some other level Twos. "Yes, but I was just leaving."

"Before you go, I have to inform you of your appointment tomorrow night."

Concern flittered in her mind. "Another night with Mekai. Yes, I already know."

He shook his head. "No. Mekai is only scheduled for tonight. You will have a new client tomorrow night. An Elikashe, like your previous client."

"But Mekai hasn't left yet. Why can't someone else take the appointment?" She couldn't get over Mekai that fast. No, she needed more time.

"To begin with, you said the same thing before you met Mekai. And I told you already that we are completely booked for this week. I don't have any spare Suavitas. Do you have a problem with that?"

Garesh's tone had turned authoritative, something she didn't often hear. Which meant no chance to disagree. "No, sir."

She slumped away, eager to get away from everyone, including Mekai. She couldn't see him again. Not if she wanted to recover from her broken heart before her next appointment. It would be easier to avoid him rather than tell him their time together had to end. But could she truly get over him without saying goodbye?

Mekai sat on the lush hillside, brushing his hands through the soft grass. They didn't have grass on Carbae, only rock. A lot of rock.

Would Nixie be happy there? Or would she regret her decision to live there with him? But what about his parents? Would they accept a Terran girl as his bride-to-be when relations with Earth remained tense? Perhaps their union would help.

He thought too far ahead. She hadn't said she would return with him. She hadn't even arrived.

He'd only been waiting a short period of time, yet his gut compressed in anxious anticipation. He would proclaim his love, present her with a ceremonial crown—

and make sweet love to her.

Fingering the crown on his lap, he sighed. In the marketplace, he hadn't found anything close to the elite mistrite crowns his family wore on Carbae. The precious metal was mined from the rock and forged into exquisite pieces of jewelry. He'd never cared to wear one, but Nixie would so everyone would know she was his princess. He didn't want anyone else.

For now, she'd have to settle for the crown he'd hand-woven using thin branches of from the flowering tree beside him. Either way, no one could be as beautiful as she, no matter what she wore.

Clothing swished behind him as someone approached. He spun around and smiled. "I'm glad you came." Reaching up, he helped her to sit beside him.

A light breeze tousled her dark locks. But the happiness he'd seen in her eyes during his week on Schedar had disappeared.

"What's wrong, Nixie?"

She shook her head and laced her fingers with his as she stared out over the city.

Tourists meandered through the marketplace, some on the backs of slow, hairy uidisses. No one seemed to be in a rush, quite different than on Carbae where no one relaxed until their daily responsibilities had been fulfilled. Even as the prince, he had his own chores to do. His home had never been a vacation destination—more like a hidden colony—but with Nixie by his side, life on Carbae would be a dream come true. If, that is, she agreed to return with him.

He breathed in her scent: bimon, a citrusy fruit found on Ubetron. The fragrance suited her better than ipsum floating around the planet. Bimon was a marking of his own heritage, giving him hope she would travel home with him. But how had she washed away the ipsum when the drug flowed through the water? And where had she found the bimon? Exporting the fruit had been banned long ago.

Had she found the scent for him, worn it to indicate her feelings for him? He glanced over at her, filled with optimism. "Nixie, I want to take you home with me. I want you to be my princess."

She gasped, and he caught the tears streaming down her cheeks. He couldn't tell if they were tears of joy or sadness. Perhaps both.

"I can't. I'm not a princess. I'm a Suavita. I have a life here, people who care about me, who have always been by my side."

His gut clenched. Had he misread her? He stroked her face, needing some contact. He refused to let her go. "You're the most beautiful woman I've ever met, inside and out. Every time I see you, my heart skips a beat." Revealing the crown of branches to her, he smiled. "Will you return to Carbae with me? Will you marry me and be my princess?" He hadn't asked Madelia to marry him—still a custom on Carbae even when betrothed—saving the honor for the woman who would capture his soul. And now he'd found her, he could never love another, no matter what decision she made.

"Mekai, I want to. It's just—"

"I don't care if you're Terran. We can make this work. All I need to know is if you feel the same way, if you love me."

She nodded, wiping the tears away.

"Then say you'll marry me."

"Yes, I will." She bowed her head.

With his insides cartwheeling, he presented her with the crown and then pulled her onto his lap. "Gods, I love you so much. I never thought I'd ever feel this way until I met you. Why don't we leave right away, start our new life together?" He kissed her with hunger, engulfed in her intoxicating essence. His life was now complete, perfect.

She pulled away, gasping. "Mekai, I need a couple days. I have some things I need to take care of first."

"That's fine. I'll help you." He wanted to spend every

minute with her, didn't want to let her go until he had her on Carbae with him. Even then he would do his best to be away from her as little as possible. And if his parents disapproved, he'd settle elsewhere, anywhere, as long as Nixie remained by his side.

She placed her hand on his chest. "No. I need to do this myself." She wouldn't meet his gaze.

What could she not need his help with? "Nixie, what—"

She stroked his face. "I'm going with you. I just have a promise I have to keep tomorrow night. Then I'm all yours. We can leave the next morning."

Pangs of guilt tore through her. She'd promised her heart, her life to Mekai, yet she would take one more client? *It's your job, and he knows it.*

He lifted her chin and stared into her eyes, her soul. Could he tell she was hiding something from him?

Taking a deep breath, she smiled. She needed to change the topic, disintegrate the tension between them and forget her guilt. "Do you remember the first time we came here?"

She hadn't been able to wait to practice some new techniques on her repeat client, having asked other Suavitas what their clients enjoyed. She'd spent so much time with him, and he'd showed her pleasure was just as fun to receive from a client as it was to give. But when she'd arrived, he'd worn a somber expression rather than the one full of lust she'd come to expect when she'd meet him in his room.

"What's wrong?" she had asked.

He'd gazed up at her and reached for her hand. "I'm falling in love with you, Nixie. I don't want to ever leave you."

She couldn't help but beam with joy. Finding a regular client as a level Two was rare, yet she'd done just that. "I'll always be here for you when you visit. You'll have priority over everyone else." With the promise of his return, she could get through life, take other clients, picturing him during each session she was with another. She'd rather travel with him, but knew that dream wasn't possible, not with the history of animosity between their cultures.

He'd leaned down and kissed her with sweet passion. And there on the hill, they'd made love, their time together not about her bringing him heightened pleasure, but to simply be together, as equals.

"I will never forget a second with you." As he did their first time together, and every encounter thereafter, Mekai worshiped her body with his hands, mouth, and ravaging tongue.

He kissed his way up her stomach, and she drew in a quick breath. "Please don't ever leave me."

"I promise I'll be by your side for the rest of my life. I love you, Nixie." Hovering above her, he joined his body with hers.

She moaned, oblivious to everything but this moment. She hoped he kept his word, for she could never give her heart to another. She would always be his.

BEYOND REACH
CHAPTER EIGHT

Nixie sighed as she left the suite. She hadn't been apart from Mekai for even a day, and now emptiness washed over her. And guilt continued to build. What would he think if he knew she was about to service another man? The idea tore her up inside. Yet, she had to go, had to keep her word to Garesh.

With each measured step, she tried not to falter. How could she even think about keeping this appointment when she'd given her heart to Mekai, accepted his marriage proposal and beautiful, hand-made crown? She leaned against the wall in an effort to regain her composure. She couldn't show up with hunched shoulders and a quivering lip. No, she had to be happy, filled with lust, ready to fulfill her client's desires. Reaching into her bag, she pulled out a bottle of ipsum massage oil and rubbed it onto her face. Anything to improve her mood.

Taking a deep breath, she stood up straight and attempted a smile, one she couldn't make happen. *No! Do this for Cyresse and Garesh.* They'd always been there for her. She had to make them proud.

Reining in her guilt, she continued down the hall. This was her last appointment. She could do this for her makeshift family. The client hadn't booked her for the entire night, so she'd be in long enough to give him a massage, release his arousal, and then she'd be done. And if her life didn't work out with Mekai, she could return, become a level Four Suavita.

She arrived at the door and retrieved her card from her bag to disengage the lock. But she couldn't. The man on the other side of that door would not be Mekai. She'd already promised him she would be with one man for the rest of her life, a promise she'd break almost immediately if she stayed.

Mekai mattered more to her than anything. He held her future. No, she would have to go back on her word to Garesh. As she turned to leave, the door opened.

An older man, covered in scales, stepped from the suite. He wore nothing but a towel around his waist. "Are you my Suavita? I've been anxiously awaiting your services since my quarantine period ended."

A tear trailed down her cheek. She couldn't leave now. "Yes, sir. Let's get started." She followed him inside and set up the massage table.

The sooner she finished, the sooner she could return to Mekai and discover what her future held.

Mekai turned the corner as Nixie followed an almost naked Elikashe man into his room. The door slid closed behind them.

He narrowed his eyes. Fire burned through his body. How could Nixie keep clients after what they'd shared? After agreeing to return with him? His heart ached as if splitting in two. Would she ever be able to leave this lifestyle behind, or would she continue to service others on Carbae? He couldn't bear the thought.

Clenching his fists, he spun around, marched back to his suite, and packed his belongings. He had to leave, to get out. To clear his head, or for good, he wasn't sure which. Why had he come here anyway? How could he have thought a Suavita would fall in love with him when obviously he'd been just another client to her? Not the woman of his fantasies, but a fake. He stormed through the halls, down the stairs, and out into the street. The air in the hotel was so thick with ipsum, he couldn't think clearly. Yet, his anger cut through any desire.

All around him, blissful tourists and Schedarn citizens paraded around. Their joy only made him angrier. He had to get away, find some place secluded where he hadn't shared tender moments with Nixie. As he raced through the streets, his heart pounded. Why did she have to betray him? And to think, he'd been willing to give up everything for her, including his parents' blessing. For they would never accept her as his future wife. Most likely, they already had him betrothed to another.

Reeling to stop, he sank to the ground. Why hadn't he thought this through? Nixie could end up shunned on Carbae. She'd never forgive him, then. Even if he forgave her first.

"Hello, handsome."

Mekai took in miles of blue legs coming to a halt underneath a short, black leather skirt. As he continued his gaze over her flat stomach and barely-covered breasts, he cock stirred. Until he saw her face. "Madelia, what are you doing here?"

"Having a good time with Ben. You can join us if you're interested."

"No, sorry. I like the outfit, though."

She grinned, swaying her hips in front of his face. "Ben looks even better in leather. I must thank you for setting us up together. I never expected him to enjoy taking orders."

He cringed. "I didn't need to hear that."

"I thought you two knew everything about each other." She eyed him up and down. "Every intimate detail."

"We weren't that close." Could she darken his mood any further?

"Hey, don't be grumpy with me. This *is* Schedar, the planet where all of your desires can come true. Go find yourself a Suavita."

"I already have." *And she broke my heart.*

"Well, go find another to wipe that scowl off your face. The first one obviously didn't do her job."

She'd done more than just her job; she'd loved him, made him fall in love with her.

He winced. *Nixie.*

No matter what he'd seen, he had to get back to her rather than let her be with another man. He loved her too much to give up without fighting for what he wanted. "I've got to go."

"Well, be quick about it. Your parents are here, too, looking for you."

"Shit." He rushed back to the hotel, peering around every corner first to ensure he would not run into the king and queen of Carbae. Not before he claimed Nixie as his, and his alone. For he could *never* share her with another.

BEYOND REACH
CHAPTER NINE

As Nixie rubbed the oils deep into the man's scaled body, tears slid down her cheeks. She didn't want to touch this man, be anywhere near him. Not when Mekai waited for her back in his suite. Why had she told Garesh she'd take this appointment? And now she'd have to live with the guilt of pleasuring another man after promising herself to her one true love.

"Oh, dear Suavita, you know how to relax my body." The man rose onto his arms. "But I want you to fulfill my desires. I want to feel your hands and mouth on my cock. And if you're really good, I'll let you go for a ride."

She shuddered, her stomach threatening to depart with its contents. She couldn't stay in this room any longer. No, she had to leave.

The man swung off the table and sauntered toward his bed, stroking his shaft as he went. "You coming?"

Backing away, she tripped over her appointment bag. *I can't do this.*

She regained her balance before she fell, and raced for the door. Nothing could make her stay. Waiting for the door to open, she realized she'd left her bag behind. She considered returning for it. No, she wouldn't need it again. *Get out!*

Escaping into the corridor, she fled for Mekai's room.

"Suavita, get back here."

Peering over her shoulder, she cringed as the man stood outside his room in the buff, shaking his fists. How had she thought she could handle going from one man like him to another, star cycle after star cycle? Even without Mekai, she would need to settle down, for that's what she'd desired all along.

Out of breath, she slid her card through the reader to Mekai's suite. If he asked her to leave now, she would. She had to get away from this life, this planet. Leave it all behind.

The door opened, revealing an empty room. She went farther inside. Maybe she'd find him in the shower. She'd join him and wash away all signs of the other man. But Mekai had left. Even his bag was missing.

Dropping to the bed, she grabbed the pillow, which still retained Mekai's scent.

She pulled it into her chest as sobs wracked her body. He'd abandoned her.

But why? Had he changed his mind, decided he didn't want a Terran girl like her?

The world spun around her. She couldn't go on like this, refusing to take clients or become a level Four. No, that option ended when she'd walked out of her last appointment. But without Mekai, she had nothing.

Help me!

She sucked in a breath. *Cyresse?*

Her mentor's cry came again. Those two monsters she'd left Cyresse with could kill her. She had to help, even if it meant her own death.

The door to the suite burst open. Garesh stood in front of her, his eyes bulging, his hair and clothes a frenzied mess. "Your client, he's mad, but, oh gods…. Nixie, it's

Cyresse. She was found crawling out of her domus. We need to get to the valetudenarium."

She wiped her eyes, then leaped from the bed. Nothing meant more to her now than the woman who'd raised her. Besides Garesh, she had no one else. She never had. "What happened?"

"I can only guess it was a client. They found her covered in blood, cuts all over her body. Oh gods, I should have convinced her to retire."

If she took the time to comfort Garesh, she would break down, too. Grabbing his hand, she bounded down the stairs and raced outside. As she ran, she tried to mind-speak with Cyresse, but once again failed. With so many tourists around, they had to dodge to the alleyways to reach the valetudenarium faster.

The tall building loomed in front of her. The valetudenarium was usually filled with tourists who'd pushed their bodies past their limits. What condition would she find Cyresse in? Would she lose someone else she loved? With Garesh still too distraught to tell her anything, she had to get in there and find out for herself.

Altrix rushed through the halls, traveling from patient to patient. In the waiting room sat Suavitas, soothing those worried about patients.

"Are you Nixie?"

She spun toward the firm, female voice. "I am."

"My condolences to you." The woman in blue scrubs placed a hand on her shoulder.

Nixie gasped. "What do you mean? What happened?"

"She lost so much blood." The altrix nodded to a young Suavito in the far corner. "When he found her, she was barely hanging on. We just couldn't save her."

"No." Her heart filled with dread. "I don't believe you. Let me see her."

"Follow me then." The altrix opened the sealed doors, ushering Nixie into the world beyond. Patients lay in beds attached to various tubes and monitors. The sexual energy zinging around the rest of the planet failed to penetrate this space.

Coming to an abrupt halt, the altrix glared at Garesh. "I told you last time, sir, you are not recorded as family and therefore must wait outside."

His frenzied gaze turned hard and focused. He gripped Nixie's hand with more strength than she'd expected from him. Through clenched jaws, he spoke. "The woman you claim as dead is my wife. I am her husband. Just ask our daughter here."

Husband? Daughter? What's going on?

The altrix fixed her steely stare upon her. "Is he your father?"

Nixie cocked her head to the side. They believed her, a Terran, to be the daughter of a level Four Suavita, but would not believe Cyresse to have a Schedarn husband, a Suavito at that?

At the same time, had the two of them really married? That would explain why Garesh frequented their house, only leaving to spend his nights elsewhere if Cyresse had clients. But why hadn't either of them told her?

"Well?"

The need to see Cyresse for herself remained her focus, and Nixie eyed the altrix. Garesh had as much right to see the body as she did. "Yes, he's my father. They adopted me after my parents abandoned me."

Setting on her way again, the altrix called over her shoulder. "Well then, let's go."

Traipsing farther into the hospital, Nixie hoped the altrix incorrect, that Cyresse remained alive. While Nixie longed to be something other than a Suavita, the profession was never supposed to lead to death.

❧ ☙

Mekai slammed his fist against the desk. "Where is Nixie?"

Two men stared back at him, the Schedarn man who'd booked his original appointment with her, and the Elikashe he'd seen her follow into his suite not long ago.

"I'd like to know the same thing, since she walked out on me." The Elikashe glared at him. "You're going to have to wait in line, buddy. She still owes me a blow job."

Mekai saw only red and slammed his fist into the Elikashe's nose. The man slapped his hands to his face, blood now spewing down his arms.

"Gentlemen!" the Schedarn cried. "There's no need for violence. This is a peaceful planet."

Mekai pivoted toward him. "I don't care if that *is* her job. No one talks about my wife-to-be like that."

"Ah, so you're the guy she's turning down clients for?" The Schedarn man strolled over and shook his hand, squeezing hard at the same time. "You'd better treat her right."

He clenched his jaw. "I will, but I can't find her. She went into that man's room, and I haven't seen her since."

"Well, she walked out on me." Accepting a towel from the Schedarn, the Elikashe held it to his nose and inched closer. "She was just about to give me a…she'd just finished my massage when she left the room crying, and never came back."

Gods, had she gone back to the room and found it empty? She'd think he abandoned her. How could he have been so irrational? This was her job, after all. She'd sworn she'd leave with him after tonight. But where could she have run off to? "Well, where is she?"

The Schedarn ignored him, dealing with the other man. "I'll give you a full refund and find you a replacement, on the house. She'll clean you up and tend to your needs. Go back to your room and she'll be there shortly."

When the Elikashe left, the other man sighed. "She's at the valetudenarium. Her mother's been murdered." Then he walked out of the room.

Murdered? She must be a wreck right now. First I'm not there for her, and then she finds out about her mother….

"And where is the vale... whatever?" Mekai called after the man, but his question went unanswered.

Mekai sprinted from the building. He would comb the entire planet to find her. He'd vowed he wouldn't leave without her by his side. And with his parents now on Schedar, he had even more reason to find her as soon as possible.

BEYOND REACH
CHAPTER TEN

"There was nothing we could do to save her." The altrix unzipped the body bag and exposed the corpse to Nixie. "She arrived covered in blood, scratches all over her body, and the left side of her face was bruised and swollen."

Nixie gulped, fighting back tears. Her mother was gone, the shell of the woman she'd known left behind. Although her body had been cleaned of the blood, nothing could hide the deep cuts across her chest—far from scratches—like some kind of sacrificial markings. Her left eye was barely visible under puffy blue skin. If only Nixie had stayed with Cyresse, she could have prevented this. Or maybe they'd both be dead, used and tossed aside like trash.

Garesh rushed to Cyresse, reaching into the bag and wrapping his arms around her like she was only sleeping. He kissed her forehead before rocking the body back and forth.

Nixie stood in the same spot, unable to stop him. She had no idea what to do, what to say. What was she supposed to do now? Was this what she could expect as a level Four? Would she be too high on ipsum to fight a client off, or to even care what they did to her?

Reeling back, Nixie prepared to run. She'd didn't want to reach the highest level, or perform as a Suavita at all.

"We trained together," Garesh said, making Nixie pause. He stroked Cyresse's hair. "We were each other's first sexual experience, and kept in contact over the years."

Garesh glanced over at her, tears in his eyes. "It got to the point where no matter how many clients we tended to, we could only think of each other. I managed to find a teaching position first. And I'd found other Suavitas for all of her regular clients. Your mother was supposed to join me in the classroom." He lowered the body back into the bag and kissed her forehead again. "This wasn't the way we'd planned it. This wasn't supposed to happen."

The urge to run dissipated, and she found herself in Garesh's arms, sobbing. Several minutes passed before she glanced up at him. "What are we supposed to do now?" She'd never had anyone she knew die. What would happen to Cyresse's body? To her domus?

Garesh pushed her back, out of the room and down the hall toward the main part of the valetudenarium. "You are going to leave this planet, be something else, anything other than a Suavita."

She heavied her feet, halting her retreat before Garesh could shove her out of the building. "What are you talking about? You want me to just leave? What are you going to do?"

"Nixie, from the time you were young, you have dreamed of so many things that are not possible on this planet, of falling in love, and having a family." He pointed to the door. "Go get those things."

She shook her head, her eyes burning from the tears. "But you and Cyresse had that here."

"And look what happened. Look where it left us. This is not a planet to raise children on. You need to leave."

What? She tried to duck past him, return to her mother's body, but he blocked her path. "Garesh, I have nothing beyond Schedar, no one to count on other than you."

"You have me."

Nixie spun around. Her heart stopped. "Mekai?"

Garesh stepped beside her and eyed the prince. "So, you're the one who's been taking up all of her time?"

"Yes." Mekai nodded, the confidence in his face vanishing in Garesh's presence.

"Do you love her?"

"With all my heart." Mekai glanced up at Garesh. "I asked her to marry me."

The man she considered a father turned to her. "And yet you're still here? Why didn't you go with him? Why didn't you say yes? This is what you've wanted all along."

"I did, but...." Torn between leaping into Mekai's arms and running the other direction, she remained in the same spot. "You didn't leave?"

He reached out for her. "No. I thought about it, but I couldn't. I love you too much. I was just so confused when I saw you with that man."

Pangs of guilt returned. "But I didn't—"

He closed the gap between them, pressing his finger to her lips. "I know." Leaning down, he kissed her, transporting her into a world where only the two of them existed. No disappointment. No death.

A throat cleared near them, yanking her back to reality. Her cheeks warmed. "Sorry. Mekai, this is my father, Garesh. He's the reason I cannot leave with you. Not now. Not after Cyresse's death."

Garesh clasped her shoulders. "I am not your father. With Cyresse gone, we are no longer family."

Nixie stopped breathing, shocked by the man's words. "What are you talking about? How can you say that?"

"Nixie, you walked out on a client. Therefore, you probably do not have a job to go back to. And with

Cyresse gone, you no longer have a home." He spun her around to face the door. "Leave. Get off the planet while you have the opportunity."

Her throat became tight while her heart broke. How had she lost everything in one day?

A hand touched her shoulder. "Nixie, I'm very sorry for your loss." Mekai lifted her chin until her gaze met his. "I can give you what you desire. I love you, and I want you to come with me. But, if you don't feel the same, I can take you anywhere you want to go. Anywhere."

She looked away, unwilling to acknowledge her feelings for the prince. Not when she hurt so much. Yet, she had no other choice but to go with him. The money she had already saved would only provide her a one way ticket away from Schedar. She'd have nothing left to live on, be forced to pleasure others again to survive.

After one last glance at Garesh, who turned his back to her, she grasped Mekai's hand and left the building. "Let's go."

BEYOND REACH
CHAPTER ELEVEN

Surveying the street before him, Mekai sighed with relief. His family was nowhere to be seen. Could he get back to Carbae without them finding him, or would they discover his whereabouts before he had the chance? He inspected the view once more before setting Nixie down and holding her by the hand. They had to reach his PSTV at the edge of Sturban as quickly as possible. If they made it to Carbae, surely his parents wouldn't turn her away.

"How do you think they're going to react when you bring me to meet them?" She chewed her lip and clasped his hand tight. "I mean, our cultures have been enemies for ages. What if they don't approve?"

The same thoughts had rolled around in his head during their entire time together, but he couldn't let her worry. He'd remain by her side, no matter where they were. "They're going to love you, because I love you. Nothing else matters."

He raced with her, hand in hand through the streets, toward the waiting spacecraft. He finally had his love, and he would never let her go. After so many star cycles, he could finally be happy living on Carbae. He only hoped she would be happy, too. He remained thankful Garesh had insisted Nixie leave the planet, made her see—albeit somewhat harshly—that leaving proved her best option. Yet, he yearned to take away her hurt, make her understand the man had only said those words to get her off planet. But, not until he had her safely in his PSTV.

"Well, well, well, look who I ran into again."

Mekai came to a grinding halt and grasped Nixie so she wouldn't fall over.

Madelia stood in their path, her arms crossed and feet spread apart. "And toting a Terran woman, none the less. What are your parents going to say about this?"

Nixie tucked herself behind him. Like she didn't already have enough to deal with without the woman he was supposed to marry showing up out of nowhere.

He sucked in a sharp breath. "What do you want this time?"

"Hmm, let's see. How about revenge?" His former betrothed smirked. "Because, as much as I am unbelievably happy with Ben, you still set me up. I would have gone along with your plan had I known, but no, you didn't trust me. And now I'm going to make you squirm."

Nixie whimpered as Madelia pulled her out into the open.

"Honestly, Mekai, I didn't expect you to consort with the enemy." She circled his lover, examining her. "I hope you're completely in love with him, because your life is about to take an unexpected twist. Trust me."

He couldn't stand the way Madelia glared at Nixie, and he clasped his future wife by the shoulders. "Madelia, I'd like you to meet Nixie. She is the woman who finally captured my heart, the woman I'm going to marry."

Nixie pressed against him, hiding her face in his chest.

Madelia whistled, halting all movement on the street. "Oh, Thornton! Please bring the king and queen here. I've found the prince."

Eyebrows furrowed, he clenched his fists. "You wouldn't. C'mon. She just lost her mother."

She grinned. "I just did. No one messes with me and gets away with it."

Mekai willed his feet to move, to escape his parents' scrutiny, even for Nixie to pull him away, but they both stood frozen to the spot.

With his gaze on the approaching entourage, bile rose in his stomach. *Oh shit.*

Nixie dared a glance at the prince's parents, the royal couple dressed in majestic garb that dragged along the ground, and hugged their round bodies. Was Mekai really their child? She didn't have time to ask, the pair only stopping to gather her and Mekai in their group before ushering them down the streets of Sturban.

"We cannot talk here," his mother said. "Everyone is watching."

When they finally halted, they stood on the steps of an elegant palace, one she'd never had the opportunity to visit.

Nixie followed Mekai through the great hall, dragging her feet, trying to delay officially meeting his parents. Even with his words of reassurance, the tension in his body revealed his misgivings.

What if the king and queen of Carbae disapproved of her? Would Mekai bow under their condemnation and leave her on Schedar? She hoped not, but couldn't be certain. She had nothing left but his offer, no one to go back to.

Mekai ground to a stop and grasped her hands in his. "No matter what happens in the next few minutes, I will always love you. If we can't be together on Carbae, we will go elsewhere. I will never leave you." Drawing her in for a kiss, he shuffled her against the wall.

All of her worry melted away, his hungry mouth weakening her. She had no time to register his movement before he yanked her into the ballroom, as she gasped for air after his kiss.

"Mother, Father!" He pulled her along behind him, and within moments, she stood before his parents, the royal couple of Carbae. Squeezing her hand, he took another step forward. "I'd like you to meet Nixie, my bride-to-be."

She froze as Mekai's mother gasped and slapped her hands over her mouth. His father examined her. "You brought a Terran before me? What were you thinking?"

The king's reaction felt like a fist slamming into her gut. Why did Mekai think this would work? If he hadn't held her to the spot, she would have bolted. Nothing could hurt worse than being denied love.

The queen stood. "Leandor, look at her. Don't you realize who she is?"

Leaning forward, he examined her. As he gasped, his blue face lost all color. "It can't be."

What did they mean? Her hands trembled, even with Mekai holding one. Mekai had promised to stay with her no matter what, but would he ever be happy without his parents' approval?

His father stood and inched toward her. He placed his hands on her arms. "It is you." His voice hitched. "You look just like your mother. Oh, Nadia, where have you been all these years?"

"No, Father, this is Nixie. She lives here, on Schedar. We're in love and going to get married."

Mekai's mother joined them, wiping away tears. "It's no surprise you love her. You two spent much of your second year together on Ubetron."

"What?"

Mekai's question echoed hers. "What's going on here?"

"Thornton," his father bellowed.

A stout Terran man scurried into the room, huffing to catch his breath. "Yes, Your Majesty?"

Terran? I thought Ubetrons and Terrans didn't get along? What is this man doing with the royal family?

"My son has returned," the king announced.

"I see, and I am most thankful." The man nodded, wringing his hands together.

"Yes, yes." The king waved his hand as if he was insignificant. "But look who he's brought with him."

Nixie went immobile under everyone's inspection. Who did they think she was? Did they somehow know her real parents? Would she be forced to face them? Her heart hammered in her chest, and she licked her dry lips.

"Impossible." Thornton circled her and Mekai. "I thought you were dead. If I would have known…."

She couldn't take the mystery any longer. "I'm not who you think I am. My name is Nixie and I was abandoned by my parents here on Schedar when I was a baby."

Thornton winced. "No, your parents love you very much, Nadia. My sister and her husband, your parents, were visiting Ubetron, forging an alliance between the two planets. You were kidnapped from the government building on my watch." He took her free hand. "Please forgive me. I only went to the washroom. When I returned, you were gone."

Taking a step back, he stared at the floor. "We looked everywhere for you. We thought they killed you. Oh, gods, why did I stop looking?"

No, this couldn't be. If she were someone else, then everything she'd believed her entire life was a lie. She wasn't abandoned, but stolen away from her parents? And she'd hated her parents her entire life.

She swallowed the lump in her throat. "I…."

Mekai wrapped his arms around her. "If she is someone I should know, how is it I've never heard you mention her name until now? I mean, I've had dreams about a Terran girl my entire life, but you told me I made her up, that she never really existed. Are you telling me now that I was betrothed to Nixie before Medalia?"

She lifted her head from the prince's chest and listened for their explanation. But when the queen scurried away sobbing, bile rose in Nixie's throat. What would happen to her now?

"Nadia? Nixie?" the king said. "Will you look at me, please?"

Stepping away from Mekai and toward the king, she braced to hear what he had to say.

"It was always too painful to talk about them before, but your parents were our closest friends back on Ubetron. When they lost you, everyone's lives turned upside-down. Sure, Thornton stepped away from you for a moment, but it was one of my people who took you. I shouldered the blame and fled, unable to face your parents or the rest of Ubetron." The king wiped a tear away. "Some came with me, such as your uncle, but life was never the same. If only we'd known where you were."

He paced in front of them. "We searched every nearby planet, halted all traffic in and out of the Petrogeous galaxy. No one had seen you." Coming to an abrupt halt, he spun on his heels and stared at her. "I'm so glad Mekai found you. I only wish it had been sooner."

Mekai joined her in front of the king and stared into her eyes. "I dreamed about you all the time, for as long as I can remember. We grew up together while I slept, fell in love. I didn't realize you existed in reality until I ran into you here. If I'd known you were here, I would have come sooner. Long ago."

But why didn't she remember him? No, the stories didn't jive. She remembered her parents leaving her behind on Schedar. They were Terrans, not anyone from Ubetron. Maybe Mekai's family did know her real parents and planned to hold her for ransom. And she'd fallen into their trap so easily.

With a huge grin, the queen stood in the doorway, gripping an object in her hands. "I have something I want you to see. Nadia, it's a picture of your parents."

Although part of her yearned to look, her feet never moved. She waited for the queen to come to her, and even then, she was afraid to gaze at the picture, relive the moment they walked away from her, their child.

"I've kept this picture with me for years." The queen held out a color imagescreen.

Nixie stared at the three people in the picture: a man, woman, and a baby. Blinking, she took in the couple again. "That's not my mom. Or my my dad."

Hands rubbed her back, not Mekai's, but the queen's. "Yes, they are. They're wonderful people who love you with all of their hearts."

Gazing up at the woman, she felt tears burning her eyes. "But... they're not the Terrans who brought me here, the ones who left me behind. Oh gods, was I really kidnapped?" Her knees wobbly, she took a seat and tried to process the information.

The queen sat beside her and set the imagescreen on Nixie's lap. "You were. Your parents would never have abandoned you."

Nixie lifted the screen and stared at the couple again. "Will you tell me about them?"

"I will. And we'll even contact them for you. It's about time we put our differences to rest." She squeezed her arm. "But later. We have a double betrothal ceremony to attend back on Carbae, followed by the biggest celebration ever. For Nadia, our future queen, is not dead, but very much alive."

Tears streamed down her face, even as she smiled. Mekai pulled her into his arms and snuggled his face into her neck. "I don't care if you're Nixie, or Nadia," he whispered. "I love you, and I'm going to marry you as soon as possible."

Grasping his shoulders, she jumped and wrapped her legs around his waist. An unbelievable joy radiated from deep inside. For the first time in her life, she knew who her parents were, that they hadn't abandoned her, and had a man who would do anything for her. No one would ever take that away.

⁂

As the freighter launched out the other side of the fold, towing his PSTV behind, Mekai held his sleeping wife-to-be in his arms. Leaving Schedar, she'd wept as he held her, until exhaustion took over. And now they were almost home, with a life together to look forward to.

He held her closer, but flashing red lights throughout the cabin interrupted his contentment. *What's going on?*

A crackle echoed through the communications system.

"We know you've got her!" The booming voice filled every corner of the room. "I want my daughter back right now."

Nixie stirred against Mekai, then sat up. "Daddy?"

"No, wait!" Mekai held her hand tight, glancing around for the source of the voice. "I found her living on Schedar. Come on board and we'll discuss what happened to Nixie." He'd just found the woman who'd haunted his dreams for many years. There was no way he was going to let her go.

"My daughter's name is Nadia." A Terran man appeared on the view screen. "And after you held her captive for so long, forced her to work as a sex slave, there is no chance of a discussion."

Jumping from his lap, Nixie rushed to the screen. "Daddy, it wasn't like that at all. I wasn't anybody's slave, and I just met Mekai."

"Nonsense," the king bellowed. "You are experiencing Stockholm syndrome. Nothing more."

Mekai's mother bustled in front of her. "You listen here, Nicolas Liberté. We used to be friends, and you know there is no way we would ever do such a thing to your daughter."

Nixie's father didn't blink, only stared harder. "I used

to believe so, Larabet. That is, until I found out you were on Schedar with my daughter in your custody."

"Dad!" Nixie pressed her hand to the screen. "Will you please listen? They rescued me. They had nothing to do with my disappearance."

"I wish I could believe you." The Terran man nodded to someone else on his own ship.

Nixie began to fade in front of him as though becoming invisible. Her father was beaming her off the ship. Mekai lunged for her, but fell through the empty space, landing on his chin. He waited for the pain. Instead, a cold rush filled him and his vision wavered. One second he saw his parents kneeling in front of him, and the next, a white room. Completely empty.

The cold quickly disappeared, replaced by the thunderbolt across his jaw. The metallic taste of blood covered his tongue. He must have bit it when he fell. With a groan, he rolled over and wiped his eyes. Where had he been transported to? A second glance around proved he was alone, stuck in some room with no furnishings. White walls and a clear front.

Terran men and women dressed in the same multi-green uniform walked past, none of them giving him a sideways glance. Could they see him? He stood, but nearly fell back to the ground, his head spinning as if he'd rolled down the snow-covered hills of Carbae.

He stumbled toward the closest wall, trying to steady himself until the sensation passed. By the time his vision cleared, another person had entered the room. No one he recognized, but the Terran scowled at him. If the man believed the same lie as Nixie's parents, Mekai dreaded what he had to say.

"Where is Nixie? I demand to see her." What had they done to her if they were keeping him locked up here?

"It does not matter. You will never see her again." He said the words so matter-of-factly Mekai's stomach twisted.

"We're to be married. I love her, and she loves me." Just when he thought he finally had everything he'd always wanted, she was stolen from him.

"Did you or did you not pay to have sex with Nadia?"

"Yes, I mean, no. It wasn't like that."

The man gave him a hard stare. "Then how was it?"

"I paid to receive an erotic massage from a Suavita. I didn't know it was Nixie, I mean Nadia, until she arrived." Though he couldn't imagine what his stay would have been like if anyone else had arrived in his room. He likely would have spent the rest of his time on Schedar searching for her.

"So, you paid to have sex with any slave. It didn't matter which one."

"A massage, and they're not slaves." He would never force himself on anyone. He enjoyed giving pleasure as much as receiving it, but he wasn't about to share that information with his captor.

"Are they not drugged? Are they not told who they are to have sex with regardless of whether they want to or not?"

"No, it's not like that there. Nixie told me that some of her friends left the planet. They have a choice as to whether they want to enter into the erotic arts or not."

"Really?" The man furrowed his brows. "So, you're saying Nadia wanted to have sex with all those people. That's funny considering she told us about the slavers your parents dropped her off at, how the man raped her before forcing her to be with others, and how his supposed wife was killed by other slavers after they raped her."

Mekai cringed at the false accusation toward Garesh. He'd been instrumental in convincing Nixie to leave Schedar, would never have hurt her. "You lie."

He clenched his fists, the sickening twist of his gut making his blood boil. Fighting the man in front of him wouldn't win him any favors, but he couldn't stop himself from lunging forward and punching him in the face. Only he missed. Or rather, his fist only met air as it traveled through the figure. The man they'd sent to interrogate him wasn't really there. Just a hologram.

"Temper, temper, boy. I'll have to let the king know you not only raped his daughter, but you also beat her. I'm sure your punishment will be swift and just."

"No," Mekai screamed as the figure vanished. He ran to the clear wall and pounded on it with his fists. He had to get out of the room. Then he had to find Nixie and get off the blasted ship before they punished him for lies they insisted as the truth. But, the more he banged against the wall, the more hope he lost. No one heard him. Not one person walking past turned to look at him. He was locked in a soundproof box with no one to hear the truth, convince Nixie's father what really happened to his daughter on Schedar.

BEYOND REACH
CHAPTER TWELVE

Nixie screamed, trying to shove the burly men out of her way to get a glance of Mekai. Her mother had let information slip about her fiancé being transported onto the ship after her, but no matter how hard she tried to sneak past her guards, she hadn't been able to find him. Having no recollection of the layout of the ship didn't help either. How she wished Mekai's parents hadn't contacted her own, simply took her back to Carbae where she could marry Mekai and live on Ubetron's moon with the man she loved. She didn't know the people who claimed to be her parents. And all they'd done was take her away from the man she loved.

One of the guards grabbed her shoulders, and out of instinct, she kneed him in the groin—a move Garesh had told her to use if she ever felt threatened. He was the man she thought of as a father, the one who'd taught her to survive. The guard released her as he doubled over, but the second one caught her and held her to his side, no chance for her to try the same move.

"I don't know why you fight us," her supposed father

said as they walked down the ramp of the ship. "That Ubetron is no good for you. You've been brainwashed to believe you love him."

Quite the opposite. She never believed love possible until she'd met Mekai. But, arguing had already proved futile. Her parents refused to believe Mekai's family had nothing to do with her kidnapping. "Just take me to my room."

She studied every corridor they passed through, every single part of the castle they traveled, waiting for the moment she was left alone. The sooner the better, because she needed to find Mekai and escape from the planet called Earth.

Her parents led her through a set of double doors, the guards never leaving her alone with them.

"This is your room." Her mother grasped her hand and pulled her into the monstrous space, a room larger than Cyresse's entire domus back on Schedar. "You have a bathroom in here, a walk-in closet, and you can contact anyone in the castle from this console over here." The woman led her over to a desk with a com unit built in, buttons with various unfamiliar names lighting up the screen. "One of your guards will let you know when dinner is served."

"So, I'm a prisoner here?" They might as well have put her with Mekai. At least she would have someone familiar around.

"No, not at all." Her father stepped into the room and closed the double doors behind him. "You have everything you need here, and until you become familiar with the castle, it's best you stay here for your own safety."

"And when do I get to see Mekai?"

The man spun to stare at her, his eyes hard, as if ready to shoot fire. "You don't."

Nixie darted around her parents toward the door. She slammed into the wood blocking her way, expecting it to burst open, but it didn't budge. She was locked in for who-knew-how-long, stuck in a strange room with strange people on a strange planet. Not at all where she wanted or needed to be.

"Have a look around." Her father held a hand out and spun in a circle, as if showing her the room all over. "You will find it to be everything you've ever dreamed of."

"You keep telling yourself that." Nixie shoved past the man and flopped onto her bed. The mattress had more give than she was used to. She held back a scream, afraid the bed would swallow her up.

"I get it. You want us to leave you alone." Her mother patted her leg. "Take time to get used to your new room. I'll be sure to have someone escort you down for dinner."

She wanted to say, "Don't bother." But, that might have led to more conversation when all she wanted was to be by herself for a change. She needed time to plan hers and Mekai's escape.

At the click of the door, she released a sigh. They'd finally left her alone. Now, she needed to find a way out.

Putting his hands out did nothing to stop Mekai's fall. He jarred his right shoulder and rolled to his side on the cold, dirt-packed floor. Metal doors clanged shut, and the men who'd thrown him inside walked away without a word, as if they'd tossed away nothing more than trash. Though with the soured stench, he wouldn't be surprised if garbage rotted somewhere nearby.

In the dim light, he couldn't see beyond the metal bars of his new prison. Using his left arm, he pushed onto his feet to get a better view of his new accommodations. The minute amount of light came from a small window carved out of the back concrete wall. If he managed to yank the bars out, he wouldn't be able to fit through the space. Tools might help him chisel out a larger hole, but the grime-covered plastic bucket and the stained mattress pad with cotton pouring out of a variety of holes wouldn't help. How he wished to be back in the sterile room on the ship rather than this rundown prison. Had they left him there to die? Or would he meet up with his interrogator again?

Mekai sat in a corner, his back against the hard wall rather than the bars. The dampness didn't bother him, only reminded him of home, the place he was supposed to be with Nixie as his wife. Straightening his legs and leaning his head back, he closed his eyes. Picturing his fiancé, whether smiling at him as they sat on the grassy hill, or face flushed after he'd brought her to orgasm came easy. But, would he ever get the chance to see her again?

BEYOND REACH
CHAPTER THIRTEEN

Nixie stared at the now-cold food on her side table. Regardless of how much her stomach rumbled, she would not eat it. After she'd refused the guard's request to join her parents for dinner, he mother had brought up some of the most beautiful food she had ever seen served on a plate. But she would starve before she put any of it in her mouth. Or not until they agreed to let her see Mekai.

No matter how many times she'd insisted his family had nothing to do with her kidnapping, that the people who left her on Schedar were Terran, they turned a deaf ear to her, confident in their own beliefs of what happened to her all those years ago.

The sun had already disappeared below the horizon, covering the castle in darkness. But in her room, a few lamps had flickered to life on their own, as if sensing the absence of light. Not ideal for sleeping, yet the glow didn't stop her from leaning back on her bed and imagining Mekai there with her. She yearned for his arms around her, his whispered words of love. Would she ever see him again?

A faint knock drew her from her thoughts. She sat up, but did not cross the room to answer the door. She'd had enough of her parents and the guards they'd posted outside her bedroom for one day.

The knock came a second time, and once again, she remained on her bed. At the click of the door handle turning, her heart sped up. Nixie clenched her jaw as the door creaked open. Why couldn't they leave her alone?

"Nadia? Are you awake?"

That name again. She'd grown up as Nixie, and upon finding her, everyone on Earth expected her to answer to a new name. Yet, she hadn't recognized the male voice who'd called her. Did she have new guards for the night? Did they expect sex because she'd grown up on Schedar?

She shuffled under the blankets and pulled them tight to her neck, keeping her eyes on the door.

"Nadia?" A figure stepped into her room. "Na-Nixie? Please answer me. I really need to talk to you."

She opened her mouth then closed it again. As much as she wanted to find out who had entered her room, she worried he was sent by her parents to spy.

"Fine then." He shuffled back toward the door. "I was going to show you where our parents are keeping the man you came with, but if you don't want my help...."

Our parents? She had a brother? And he knew where they were keeping her fiancé? "Wait." She threw off the blankets and leaped from the bed. "I'm awake. Please help me find Mekai."

The man rushed toward her and held out his arms as if to embrace her. But Nixie backed away. Just because he offered to help didn't mean he would, or that she could trust him.

"Who are you?" She eyed him with caution, tried to ignore the familiar upturned nose and almond-shaped eyes she saw in the mirror every day. "How can you help me?"

"I am your brother, Alexander." He stared at her, his

eyes shifting focus as if he didn't believe what he saw. "I thought I would never see you again. I thought they had killed you, and expected them to murder me in my sleep. But, you're here." He touched her cheek then quickly pulled his hand away. "I'm sorry. But, you're being here is like a dream come true."

"Well, it's been a nightmare for me." Guilt flooded her. She shouldn't be rude to someone who might be able to help her. "Sorry, but who were you talking about before when you said you thought they'd killed me?"

"Oh, Luca and Rosa Scordato." A flash of fury washed over his face. "They are the ones who kidnapped you from Ubetron. When they returned to Earth without you, I thought they'd killed you and left your body floating in space."

A tingle shot from her chest down to her limbs. Finally, she knew who'd taken her. But, why did her father and mother believe Mekai's parents responsible? "Why didn't you tell our parents? Why do they hold Mekai in a prison cell when he's not guilty of anything?"

"I did." He sat on the bench at the foot of her bed. "Before Luca and Rosa threatened to kill me in my sleep, I did tell our parents. But, they didn't believe me. They refused to believe their friends would steal their daughter away."

"Friends? I would hardly call them that if they deceived our parents." Nixie placed her palm on her forehead. "What do they look like? I remember the Terrans who left me on Schedar. If I could identify them, I could prove you right."

Alexander jumped from the bench. "We don't have time for that right now. The guards will only be unconscious for a few more minutes. We must leave now if you want to see Mekai."

"They're unconscious?" She peeked beyond her door to where the guards were supposed to be stationed. "What did you do to them?"

"It doesn't matter." Her brother glanced down the hall in both directions before pulling her into the corridor. "If we don't go now, we'll never get another chance."

She spotted the guards slumped on the floor on either side of her room. Definitely out of it, but not dead as their chests rose and fell with breath. "Fine, let's go." She followed him through the castle, heading farther down and away from her room. She quickly became lost, the trek seemingly longer than when she'd been taken to her quarters. Alexander would have to guide her back to her room, or hopefully, out of the castle entirely with Mekai by her side.

He brother suddenly stopped and held his hand up. "We're here."

Nixie glanced around the stone hallway. Torches lined the walls, but when she placed her hand on the stone, she felt it's wetness. She shivered as a chill crept through her. Where was Mekai? Three openings lay ahead, and she hoped to find him behind one of them. Or maybe she'd been led into a trap, trusted the guy who claimed to be her brother too easily with the hope of seeing her fiancé again.

Alexander placed his finger on his lips then leaned ahead and peeked through the closest archway. When he came back to her, his face had paled. "He's in there, but he doesn't look good."

Mekai leaned against the cold wall, sucking in air through his teeth. After the multitude of slashes he'd received across his back, every position he'd tried to make himself comfortable only enhanced the sting of his punishment. Punishment for telling the truth. No matter how many times he'd told Nixie's father and the man with the whip that his parents had nothing to do with her disappearance, they refused to believe him. He'd rejoiced when they finally left. Yet the open wounds on his skin still brought him torture. Regardless of the pain, he didn't regret meeting Nixie. His short time with her—even if that's all they had—proved the most fulfilling days of his life. He only hoped she found happiness on Earth without him.

A shuffle from beyond the entrance caught his attention. Had his torturer returned for another round? Mekai lolled his head to the side and closed his eyes, hoping his visitor would assume him asleep and leave.

When his visitor rattled the bars of his cage, he sneaked a quick glance. Yet neither the king nor the man with the whip stood outside his prison. Maybe he had fallen asleep, because the most beautiful woman in the universe stared at him.

"Mekai?" She gripped the bars, reaching one hand through, toward him. "Are you okay?"

"Nixie?" He struggled onto his feet, unsure whether to believe his eyes. "Is it really you?"

Even in the faint light, he caught the reflection of her tear as it slid down her cheek. Sucking in a deep breath, he ignored the pain as he made his way to the bars. Placing his hand on her cheek, he wiped away the tear. "You shouldn't be down here." She didn't need to see what had been done to him.

Pulling away, she moved to the door and rattled the bars. "I have to get you out of here. We need to leave."

As much as he yearned to escape with her, he'd already tried every possible way to break out he could conceive. "It's not going to happen. I'm stuck in here until they kill me or I die of starvation."

"No!" She shook the bars harder, the whimper in her voice breaking his heart. He wished they had a future together, but it wasn't meant to be.

Reaching through the bars, he pulled her toward him until their lips met. He kissed her with everything he had, hoping she'd never forget their last moment of intimacy. Then he shoved her away. "Now leave. Go, and don't ever come down here again."

"Mekai." Her voice cracked. "How can you say that?"

More tears, but he couldn't let them change his mind. "You need to move on. We were never meant to be."

Footfalls from the hallway echoed into the room. Then he heard the distinctive whistle of his torturer. His stomach sank.

"Hide." He pointed to some crates on the other side of the room. If the man with the whip caught Nixie down there, his life was over, and he dreaded what his torturer would do to her.

BEYOND REACH
CHAPTER FOURTEEN

Nixie dove behind the wooden boxes. As much as it tore at her heart to leave Mekai at the mercy of the person who had broken his skin and left him bleeding, she wouldn't find a way to get her fiancé out if she was caught.

The footsteps grew louder, and something sharp hit the ground. A whip. Whoever had entered the room planned to hurt Mekai again. Where was Alexander? Had her brother brought the torturer down? Or maybe the visitor had already killed her brother, just as the man who'd kidnapped her had threatened to do to him.

Nixie dared a peek. The torturer faced away from her, so she couldn't confirm or deny whether he was the one who'd abducted her. Reaching into his pocket, the man pulled out a key and slid it into the lock on the prison cell. The door clicked open, and the man let himself inside, dragging his whip along with him.

"You ready to confess yet, Deadskin?"

Nixie covered her mouth to hide her gasp. She'd heard the derogatory term for Ubetrons before, but such words were punishable by law if spoken on Schedar.

"Never." Her fiancé stood up straight with his hands behind his back, as if he hadn't already felt the bite of the whip. "I cannot confess to something I didn't commit."

"Wrong answer."

The whip hit him hard, drawing blood in a straight line across his chest.

Nixie swallowed a cry. She couldn't bear to watch the man hurt Mekai, but she needed to know his identity.

"Let's try this again." The man drew the piece of leather across his palm. "Admit that your parents kidnapped Nadia and took her to Schedar to work as a sex slave, and that you raped her until she believed she loved you."

Mekai rushed the man, screaming as he lunged. But an ill-placed boot stopped him. He crashed to the ground.

The man lifted his whip. "There's no escape." The leather came down across Mekai's back, chewing up his already bloody skin. The man stood on the back of his neck, pushing Mekai's face into the ground. "I don't care if you did it. You will confess, or you will die."

Bile rose to Nixie's throat as the whip hit Mekai again. Her fiancé jerked with every strike as they came faster and harder until he ceased all movement. Tears streamed down her face. She couldn't watch anymore, couldn't bear to see the love of her life killed. Pushing up from the ground, she yelled, "Stop!"

The man with the whip turned to face her, and she recognized the scar on his lip and his crooked, hooked nose instantly.

"Well, well, well, if it isn't the tainted princess herself."

"Leave him alone, Luca." Nixie left the safety of the boxes and approached the man she had long believed to be her father, the one who'd left her on Schedar. "Let Mekai go. You know his family is not responsible for my kidnapping."

"Ah, so you know my name." He drew the piece of

leather across his palm. "That means you either have a great memory, or your brother told you. Seeing as you somehow managed to get past your guards, I would bet Alexander is somehow involved. I should have taken him out long ago."

"I remember you." She stared him down, hoping to keep his mind off her fiancé and her brother. If Alexander hadn't been caught, he could still help her and Mekai. If he hadn't abandoned them. "You and your wife took me to Schedar. You left me in a bar. All by myself."

"Yes, but do you remember what I said to you all those years ago, when I left you to rot on that filthy planet?" Luca exited the barred cell, his eyes in slits, reminding her of kans—creatures on Schedar that slithered around on their tiny legs. When he grabbed the back of her hair, she winced.

"I told you..." He learned into her ear. "...that making a deal with the Deadskins would bring ruin to our planet and if you ever returned to Earth, I would kill you."

"You will do no such thing!" A loud voice boomed, and Nixie jumped back.

Luca's face paled, and when her father entered the room, the torturer glanced around as if looking for an escape route.

"Guards, arrest Luca Scordato. When he is secure, hunt down his wife and lock her in the cell next door. And take that poor Ubetron boy to the infirmary." Her father tightened his jaw. "I guess I owe his parents and apology."

Finally, her father knew the truth. But would Mekai's parents torture her for what had been done to their son? Would they blame her because Mekai fell in love with her?

Men and women in multi-green uniforms rushed to and fro, the room becoming a flurry of activity.

The two guards stationed to her room had recovered and dragged Mekai's limp body from the cell before shoving Luca inside. Nixie rushed to her fiancé's side, unsure if he'd survived that last round of torture. But two women in white uniforms shoved her away before they loaded him onto a stretcher and carried him away.

"Is he okay?" she called out, but received no answer. When she tried to follow, her father caught her arm and held her back.

"Our best doctors will work on him. Until I find out more, you will stay with me. We have a lot to discuss."

She jerked from his hold. "I have already told you everything, but you chose to believe your supposed friend over your own family." Turning from her father, she raced out of the room, searching for Mekai. But the stretcher and the women in white were gone. She had no idea if he'd survived the torture. If only she'd stood up sooner.

Mekai clawed his way toward the light, struggling to reach the surface. Though he swore he was underwater, he could still breath. When he emerged, heat penetrated every part of his body, taking away his chill. He opened his eyes to find himself back in the white room of the ship belonging to Nixie's parents. Only he wasn't alone. A woman stood nearby, her loose-fitting white outfit dotted with blood. His? Pulses of electric pain raced across his back. He rolled onto his side, trying to escape the torture.

"Whoa there, Mekai." The woman rushed to his side and yanked steel bars up in front of his face. "We don't want you falling out of bed."

Bed? The Terrans had actually given him a bed rather than making him sleep on the floor like an animal?

Bustling away from him, the woman returned with a cup filled with a clear liquid. "It's purified water. Drink some, and then we'll talk."

Talk? No. He'd done enough talking. And no one believed him anyway. He turned his head.

"Fine." She pulled a metal holder from the bars and set the cup inside. "Then just listen to what I have to say."

Sounded like a great idea. If only someone had shown him the same courtesy on Earth.

Without warning, the top half of his bed began to lift up, making it impossible for him to remain on his side. He rolled onto his back, only to feel the fiery pain again. Sucking in air through his teeth didn't help, but it seemed to get the attention of the woman in the room with him.

"Oh, sorry." She rolled her thumb across some tube. And that's when he noticed it was attached to the back of his hand under a bandage.

He grabbed the tube to yank it out, but stopped when the pain disappeared, replaced with a cold sensation. Much more bearable. "What did you do to me?"

"I upped your dosage of pain medication." She released the tube, and stared at him. "It should make you more comfortable and help your body heal after what that asshole, Luca did to you. He fooled us all." Holding a hand over her eyes, she drew in a deep breath before turning her back to him. "Nadia will be in soon to see you."

Nixie was on the ship with him? Going back to Carbae? Maybe something good would come out of the torture he'd received. But would she be accepted, or receive the same punishment he had on Earth? He wouldn't allow it. He'd rather receive a thousand lashes than to see her experience any bit of pain.

Mekai's eyelids suddenly became heavy. As much as he desired to see his fiancé again, he couldn't help but succumb to the demands of his body.

At the gentle press of someone's finger on the back of his hand, Mekai pulled away. He didn't want the woman in white to remove the medication, needed another hit as he opened his eyes. Instead of the woman he expected, he laid eyes on his beautiful fiancé. Though the lines across her forehead made his gut clench. He braced for bad news.

"Hi." She folded her hands in front of her instead of touching him, a sure sign something had changed between them. "I'm glad you're awake. Are you okay? Do you need more pain medicine? The nurse... altrix showed me how."

He nodded, too afraid a single word would lead to her saying what she had to, then leaving him forever.

Nixie pressed a button on the tube then reached out to him, but never made contact. Was she really ending things after all they'd been through?

Thrusting his arm out, he grabbed her hand and placed it on his chest. Over his heart. He refused to let her go so easily.

"A lot has changed since we left Schedar." A tear slipped down her cheek, a sure sign of their doomed future.

He shook his head. "Nothing's changed." His words came out in a cracked whisper, but he didn't want to lose her. "I love you."

More tears fell. "How can you love me after what my family did to you? I hate them for it, for not believing you and me, and especially Alexander."

Alexander? He recognized the name, but how? Was she leaving him for that man? He'd fight for her even from the bed if he had to. Kissing the back of her hand, he repeated his words. "I love you."

She chewed on her lips then sighed. "I don't think it will be that easy for us. My dad and Alexander have traveled ahead to Carbae, but I don't think your parents will be so quick to forgive."

Mekai released her hands and blinked hard. She was making excuses. "You want to marry Alexander." Perhaps she'd told him while he slept, the reason he'd recognized the name.

"No!" She scrunched up her face. "Alexander is my brother. My older brother. He was with us the day Luca took me, and tried to tell my parents. But, they didn't believe him either."

So, she worried about his parents, what they'd think of her because of the treatment he'd received. It didn't matter. He didn't care what anyone thought. Reaching over the bars of his bed, he cupped her side. "We don't have to live on Carbae, but we will be together, and we'll get married. I promise."

BEYOND REACH
CHAPTER FIFTEEN

The ship came to a sudden halt, sending Nixie flying off the chair in Mekai's hospital room. When it accelerated in the opposite direction, worry twisted through her stomach. They had almost reached Carbae. Had something happened to her father and brother? She rushed down the hallways in onto the bridge. "What's the matter? Where are we going?" she asked the captain.

The second-in-command shrugged. "We're heading to Ubetron. That's where your father told us to meet him."

Ubetron. Had he fled there after Mekai's parents had threatened his life? What about Alexander? He didn't deserve any sort of punishment. But neither had Mekai. They'd both told the truth all along.

Glancing at the view screen, she spotted a small planet in the distance.

"How far away are we?" If she could get Mekai to an escape pod, they could land separately from the ship before escaping to another planet far away from both their families and her past. Exactly what they should have done when Mekai asked her to leave Schedar with him the first time.

"Maybe thirty minutes, if that."

Nixie bolted from the bridge, back to her fiancé's room. They had only a matter of minutes before the ship reached the planet's atmosphere, making any pod escape impossible.

Dashing into Mekai's room, she grabbed a crew suit and tossed it at him. "Get dressed. We've got to go right now." Thank goodness the doctor had already removed all the tubes attached to his body.

"Why? What happened?" He shucked off the gown, making her wish she had more time to touch his muscular body, make love to him as she had on Schedar. But his wince when putting on the suit reminded her of his scars and their urgency to get off the ship.

"We're not going to Carbae now. My father redirected the captain to Ubetron."

His face drained of color, affirming her doubts about their change in destination.

She grabbed his hand before he had the chance to zip the suit over his chest. "We can leave in a pod before we reach the atmosphere, land faraway before hitching a ride to Gophandoreon, or some other distant planet."

"Good plan." Mekai sped up, keeping pace with her around corners, and up lifts. If not for the time she'd spent wandering the halls while she'd waited for him to regain consciousness, she wouldn't know where to go.

The pods were in sight when the cold tingle of a transporter beam gripped her body. She reached for Mekai, never wanting to be separated from him again.

Mekai stared at the leaders in front of him, two men and one woman he never expected to be found on the same planet, let alone all three within feet of each other. Gripping Nixie's hand, he willed the sight to be a dream.

No, it was the beginning of his worst nightmare. Because sworn enemies never smiled in the presence of one another.

Laravette, the leader of Ubetron stepped forward, holding out her hand. "Welcome home, Mekai."

Home? Although he'd once lived on the planet, he didn't remember anything—except for the visions of Nixie—before Carbae. He ignored the leader's gesture and glanced at his father. "Wanna tell me what's going on here?"

Nixie squeezed closer to him, seeming as anxious to be there as he was. "Don't trust them."

He wouldn't, especially her father. How could his own dad stand beside the man without wanting to seek revenge. Though Mekai refused to let anyone near his fiancé.

"Mekai...." His father removed his crown and tossed it away, a sure sign the situation wasn't real. "There's no need to be afraid. No one is going to hurt you anymore."

He wished he could believe the man. "Why are you here? What's going on?"

Laravette's smile faded, as if ready to reveal the nightmare they had entered. "A treaty has been signed between all of our worlds."

A treaty. And he was part of it if she was welcoming him home. Tenebrae, if only he and Nixie had had the chance to escape. "And?"

"Carbae is now a territory of Ubetron," the former king said. "The people are free to travel and move between as they wish. Those leaving Carbae will receive assistance in finding employment and living accommodations here. It's a process that will take time, but it will benefit all involved." His father stared down, suddenly interested in his shuffling feet. "As part of the treaty, you will live here, too."

"No." None of them could make decisions for him. Their parents had been the cause of this mess in the first place.

Nicolas, the last to advance toward them, placed a hand on his daughter's arm. "You will live here, too, Nadia, as an act of good faith. A large house had already been secured for you both. But first—"

"Wait." Nixie glanced around. "Where's Alexander? What did you do to him?"

"I'm right here." A man not much older than Mekai strolled forward with the same raven-colored hair and upturned nose as his fiancé. He was hand-in-hand with a woman about the same age he recognized from Carbae. "The treaty is a good thing if you'll just listen without interrupting them. It's what should have happened before Luca took you. Only dad has some extra debts he had to pay."

Nicolas nodded, holding his hands behind his back. "I can't say enough how truly sorry I am for what happened to you."

Mekai glanced from one person to the next—including Thornton who stood in the crowd—waiting for one of them to break his bubble of hope. Did he and Nixie actually have a chance at a life together without running from their families?

"You will be married tomorrow," Laravette announced. "And during the broadcast of your union, the treaty will also be announced."

Nixie squeezed his hand, and when he looked upon her, she nodded, smiling for the first time since they'd left Schedar. "Yes," she whispered.

"Okay then." All his objections scattered. If his fiancé agreed, he would, too. "Let's get ready for this wedding."

Nixie stared in the mirror, taking in the white satin and lace dress she'd been married in. So plain compared to the extravagant outfits worn by the crowd at her wedding. Yet, they had all told her how beautiful she looked, and shared their excitement about the new treaty.

Her father refused to tell her what extra obligations the treaty meant for him, but she couldn't dwell on something he'd agreed to.

Slipping off the dress and her undergarments, she wore nothing but the gold band Mekai had placed on her finger, a symbol not only of his love and commitment, but the uniting of their people after so many years of angst. And all it took was one chance meeting.

She opened the door and found her new husband lying naked on their bed. As if truly seeing Mekai for the first time, she shuffled to the bed, her cheeks blazing hot. Even with all the muscles proving his strength, she knew the sweet man that lay underneath. She couldn't imagine being with anyone else.

Getting up from the bed, he stood in front of her. He tucked her hair behind her ears then pulled her hips until she was pressed tight against him. So close, she barely remembered to breathe, her head spinning. Yet, she never wanted to be anywhere else.

"Hello, my wife." He kissed her with gentle passion as he spun her around. When the back of her knees hit the bed, he laid her on the sheets. "I've been waiting a long time for this."

"Yes, we haven't made love since on Schedar." Her body didn't forget his touch, his gentle strokes making her thrust into the air, craving his sweet invasion.

"No, that's not what I mean." He slid his fingers between her legs, into her already evident arousal. She couldn't help herself with his touch.

"Then what do you mean?" She slid up the bed and spread out for him, too impatient for his foreplay.

"My dreams." He lay over her, and lined the head of his cock to her entrance. "I've dreamed about you for as long as I can remember, about being with you, loving you." He touched his lips to hers, drawing her into his kiss. But when she grabbed his ass to push him into her, he pulled away. "And now we're finally together. For good. My dreams have come true."

He slid into her, filling her body, mind, and soul. Their union was sanctified. And no one could ever separate them again

Her plans changed in an instant…

Once finished college, Leanne intended to take over her family dairy farm, let her father retire and finally take a vacation. After one tragic night, her dreams go up in smoke. She loses the ability to do the most basic of things.

And brought him closer…

Jake, the farm hand who lives down the road, refuses to let Leanne give up on her goals. He remains by her side throughout her healing. But, when he confesses his true intentions, their friendship takes a drastic turn.

If only she'd known before she lost her arm.

ACCIDENTAL ROMANCE
CHAPTER ONE

Leanne ducked, trying to avoid the apple flying toward her. With its speed, it stirred her hair, but she avoided contact. Instead, the fruit smashed against the wall then fell to the floor, a mess of brown pulp and skin. She stood and glared at the source of the flying object. "Jake, you're such an ass."

He grinned at her from across the milking parlor, tossing into the air another rotten apple he must have grabbed when he put the cows out to pasture. "You'd better be nice to me, LA, if you want me to do your chores tonight."

With a huff, she rolled her eyes. "Whatever. I wasn't the one who threw fruit at your head." She cursed him several times a day for such pranks. Often he'd tossed her in the manure pile or turned the pressure hoses on her. He lived with his family down the road, and if their parents weren't such good friends, she would have told her father to fire Jake years ago.

"What do you have planned for tonight anyway?" He sauntered toward her, gripping the other apple so hard, she expected pulp to squeeze between his fingers. "Going out with your *boyfriend*?"

She cringed, hating how he mocked her with the word. "Jealous, much?"

Taking a step back, he scowled. "You wish. Why should I care who you date? You're a grown woman."

"I'm glad you noticed." She reached down for a piece of straw and poked him in the chest with it. "So, why is it such a problem?"

He shrugged his shoulders, his expression suddenly indifferent. "I think you can do better."

She poked him again. "What, like you?"

He leaned closer, his face only an inch from hers. His musky scent overpowered the sweet stench of the barn and filled her senses. If he hadn't been a constant pain in her ass, she might have thought he was going to kiss her.

"In your dreams."

Should have known. She chuckled and tapped his cheek a couple times with her palm. "I can honestly say you have never been in any of my dreams. Not even my nightmares. And if you must know, I'm going out with my friends from college." She spun around and called over her shoulder. "*Tomorrow* I'll be with Scott." She headed out of the barn. A field of wheat waited for her, and she had to harvest it before she went out.

Leanne slammed the door of the bright green tractor then slid to the ground. *Stupid auger.* Yet another delay in her chores. She hadn't seen her friends since she'd graduated from the business administration program and moved back home three months before. But if her day kept going to shit, she wouldn't see them at all.

All she had to do was get the damn grain in the corrugated bin. She hoped things would run smoother when she officially took over the farm than they had today.

First, the cows had gotten loose after Jake had put them out to pasture. Some punk kid had cut the chain on the gate, and the herd of course found the opening and made a run for it. Thank God, Jake and his four-wheeler had been there to round them up. And then the freakin' auger had a bearing seize, making it impossible to get the wheat up into the grain bin. She'd had to head to the farm a mile and a quarter over to borrow an ancient version, and now the piece of shit was jammed. *Fuck!*

She didn't bother to turn the tractor off. She could probably shake the clump of grain loose and be back to filling the bin in minutes. As she stormed over, she rolled up her sleeves and grabbed a stick in case the blockage needed some extra oomph to break it down.

Her phone vibrated against her leg. She plucked it from her pocket and stared at her boyfriend's smiling face. *Scott.* At least he could brighten her day.

She stuck the cell to her ear. "Hey, babes. What's up?"

"Are we still on for tomorrow?"

"Of course. I'll be there around noon after I finish morning chores." She hadn't seen him all week, having been too tired to drive into the city every night after taking care of the farm.

"Good, 'cause I miss you."

"I miss you, too, but I've gotta go. Stupid machine here is jammed."

"You know, if you moved into the city with me—"

"Scott, we're not having this conversation again." Living there for two years to attend college had been stressful enough; she was a country girl through and through. While she doubted he would ever join her on the farm, she planned to enjoy their time together while they lasted. "I said I'll see you tomorrow. We'll have fun." *Sweaty fun.*

"No, Leanne, we *are* having this conversation. You can't keep darting around it."

She groaned. She didn't have time for this shit. "Can't

we do this tomorrow?"

"No. What's the point of me setting a whole day aside for you if we have no future?"

Clutching the phone, she sighed. *Not this argument again.* "Well, I'm sorry if I'm such an inconvenience, interrupting all your precious plans, but I wasn't the one begging you to come over all week, was I? And it's not as if you ever come to visit me."

"You know I hate the country."

"Well, I hate the city. And so you know, I'm never going to live there. Ever." She'd had enough of catering to him, and he'd caught her on a really bad day. If their relationship wasn't going to work both ways, she didn't want to continue. Might as well set him straight now.

"Then I guess we're through. You were a nice fuck while you lasted."

She vibrated with anger. *Mother fucker!* Should have known he'd be an ass. All those wasted months. She could have been focused on something else—like sleep—rather than making him happy. Jake was right. She could do better. At least tonight, she could enjoy the time with her friends without worrying about what her boyfriend thought. If she ever got the auger working.

"Scott, you're an asshole. Good riddance." She flipped the phone closed and shoved it in her pants pocket, setting her sights on the clogged equipment. Something else giving her shit tonight.

The grain in the hopper piled up. She banged on the side of the auger in an attempt to shake the blockage loose. *No such luck. Time for the stick.* Leaning over the hopper, she rammed the piece of wood into the spinning blades. With a snap, the twig broke and managed to dislodge the clump of grain. The hopper began to empty again. She pushed off the edge of the plastic tub, but couldn't get any traction. Her feet slipped on spilled-over grain. She fell forward, thrusting her hands out in front of her. She caught the edge of the hopper. Her upper body continued forward, twisting around. *Oh God.* She tried to stop herself, pull her body over to the edge, but couldn't halt the inertia.

Her hand slid past the rusted old guard and into the spinning blade. The steel sliced her fingers apart, spraying blood across the grain and up into her face. She couldn't fathom the sight. Pain sang along every nerve, firing from her mangled fingers to her brain. Darkness flooded her vision. A cold sweat washed over her. She cried out, tears filling her eyes. As hard as she fought, she couldn't pull free.

Molten agony continued through her body. With one final effort, she threw all her weight back, ripping her shredded limb from the auger.

On her back, she stared at the mutilated hand, her vision wavering. Strips of torn flesh with bone poking out. So much blood, and it kept pumping out. Her stomach churned, bile burning her throat. She couldn't turn her head in time and puked all over herself. Then everything went silent except the high-pitched ringing in her ears. Her body grew numb to the pain. Bright lights danced behind her eyes.

A warbling sound broke through. It kept repeating until she heard it clearly. "Leanne, are you okay?"

She tried to answer, but her body wouldn't cooperate.

Something touched her face. "Stay with me, sweetheart. The ambulance is on its way."

Daddy?

A calming weight pressed down on her until she felt nothing, and she disappeared into the void.

A million needles pierced her wrist. She had to get away from the fire. Leanne flicked open her eyes, screaming, longing for the agony to stop.

White walls surrounded her. Machines beeped. Taking in the new scenery, she closed her mouth, the pain forgotten. Bags filled with clear liquids as well as blood hung from a metal pole. She followed the tubes from the bags into her left hand. Was that where the burn came from? She glanced at the other arm, the end of which was wrapped in thick bandages. The image of spinning blades and her mangled flesh flashed before her eyes. She screamed again, tears falling down her cheeks. *This can't be happening.*

Bodies rushed into the room, many in scrubs. With her vision blurred, she didn't recognize anyone. All strangers. She was in the foreign place by herself. A nightmare. Had to be.

"Shh, calm down, sweetie. You'll be okay."

A familiar voice. She glanced to her other side to see her mom standing beside her, her eyes glassy. She held her hand, but Leanne couldn't feel it, only the throbbing which had returned to her other one, the one that was…gone? She groaned, turning on her side, and pulled her knees up to her chest.

"Mom, is it really…?"

She brushed her fingers over her forehead. "Don't worry about it right now. You need to rest."

"It hurts so bad."

"I know." Her mom stroked her face again. "But the nurses will help it go away."

"Leanne," one of the nurses hovering around her said. "I want you to take deep breaths and count backward from ten."

"Ten." She sucked in air and cried out in agony. *Fuck!*

Between clenched teeth, she continued. Anything to stop the pain. "Nine."

Ice traveled through her veins. "Eight."

The throbbing slowly ebbed away. *Seven.*

Darkness swept over her and pulled her down with it.

"Sweetheart, are you okay?"

Daddy?

She'd had the worst nightmare, losing her hand in an auger. She wiggled her fingers, needing assurance it wasn't real. They all responded. All of her fingers worked. Just a horrendous dream.

Opening her eyes, she lifted her arm and stared at the end, all wrapped in bandages. "No, tell me it's not true."

"Honey, I'm so sorry."

She glanced over at her father.

Dressed in a clean pair of farm coveralls, he ran his fingers through his already disheveled hair. "But everything will be okay. You'll be fine."

"Daddy, my hand is gone." Her chest heaved and she struggled to breathe. "It's gone. Nothing there. How am I supposed to take over the farm?"

"We'll worry about that when you get out of here. Right now, you need to calm down. Relax." He squeezed her shoulder, but his touch brought no comfort.

Her hand was gone. The hand she used to write. To eat and brush her hair. To do everything. And she could never get it back.

Tears of loss trickled down her face. She stared at the bandages. What did it look like under there? Just a nub? What was she supposed to do with that? "Daddy, where's my hand? What did they do with it?"

"It's gone, sweetheart. They couldn't save it." He moved a chair closer to her bed and sat in it, stroking her hair. "I'm so thankful your hand was all you lost. It could have been much worse."

"My hand is gone. How could it be any worse?"

"People have lost their lives in auger accidents. If Jake hadn't been there…."

"Jake?" She tried to recall the night of the accident, what had happened, but everything blurred together. She remembered the spinning blade, her feet slipping…. *Oh God.* And a voice. Someone there beside her. "You were there. I heard you."

"No." He glanced away. "I wish I had been. I might have prevented it. But your mother and I didn't see you until after you'd already arrived here. Jake found you. He turned off the tractor and called 9-1-1. He stayed with you the whole time. I owe him for saving your life."

Jake. He'd saved her life. How could she ever repay him? As the farmhand, he helped her out every day. Now he was probably working night and day to cover her absence, and her father's.

"I need to see him. Thank him." Her mind wandered to what she'd been doing that night. She was supposed to meet the girls. She didn't even know what day it was. "Did you tell my friends? They're going to think I abandoned them."

Her chest constricted. What would they think of her now? They'd probably look at her differently, treat her like she'd somehow changed. Maybe it was best they didn't know.

"I did. They are all anxious to visit. If you're up for it, I'm sure they'll be up later today or tomorrow. Scott, well, I didn't like him anyway."

Would have been nice if he'd told her earlier he didn't like her boyfriend. "We broke up."

Gripping the arms of the chair, her father sighed. "It's for the best." Then he stood and kissed her forehead. "I've got to get back to help with chores, but I'll let Tina and the rest know you're awake now. Mom will be up later today. And I'm sure Jake plans to visit before you come home."

But when would that be? She reached for her father as he left the side of her bed. She didn't want to be alone. Not in this strange place in the city, so far from everything she knew. "Please stay."

But he ducked out of the room without an answer. Had he even heard her? She sighed. Her next visitor couldn't come soon enough.

Grasping the railings of the bed, she tried to pull

herself up. Blinding pain shot up her arm. She cried out. *Fuck!* She would never get used to having only one hand. She could live without a finger, an ear, but a whole hand? Life as she knew it was over. Everything had changed.

A nurse rushed into her room. "Are you okay, Leanne? What do you need?"

She winced as she held up her arm, the pain beginning to dull. "I forgot."

"Yes, that will happen. I'm Tory, and I'll be here for the next few days." She examined her bandages. "Looks like we're going to need to change these. Have you gone to the washroom yet?"

Leanne shook her head, suddenly aware of her full bladder.

"Well, let's take you there first, and then I'll change your dressings."

Supporting the elbow of her damaged arm, the nurse helped her off the bed and rolled the steel pole with all the bags behind her.

Once in the bathroom, Leanne inched down her underwear and easily sat on the toilet, with only a hospital gown to hold to the side. Business done, she reached for the toilet paper. *Shit! Wrong hand.*

With her left, she yanked on the tissue, hoping to roll off enough to do the job. But the paper didn't stop. It just kept coming, falling in heaps to the floor. Tory reached over and tore a length for her, spinning the rest back up.

Leanne burst into tears, burying her face in the crook of her arm. "I'll never get used to this."

"It'll take some time," her nurse said. "And when everything is healed, you can have a prosthetic arm made, if you want. It won't be quite the same, but pretty close."

Prosthesis? She hadn't thought past getting out of the hospital, still coming to terms with her missing limb. As long as she wasn't given a hook. She would more likely hurt herself with it than find it useful. She'd get the thing caught in her hair trying to put in a braid.

She finished on the toilet and, pulling up her drawers, gave herself a wedgie. With a little yanking and shifting, she had the material back in place and stepped over to the sink. Washing her hand. *This should be easy.* She turned on the faucet, squirted on some soap, and then stood there, trying to figure out how to rub the soap in. Tory leaned over the sink and scrubbed her hand, reminding her of when she was a kid and her mother helped to wash up.

She was a child again, having to learn the basic movements in life all over. Even with the prospect of an artificial limb, she still had so far to go. The quick glance at herself in the mirror didn't help either. She wasn't one to preen and primp for hours on end, but her usual French braid had come loose, and her blonde hair stood out in every direction. No way could she fix it herself. Tear stains crossed her cheeks, and snot crusted under her nose. Not how she wanted anyone to see her, even after the accident.

She turned to her nurse. "Can I please have a shower or something?" A thin film still covered her from working out in the field, and her body odor left her eyes watering. Anyone who saw her would run the other way. Well, except Tory, who was paid to help her, and her parents who obviously loved her unconditionally.

"Sure. It's too soon to get you in the tub, but I'll help you wash off and then change your bandages."

Thank goodness. Anything to make her feel half normal again.

"Leanne, oh my God, I can't believe you ditched us for the hospital."

She managed a soft smile at Tina, who stood in the doorway. If anyone could make her feel better, her best friend could. Her mother had come in yesterday as the nurse sponged her off, but even with her hair back in place and her skin scrubbed clean, she couldn't shake the depression consuming her. Her life would never be the same.

Tina could at least make her forget. At five-feet-nothing, she couldn't be more different from Leanne. Her short brown hair stood in well-coifed spikes, and she wore practically nothing over her curvy body. Yet, they'd been instant friends since the day they met, when they learned they would be roommates during their first year of college.

"Why would I wanna hang with you when I can sit on my ass here all day, and I even get a sponge bath?"

Tina rushed over and wrapped her arms around her, seemingly not bothered by her bandaged arm. Thank goodness her IV had been removed. The needle had felt like a zillion bugs trying to burrow under her skin, and it always got in the way.

When Tina pulled away, her eyes had lost their sparkle. "I can't believe I almost lost you. If Jake hadn't been there, who knows what could have happened."

"Jake, again." Her parents mentioned him every time they drove over to visit her, even had her surgeon citing his heroism. And now Tina. Yet, he hadn't bothered to visit her or even call.

"He saved you, Leanne."

"Yes, and when I see him next, I'll be sure to thank him." If he ever wanted to talk to her again. He probably thought her useless now and couldn't be bothered. She leaned back against her pillow while Tina sat in the chair beside her bed. "So, did you have fun Saturday night?"

Her friend stood and reached for her hand, grasping her bandages instead. "I'm sorry." She shook off the mistake. "Please don't hate me for what I'm going to tell you, but everyone thought it best you find out from me. If Scott didn't tell you first."

Dread washed over her like the sting of acid rain. As if her life hadn't taken a turn for the worse already. Did she have some kind of STD, too? "What?"

"On the night of your accident, Jake used your cell

contact list and phoned everyone, including Scott, to let us know what happened. If he hadn't, we would have been so worried. Heck, we were after we found out." She shifted from one foot to the other. "I didn't end up going out, but Crystal did. And at The Mirror, she saw Scott making out with some chick. Then they headed for the back room."

Leanne groaned. She'd known her relationship with Scott was over, but she'd never expected him to move on so quickly. If he knew what had happened to her, he could at least have come to visit. Their relationship must have meant absolutely nothing to him.

She reached for her phone, but Tina grabbed it first. "Leanne, don't."

"We broke up Saturday night, before my…accident," she said. "I want to remove him from my contact list."

Tina handed the instrument to her and Leanne thumbed through her contacts to find Scott's number. With the press of the delete button and the resulting beep, she erased him from her life forever.

Tina gathered her in a hug, rubbing her back. "I'm sorry."

She reveled in the fact her friend didn't say I told you so or tell her she deserved better. Tina was simply there, everything she needed at the moment. Loosening her grip, Leanne took a deep breath and leaned back on the bed. "Thank you for being here. And thanks for not being put off by the fact I'm no longer whole."

"Why would I be anywhere else?" Tina gripped her arm again. "You're still the same person. So what if you're one hand less." A tear trickled down her cheek. "Anyone who can't see you're still the same beautiful Leanne is an ass."

"I agree."

Leanne turned her head toward the doorway at the sound of the familiar husky voice. But the sight was not what she was used to at all. Instead of his dirty and smelly farm coveralls, Jake had on a T-shirt that stretched across his ripped chest, and his blue jeans hugged all the right places. He'd left the ball cap somewhere else, revealing the wave in his dark brown hair. When had he grown up from the teen she remembered in high school? His blue eyes were fixed on her as if she'd disappear if he glanced away.

But she wasn't going anywhere. He might have saved her life, but she'd never be the same. Her dream of taking over the farm was shattered. She'd never work by his side again.

Tina leaned down and hugged her. "Well, I think it's time for me to leave. You have a hero to thank."

No. For some reason, she was scared by the idea of being alone with Jake. He'd never hurt her, but something else worried her. She reached for her friend, but Tina had already made her way to the door.

"I'm glad you were there, Jake." Tina smiled as she passed him. "Thank you for saving her."

He nodded, but his gaze remained on Leanne, not following her friend as she'd often caught her boyfriend—ex-boyfriend—doing. She needed to say something, thank him, but there was a problem between her mind and her mouth. She suddenly couldn't talk. Oh God, she was a teen again, crushing on a boy. No, a man who she saw clearly for the first time.

Then she remembered. She was damaged goods. No man would ever want her. Especially Jake.

ACCIDENTAL ROMANCE
CHAPTER TWO

"So, how are you feeling, LA?" Jake sauntered into the room, his worried expression replaced with a cocky grin.

God, she hated that look. It meant he was planning something, ready with another prank. And using his nickname for her, LA, another sign he was up to no good. Things were different now though. She wouldn't be working with him every day, and the thought made her stomach twist.

"Oh, fine, Jake-a-roo. I'm missing a hand, but otherwise, just peachy."

"Great, then get the hell out of bed."

She drew in a quick breath. How dare he talk to her like that. She was in the hospital. "Did you not hear me? My hand is gone." How could anyone forget? She never would.

"Yes, your hand, not your legs." He shucked the blankets off her. "So, get off your ass, and let's go for a walk."

"I only have a hospital gown on. I can't go wandering

around." Reaching for the sheets, she tried to cover herself, but he refused to give them back. "C'mon Jake, this is embarrassing." She didn't need him or anyone else in shock from an accidental flash.

He finally let go, only to march over to her small closet and grab her robe. "Put this on." He tossed it at her. "Otherwise, I'm going to carry you out into the hall and plop you down on the floor."

"You're such an ass."

His shit-eating grin returned. "I know, but I refuse to let you sit around and throw a pity party." He gripped her arms and stared into her eyes, as serious as when he'd arrived. "You're not dead."

The intensity radiating from him stole her breath. She was seeing a side of Jake he'd never revealed before. Why? She gasped, struggling for air. What was she supposed to say? He didn't understand. She had to thank him, yes, thank her hero. "Jake, thank you. You…you saved me."

"Yes, I did." His gaze traveled down her body, leaving a trail of goose bumps. Then he glanced at the door. "Let's go, LA."

Shit, he wasn't going to give up. Might as well placate him. Pressing her hand onto the mattress, she swung her legs off the side. She slipped her feet into her fuzzy slippers and stood up, immediately feeling a cool breeze across her back. Most days, she welcomed air conditioning, but not today. "I, um, need some help with the robe."

When Jake returned his focus to her, his cheeks flushed. "Yeah, I guess you do."

He held it open while she slipped her arms into the sleeves, the first with ease, the second, not so much. The dressing around the end of her nub caught in the fleece. Pain sliced through her arm, and she yelped.

"Sorry." His face drained of all color. He yanked the robe off her bandages and draped it over her right shoulder then secured the tie at her waist. "I guess it's going to take us all some time to get used to this."

"Yeah." Except he didn't have to get used to anything. Leanne wouldn't return to the fields or the barn. The only time she'd see him was the occasional night her parents invited him to stay for dinner. And even then, he wouldn't have anything to do with her except friendly conversation.

"Since there's no longer a chance of you showing off your sexy pink hearts to everyone…." He winked at her. "Let's go for our walk."

Crap. He'd seen her thong. "Did you like the view?" Her cheeks warmed. She'd blurted the first thing that came to mind in order to stifle her embarrassment, but only made it worse.

He placed his hand in the center of her back and guided her into the hall. "I did. Now, let's find the cafeteria. I'm starving, and I'm sure you could use some decent food, too."

He liked the view? Did that mean he…? She reined in her excitement. What guy didn't like to look at a woman's skimpy underwear? And they were just friends, anyway. Had been since he started working on the farm, and he would always be a friend, so long as he didn't abandon her when he found her no longer of any use in the barn.

Down the hall, in the elevator, and through more corridors she kept in step with him, overwhelmed by the awkward silence. Never had they been short for conversation. Jake always had a playful remark for everything, and she was quick with comebacks. But he remained quiet, the only indication he was even there, his touch guiding her along, as if she'd stray if he let go. Yes, she'd had moments where she felt like a child since her accident, but it hurt even worse when her friend treated her like one.

She glanced around when they reached the cafeteria. Fastened-down tables and chairs were the only things static amongst the energetic food vendors selling pizza, pitas, and other delicious foods. Why had no one offered her any of these meals during her stay?

Jake sat her down and stood over her like a parent. "What can I get for you?"

As much as she hated being coddled, she couldn't ignore her rumbling stomach. "Pizza and cold green tea would be great. Thanks." And if he paid for her meal, even better.

When he left, she shivered as several sets of eyes seemed to focus on her. But when she glanced around, the people quickly found something else to stare at. She wasn't the only person in the room wearing a bathrobe, but no one else was missing their hand. Would it be like this everywhere she went? She tensed, her pulse racing. Did they see her as some sort of freak? They were at a hospital where most everyone was different from the norm. Some people were missing their hair, and other had burns across their faces. Why did everyone have to gawk at her?

Thank God, Jake returned within minutes. She wanted to eat and get back to her private room—her parents' health insurance coverage making her accommodations possible. He placed the food on the table, but she didn't wait for him to sit down, reaching for one of the slices. She salivated as she brought it up to her mouth. One would think she hadn't eaten all day. She quickly devoured the pizza, ready to quench her thirst. Grabbing the can of cold green tea, she went to pop the top open. "Shit."

Jake dropped his pizza onto the table and yanked the can from her. "I'll get it."

She drew in a quick breath. "You didn't have to take it from me." Was this what the rest of her life was going to be like, people doing everything for her? She didn't want pity. She wanted her hand back.

"Well, you shouldn't be afraid to ask for help. When you're back in the barns—"

"I won't be working in the parlor, barns, or even in the fields, Jake. That dream is over."

"Bullshit." He turned in his chair and stared at her with his deep blue eyes. "You've wanted to run the farm for as long as I've known you. You can't give up because of one little accident."

"It wasn't a little accident. My hand got shredded into tiny pieces, and as everyone likes to remind me, I could've died."

He clasped her face in his palms. "But you didn't. Thank God, you didn't."

She gasped and leaned back from his reach. Both the intensity of his gaze and the attention of everyone else in the cafeteria left her ready to bolt. She pushed up from the table. "I need to go back to my room."

"Leanne, wait."

She made it to the elevators before he caught up with her and grasped her left arm. "What's wrong? Are you okay?"

She yanked free. "No. I was normal before, never attracting much attention." Including from guys. "But since I lost an appendage, everyone stares. And you—one minute you look at me as though I'm about to break and the next like you're ready to sweep me off my feet. Everything's changed, Jake, so how can I be okay?"

The doors opened, and she rushed inside. She wanted to be left alone. But he darted in beside her. "We're friends, right?"

"Yeah, I guess." What was he getting at?

He raised his eyebrows. "You guess?"

"Fine," she sighed. "You *are* a friend. A good friend."

"Then trust I'm here for you. Now and forever."

Her chest tightened and tears welled in her eyes. As much as she wanted to hear those words from him, from everyone, she couldn't say them in return. She wasn't the same person. Heck, she hadn't even shed a tear when her boyfriend dumped her. Now she couldn't keep the tears at bay. When the elevator doors opened, she charged out, heading straight to her room.

And he followed her again, right behind her. "No response?"

She spun around to face him, tears flowing down her cheeks. "I can't be who you want me to be, who my parents want me to be. None of you seem to understand." Their bodies were are all still whole.

"I won't give up on you." He pivoted on his heel and left the room.

Fuck, she wanted to throw something at him. She hadn't chosen for her dream of running the farm to end like this.

Crawling onto the bed, she lay back and wiped away her tears. She wasn't normally one to give up, but all her hopes for the future had been stolen from her on the worst day of her life. And she could never get them back.

Leanne awoke with a pounding headache after the most restless night of sleep ever. She'd tossed and turned, several times landing on her bandaged arm to be bolted back into consciousness at the stabbing pain. And her nightmares had shown her completely alone, everyone having given up on her once she returned home. She didn't want to be abandoned, didn't want to give up on her dreams, but how could she run the family farm with only one hand? Even if she did get a prosthetic arm, she would still be limited to what she could accomplish. Her parents could no longer depend on her.

"Hey, Leanne." Her nurse, Tory, scurried into the room. "Ready to go home today?"

She groaned. As much as she wanted out of the hospital—three days of horrible food and little sleep was long enough—she didn't feel prepared to face her new life. "Are you coming home with me?"

Tory chuckled. "I wish. I'd take a hundred patients like you any day. But I'm sure you're anxious to be out in the real world with your family and friends."

Not at all. Relying on others every minute of the day

held no appeal, yet she hoped someone would always be around. Just in case.

A nurse would visit daily to check her wounds and change her dressing until her nub had healed completely, but otherwise she'd need her mother or someone else to help her for the rest of her life.

And she'd go stir crazy at home. What the hell was she supposed to do now? She would be good for nothing out in the country. She didn't want to move to the city to make a living, but even if she did, where would she find work anyway? She'd need to be whole to get even minimum wage jobs. No one would hire her.

"Why don't you get dressed? I'll change your bandages after the doctor takes one last look at your arm."

She nodded. Though getting dressed wasn't as easy as she expected. Tory helped her do up snaps and held arm holes open. Otherwise, she might have ended up in a tangled mess. What would happen after she left the hospital?

After her nurse exited the room, she managed to swallow her breakfast of tasteless eggs and toast. While she waited for her ride, her nurse gave her enough pain medication for the rest of the day, with a prescription for more. And reminded her that in two weeks, she had a follow-up appointment with her surgeon. Yet, she sat on the bed, hoping she'd been forgotten, wishing she could have one more day in the hospital before having to face her new reality.

Within minutes, Tory popped back into her room with a wheelchair. "Your ride's here, and he's a handsome one. You're a lucky girl."

Lucky? Her mother was supposed to pick her up. Who was taking her home?

She released a heavy breath as Jake strolled in. *Great!* Now she was a burden to him, as well. "What are you doing here?"

Raising his eyebrows, he smirked. "Nice to see you,

too. Your parents have an appointment with the insurance agent and asked me to pick you up. Is that all right with you, LA?"

Back to his smart-ass self. At least she knew how to act around this guy. "Well, if you're my last resort, then I guess I'm going to have to deal with it. But don't expect me to be grateful or anything."

"Nice to have my girl back."

His girl? *Um, no.* The only person she'd ever expect to call her that was her father, but he called her sweetheart. She didn't belong to Jake. She shook her head and brushed off the comment. There were so many other things for her to worry about.

She hugged Tory on her way out. "Thanks for everything."

"Not a problem, honey. You take care of yourself."

She sighed. If only she could. Seizing her bag, she headed for the door, the portal to an unfamiliar life.

Grasping her luggage from her, Jake clutched her arm with his other hand. "I believe you're supposed to be in the chair."

"Why? I'm not missing a foot or a leg."

Tory cleared her throat. "Hospital policy."

Rolling her eyes, Leanne sighed and plopped into the seat. Jake rolled her down to the front doors, but she jumped up once outside. "Leave that thing here."

"Leanne, you're supposed to—"

"I'm not helpless, Jake. I can do some things for myself." She took off into the parking lot with him in pursuit.

"I'm sure you can do many things once you get used to—"

She spun around at his truck. "What? My hand being gone? It's a hard enough thing to say, let alone get used to." If only she could go back in time, somehow prevent what had happened to her. She never should have borrowed that ancient auger. And sticking a branch in to get the intake unclogged was a stupid idea. She'd been trained from the first time her dad took her on a ride-along that the tractor always has to be turned off before removing debris from any equipment. But she'd been in such a hurry.... She swallowed the lump in her throat. It was her own fault she had no hand.

"No, I was going to say me being constantly by your side. Because, no matter how much you object, I'm going to have you working in the barns. You're not giving up on your dreams." He opened the passenger door for her.

Fuming, she stepped up and inside, mad at herself and him. Why didn't he understand how difficult things would be for her now? Even strapping herself in proved tricky. She struggled with the buckle, fighting to line the two ends up with only her left hand. Finally, she clicked them together and leaned back in the seat. *This is only the beginning.*

Jake closed the door and got in on the driver's side, tossing her luggage into the backseat. "And if you don't show up, I'll come get you and throw you over my shoulder to carry you out there."

She pursed her lips to hide a smile, remembering him doing so once before when they'd been horsing around. She really would miss working with him. But she couldn't do the things she used to. "I can't."

"So, what are you going to do all day? Sit on your ass? That's not like you, LA." He started the truck and drove out of the parking lot with a heavy foot. "You can't stop living because one of your hands is gone."

She couldn't grab the "holy shit" bar and planted her feet on the floor instead. She didn't need a lecture, just someone to understand. "And what if it were you, Jake? What if you lost *your* hand? I can't even write my own name without the letters looking like someone in kindergarten printed them."

Reaching for her hand, he intertwined his fingers with hers. Yet, he remained focused on the road, slowing down to a reasonable speed. "I wouldn't give up if it meant I could still see you every day."

She drew in a quick breath. Her body filled with a tingling warmth she hadn't experience in a long time, one she had never expected to feel again. But Jake was still by her side, calling her his girl, saying he'd never give up on her. And now, he held onto her as he drove. Had he been interested all along and she too blind to see him as more than a friend? At the moment, though, she needed someone who was simply there for her. Besides, what would happen when he realized her limitations? Would she lose him forever?

"Jake, it's best if we—"

"Shh, I know. And I'll always be here, whether as a friend, or…whatever."

She relaxed in the silence, Jake released her hand only to turn the corners then quickly clasped it again. She welcomed his touch, not dwelling on the meaning behind his actions, but finding comfort in knowing he was there. She wasn't alone.

Pulling into the lane of her parents' farm, he let go of her again. She glanced around at the fields she'd plowed and harvested for years, the barns where she'd spent every morning and evening milking the cows. How could she walk away from all of it? Maybe she could help out somehow, after some time to adjust. Jake was right. She couldn't sit on her ass all day.

Right after he switched off the truck, Jake turned to her, brushing his thumb along her cheek. "I'm giving you a week, LA. Come Monday morning, you had better meet me out in the barn, or I'll drag you out of bed. And if you sleep naked, even better."

Oh God! A rush of desire pooled between her thighs at the image he'd created.

He kissed her forehead and hopped out of the truck as if he hadn't flipped her world upside down. The warmth she'd basked in the entire ride home had turned into a blazing fire. Yet she had no time to figure out what had changed between them with Jake helping her out of his truck and her parents waiting on the porch. Did they know what he was up to? Would they approve?

Thinking about him, about what they could have had, would only lead to disappointment when he realized how much of a burden she was now. She had to focus on herself, on learning to do things all over again.

She joined her parents on the porch, with hugs all around. Jake stood off to the side, resting against the railing.

Her father approached him, clasping his shoulder. "Thank you so much for bringing my daughter home. I owe you for keeping her alive."

Jake shifted from one foot to the other. "It was nothing. I'm just glad I arrived in time."

"Yes, me, too." Her mother teared up, pressing her palm to her chest. "Why don't you stay for dinner, tonight? It's the least we can do."

"Maybe another time." He winked at Leanne. "I'm sure you'll have your hands full this evening." He strolled down the steps and around the corner of the house toward the barn.

After their drive home, she couldn't help but see him differently. He was rugged and damn sexy. And he loved living out in the country as much as she did. Was she hoping for too much, though?

"C'mon, sweetie." Her mother held the screen door open. "Let's get you inside and settled."

She sighed and headed into the house. Settled did not appear in her vocabulary, not for the next few months, anyway, with so much to think about and so much to learn. Maybe when she had a prosthetic arm, but until then, every day would be a struggle.

ACCIDENTAL ROMANCE
CHAPTER THREE

Leanne yanked her shirt over her head, trying to ignore her churning stomach. The early morning rays of sunshine had started to peek through her bedroom window, and she had only minutes before Jake would storm into her room and carry her out to the barn. He'd paid her a visit every day for the past week, stopping at the house to issue his threat. "Monday morning, LA. You, me. We're milking the cows, even if I have to drag you." He'd never mentioned entering her room or throwing her over his shoulder while her parents were around, but she didn't doubt he would follow through.

Bending her right elbow, she carefully worked her arm up inside the cotton and through the armhole, ensuring not to jamb her nub into the material. She'd done the same thing enough times already to learn from the agony it caused. Getting her left arm in proved even trickier. She couldn't hold the material out as she normally would, so her effort became a free-for-all as she wiggled like a contortionist until the shirt was on. Sweat beaded her forehead, and it was still early in the morning. At least pants required less exertion to get them on. Unable to button a pair of jeans—and unwilling to wear those her mother had with an elastic waist—she'd resorted to sweats and tights as her fashion of choice. And thank God she wasn't stacked because putting a bra on proved impossible. Sports bras twisted up worse than her underwear.

With her clothes on, she bolted down the stairs. No way did she want Jake watching her fumble to get dressed. It was bad enough the couple of nights he'd stayed for dinner, studying her as she repeatedly tried to eat with her right hand. He never laughed, only smiled as if to say, "It's okay."

She often forgot there was nothing beyond her nub, sure she could move her wrist and her fingers with the tingling sensation she felt every day. Her doctor called it phantom limb syndrome, and explained the still active nerve endings could allow her to have a cybernetic or bionic arm, if she could afford one. She couldn't wait to be fitted with a prosthetic arm, which would make her life so much easier, but her amputation had to heal first.

She slid on the brand new steel-toed Western boots she'd had rush delivered last week—she couldn't do up the laces of her old ones—and opened the door.

"Make sure you come back for breakfast," her mother called from upstairs. "Jake, too."

He came to eat each morning after the cows were milked, but she'd remained in bed, waiting until after he'd left to get up. He didn't need to see her with bed head and in her pajamas. But her mother had helped her learn to dress on her own so she'd be set for this morning. "Okay, Mom. But you know it may take longer today, right?"

"Yes, sweetie. I'll keep the food warm."

"Food?" she heard from outside.

Jake stood on the porch. He glanced over her shoulder, into the house. "Did someone mention food?"

She rolled her eyes. "Yes, Mom said to come back for breakfast, as you do every day, when we're done." And she'd use their time together to convince him to let her take the rest of the day off. She refused to disappoint him, but her failures this past week had often brought her to tears. Crying in front of Jake would only make things worse.

"Sounds great." He put an arm around her shoulder. "Hey, I didn't expect you to be almost ready when I came. I thought I'd get to wake you up."

Liquid heat rushed through her veins as she imagined how he would wake her up. And what was with the arm? Did he still want to move their relationship beyond being friends? She mentally squashed those thoughts. Jake couldn't be any more than her buddy until he knew exactly how she had changed. Until then, she couldn't hope for anything else between them. She had to shield her heart. Her new life had enough to handle without heartbreak. Spinning out of his hold, she faced him. "What do you mean, almost ready?"

He grabbed a strand of her hair. "You usually wear your hair back. Why not today?"

She held up her arm. "Missing hand. Makes it impossible to do on my own, and I didn't want to bother Mom."

"Want me to do it?"

What? "You can braid hair? Since when?"

"It's one of the many girlie things I learned growing up with four older sisters." He let go and raised an eyebrow. "So, you want me to?"

And she thought she knew him. Since her accident, she'd started to see another side of her long-time friend. "Sure, but I don't have an elastic. Or a brush."

He pulled small, clear band from his pocket. "My niece likes to leave them all over the place. Found this one in my truck."

Stepping around behind her, he ran his fingers through her hair. She moaned as goose bumps popped up across her scalp. "Wow, that feels so good."

"I'm a professional. Or so my niece tells me."

She giggled as he fiddled with her tresses. In less than a minute, he had her hair pulled back. She reached behind to feel the familiar ripples. "Not bad." More than she could do now.

He poked her side. "Would have been better if you'd held still."

God, she loved when he touched her. He made her feel special. Desirable.

Clutching her hand, he gently tugged her toward the barn. "Let's get started. Your dad's already washing the lines. He'll clean the stalls while we feed, all right?"

"I guess, but I'm going to slow you down." She glanced back at the house, wondering if it was the best place for her. "You sure you want me in there?"

"Do I have to throw you over my shoulder? 'Cos I will."

She sighed, fighting the mental images he'd created. "I know. I don't want to be in the way. I mean, how much can I really do now?"

"I'll be by your side." He squeezed her fingers, giving her some reassurance along with a rush of longing. "We'll be working as a team."

With one last huff, she followed him to the barn, squashing down her ill-timed longing. "Fine, but don't say I didn't warn you."

Increasing his speed, he tugged her behind him. "Stop making excuses. The girls are waiting."

She rushed to keep up for fear he'd pull her off her feet. When they reached the barn, she and Jake scrubbed their boots to remove any outside contaminants.

Her dad had already started cleaning the stalls, and the cart of food sat in the walkway between the mangers.

Jake grabbed the handles. "You can feed the girls. Nothing's changed in the feeding schedule, so let's get on it."

Feeding. Yes, she could do that much. Two scoops for

Donna, four for Lucy, all the way up and down the row then over to the calf pens. Jake pushed the cart while she filled the mangers. Maybe she could be of some use, but Jake could have done everything she'd done so far by himself. And probably much faster. Why was he so determined to have her out there with him?

She stared at Jake in his barn clothes, suddenly aware of how his pants hugged the curve of his ass. Seeing him in this new light didn't help matters, either. With one look or a simple touch, he left her heart fluttering. Working so close to him would only leave her wanting more. Why hadn't he made his feelings known earlier? Was he pretending in order to make her feel better about her amputation?

A throat cleared behind her. "Looking at something interesting?"

She spun around, her cheeks burning. "Are you ready to start milking, Daddy?"

He crossed his arms, eyebrows raised. "Yes, come with me into the milking room. Jake can put the food away."

Without a backward glance, she followed him. He didn't seem impressed at catching her staring at Jake. Her father had admitted to not liking her last boyfriend, but their farmhand was practically family. Maybe that was the problem. What if things didn't work out? She glanced back at Jake then shook her head. Working with him would be too awkward if they dated then broke up. She'd best keep her inappropriate thoughts about him locked away.

"Come scrub your hands." She caught her father's grimace as she stuck her hand under the water for him to wash for her. "Sorry, sweetheart."

"It's okay. I'm still getting used to it, too."

He helped her dry off, then pulled in a deep breath. "You're so brave to be back out here so soon. I'm proud of you."

She drew in a quick breath to halt her tears. His approval meant everything to her. And crying in the barn was a no-no, as she'd learned as a child the first time she'd helped birth a cow and the calf didn't make it.

"Okay." Her father turned his attention to the equipment. "I'll move the milkers out if you want to prepare the dips. You won't be able to support the milkers, so all you can do is help clean the teats and dip them after. Once you help Jake get started, though, I want you up in the mow, sending down some hay. The girls have been eating faster than ever."

"Sure." She sighed as he left the room. Milking had been her favorite part, interacting with each cow. They all had their own distinct personalities, and she would talk to them as their milk flowed through the tubes.

She grabbed the jug of teat cleaner. Wrapping her bandaged arm around the jug, she used her hand to loosen the lid. But it wouldn't budge. Someone had tightened it too much. She twisted again, grunting as she wrenched on the lid. Nothing. "Fuck!"

A tear trickled down her cheek. She couldn't help it. Even the most basic things proved difficult for her now. If she couldn't even get the jug open, how was she supposed to do anything else? She dropped it on the counter, tempted to pitch it across the room. *It's too soon for me to be in here.*

She turned to leave and slammed right into Jake. He wrapped his arms around her. "Where are you going so fast, LA?"

"I can't do this. I shouldn't be here." She began to shake against him. "I can't do anything anymore."

"Yes, you can." He stepped back and stroked her cheeks, using his thumbs to brush away her tears. "This is exactly why you need to be out here. Sure, you can't do everything, but you just fed the girls."

She focused on his chin, unable to meet his gaze, afraid what would happen if she did. "I couldn't open the jug."

"Then ask for help." He kissed her forehead then let go, squeezing past her into the room. "That's what we're here for." He pulled her over to the counter. "But don't ever give up."

With the lids off, she poured the teat cleaner and then the dip into smaller bottles. Jake held onto them for her then helped her carry out the bottles and cloths. "Okay, help me get started and then your dad wants you up in the mow. If you need a hand up there, don't be afraid to ask."

She nodded, ignoring the pun. He probably hadn't even realized he'd said it. She wanted to get the morning over with. Crouching down beside the five-year old cow, Donna, she dipped one teat at a time into the sanitizer then wiped them down. Slower than normal, but she still managed to do her job. She squirted a bit of foremilk out of each teat to check for flakes or clots, but everything was clear. Jake came up behind her with the milking cluster, holding the base in one hand, while he attached the teat cups with the other. Not a task she could accomplish by herself without dropping the unit. She moved over to Lucy and repeated the process.

"See, LA, you're back in the game." Jake squatted beside her "I knew you could do it."

For the first time since she'd arrived home, she filled with genuine hope. Maybe she couldn't do everything, but she didn't have to stay away completely. And his wide smile left her wanting to please him even more.

She leaned her head on his shoulder. "Thank you for believing in me."

"Leanne, you planning on getting that hay today?" Her father asked from behind her. "The girls are getting hungry again."

Rolling her eyes, she stood up and traipsed to the back of the barn where she took the set of stairs up to the mow. No resting with her father around. And what did he suddenly have against Jake?

From the walkway, she glanced up the ladder. Stairs were one thing, but how the hell was she supposed to climb up the wooden rungs in front of her?

Her hand tingled, the one not there anymore. And Jake's smile flashed through her mind. She would try for him. Even if she couldn't do it, she refused to give up without an attempt.

Grabbing the rung in front of her, she wrapped her amputated arm around the edge, and stepped up. One rung at a time, she climbed higher and higher until she reached the top. She'd made it. A new feat accomplished.

She swung around onto the bales of hay. Oh God, another challenge. She was used to grasping the twine of each bundle and tossing it onto the walkway below.

Now, she could think of no other way than to drag it to the edge and kick the hay over. She'd have to do the same down on the walkway once she'd sent enough down.

Clasping one rope, she tugged. The hay jerked toward her faster than she'd expected. She lost her balance and landed on her ass with a thud. If she'd been closer to the edge, she'd have fallen down fifteen feet. But she refused to give up. Jake, and even her dad, believed she could do this job. She wouldn't disappoint them.

She gripped the twine again and pulled the bale over to the edge. Then, holding onto another for balance, she kicked the hay over. The process took longer than normal, but one by one, she tossed the bales down. Twenty lay on the walkway below, and now she had to send them through the chute, and down to the main level. All she had to do was climb down. She reached for the top rung and placed her left foot onto the ladder. She swung her other foot around but slipped. Her feet flew out from underneath her. She grabbed hold of the ladder. *Shit! No hand.* She slammed her nub against the rung instead. Pain shot up her arm and through her body like the jolt of an electric fence. Stars danced behind her eyes. She was falling.

She grasped the ladder, struggling to find footing. Wrapping her other arm around the edge, she found a rung to step onto. For a few moments, she didn't move, taking several deep breaths to slow her racing heart. Then she climbed down, taking her time, until she reached the bottom.

She plopped onto a bundle, still struggling to catch her breath.

"Sitting down on the job, are we?"

She glanced up at Jake, ready to tell him off. He should try getting the hay with only one hand. But she paused at the smart-ass grin on his face. "It's not as easy as I expected."

"That's why I came up to check on you." He walked over to her and fingered the end of her braid. "Wanted to make sure you were okay."

Okay? "Well, after almost falling fifteen feet, not once, but twice, I managed to get enough down and didn't kill myself."

"Definitely a good thing." He rubbed her shoulders, making her heart pound for another reason. "You're so courageous, LA. I'm glad you never gave up."

She leaned against him, so confused as to where she stood with him. "I wouldn't be up here if it weren't for you being such a pain in my ass."

He chuckled. "And I'm going to continue being a pain in your ass. Now, let's get these to the girls."

They shoved the hay down the chutes, Jake sending more than half of what she did. And when they'd finished, she followed him back to the main floor. He returned to milking while she cut open the bales and spread the hay amongst the mangers.

"Okay, sweetheart." Her father leaned forward, rubbing his hands together. "We're done milking. Why don't you take the girls out to pasture while Jake and I clean the pens." He smiled at her. "It's nice to have you back."

It was nice to be back. Sure, she couldn't do everything she used to, but she'd missed being in the barn. And now that she'd returned, she wouldn't be kept away. She'd be back again tonight, tomorrow, and every day after. She'd lost a limb, but her farming spirit hadn't vanished. She would continue pursuing her dream, despite the everyday challenges she'd face without her right hand. And working next to Jake was an added bonus. Maybe they could eventually become more than friends. If he stuck around.

ACCIDENTAL ROMANCE
CHAPTER FOUR

Leanne glanced over at Jake sitting on the wingback chair in her parents' living room. For the past half hour, he'd sat there, twiddling his thumbs, tapping his foot, and picking lint off the chair. What was up with him? If she didn't know better, she'd say he was nervous? But why?

As if he sensed her watching him, he turned to her and smiled. All tension seemed to exit from his body as he leaned back. "So, tomorrow's the big day, huh? Getting cast for your new hand?"

"Yes." She couldn't suppress her grin. In a matter of weeks, her myoelectric prosthesis would be constructed and she'd be trained to use it to its full potential. She'd be back in the barn doing everything she used to. "I can't wait."

"I'll miss you tomorrow."

And she'd miss him. They'd become a team over the past few months, every day milking half the cows together. Eventually, they'd even managed to beat her father on the other side of the barn. And then she'd helped Jake clean the pens. She grew closer and closer to him, on the verge of crossing the line from friends to lovers. But she still worried about winding up with a broken heart, as well as her father's reaction. And she never found much time to be alone with Jake anyway.

"Just think, I'll be able to milk the girls without your help. Then we can kick my dad out of the barn and not have to worry about him popping up out of nowhere."

There'd been numerous times she'd been tucked around a corner with Jake, wanting him to kiss her and more. And as his lips met hers, her father would show up, sending them to do other chores in opposite directions. If she'd been capable of doing more, she would have objected, but her father still owned the farm and signed her paychecks.

"Sounds good." Jake grinned.

Her father stirred beside her on the couch. "I'm right here. You could at least wait until I'm out of the room."

She leaned over and patted her father's arm. "It's okay, Daddy. I still love you."

He rolled his eyes. "So you say. It's like before your accident again. You're anxious to take over."

Yes, all thanks to Jake convincing her she could still live her dream, at least with his help. And she couldn't think of a better person to share the responsibility with. If only she could find some time to be alone with him. Maybe if he asked her out, she'd have an excuse to leave the property and go on a date. What was he waiting for? He barely spent any time at home anymore, except to sleep. If he did have a girlfriend, she didn't get any of his attention. But was that why he'd never asked her out?

Her mother tucked her knitting needles away and rested a hand on her father's shoulder. "Let's go to bed, Harold."

He glanced up at her, his eyebrows drawn together. "What are you talking about? It's not even ten. Besides, Jake's still here."

Leanne shook her head. Jake had fallen asleep many times on their couch. She'd draped a blanket over him, only to find him gone when she got up the next morning. God forbid her father leave the two of them awake and alone together. She was twenty-two, for goodness' sake.

"I'm sure Leanne can see him out." Her mother winked at her.

"And so can I," he grumbled.

"C'mon, Harold. They're young. Remember when we were their age?"

"That's what I'm afraid of." But he stood and followed her.

"Goodnight, Mom and Dad," Leanne called. Maybe with them gone, she could figure out what was up with Jake. Did her father say something to him?

"Goodnight, sweetie," her mother answered. "Don't stay up too late. Don't forget Tina's coming to get you at eight."

"Yes, Mom." She hadn't seen her friend for a couple weeks, but Tina had some vacation time to use up and agreed to take her the two hour drive to her appointment. Then they would spend the rest of the day shopping. Not what she was used to, but she wouldn't complain about having Tina there for support. She couldn't ask her father to give up Jake for the day.

"Goodnight, Mr. and Mrs. Declan." Jake waved. "Thanks for dinner."

Her father spun around and glared at him. "Behave yourself, or else."

Jake shrank back in his chair with a smirk across his face. "Yes, sir."

She sighed. Would her father ever let her grow up? He hadn't seemed to have a problem leaving her with Jake before the accident. Why was he more protective of her now?

The door to upstairs closed behind her parents, which meant she couldn't hear them and they couldn't hear her.

Obviously her mother's doing.

Jake remained on the chair, rubbing his palms across his pants.

"What's up with you tonight?" She'd thought it had been her father making him nervous.

He turned to her, his face slightly green. "I want to ask you something. Can I come sit with you?"

"Of course." She'd wanted him beside her all night. If her father hadn't been in the room, she would have sat on Jake's lap after helping her mother clean up after dinner. She was tired of the friend line between them. He'd stuck around all this time, proved he wasn't going to flee because of her amputation.

He walked toward her, stiff like a pitchfork, and sat at the other end of the couch. Did she smell? Why wouldn't he sit closer?

Leaning over, he lifted her feet onto his lap. Then he removed one of her socks and dug his thumbs into her sole. She moaned and sank into the couch. "Wow, you really know what you're doing."

"Sorry, I'm nervous and I needed something to do with my hands."

"Oh, don't be sorry." He could rub her down any day. A slight cry escaped her as he ran one thumb down the center of her sole. She'd never had a massage that left her whole body tingling. "Where did you learn how to do this?"

"My oldest sister is an esthetician and thought it important I learn how to massage a woman's feet if I were ever to keep a girlfriend."

"Sounds like she has a lot of faith in you." Now was the time to find out if he had one. "So, you're practicing on me before you get to your girlfriend?"

"No." He met her gaze. "I want you to be my girlfriend, Leanne." Leaning his head back, he groaned. "God, that sounded so lame. Look, I know we've been friends for a long time, and I don't want to lose what we have, but—"

She gasped. He'd offered everything she'd wanted from him for months. "Jake, do you mean it? Are you asking me out?" Excitement bubbled up inside her. *Please, let it not be a dream.*

His deer-in-the-headlights look didn't show the same enthusiasm. "Yes, I guess. I mean, if it's what you want."

She removed her feet from his lap, leaned forward, and cupped his cheek. "Of course it's what I want. I've been waiting a while for you to ask."

"You have?" A sly grin spread across his face, turning him from a scared little boy into a confident man. The sexy man she longed for.

"And here I was thinking you'd say no, that you just wanted to be friends."

"I would have slapped you every time you tried to kiss me in the barn if I only wanted to be friends. If Dad hadn't interrupted us every time…."

Jake glanced over his shoulder. "And I fear he'll interrupt us again if we start anything now. Maybe we could go to a show next weekend?"

She refused to wait any longer. Need radiated through her body. She inched forward to sit on his lap, nuzzling against his neck. "Mom closed the door behind her. And if you listen carefully, you can hear Dad snoring. We're good."

"In that case…." He laid her back and leaned over her. "I've wanted you for years, LA, but I've always been too afraid you wouldn't want me."

"I didn't know," she whispered. She could barely concentrate with him so close. Her body hummed in silent longing. She'd never wanted anyone so badly.

He kissed her forehead, her nose, down her cheeks, and finally her lips. *Yes!*

With soft lips, he explored her mouth, lacking the desperation of her previous boyfriends. She pulled him closer then paused. Would the feel of her nub bother him?

She tucked her arm down beside her, but kept her hand pressed to his back. If he stopped, she'd be devastated.

But he didn't seem at all bothered, holding her tighter. He lined her lips with his tongue and she opened to his sweet invasion. All thoughts vanished except her longing for Jake. They'd only started to date, but she couldn't get enough. She wanted all of him.

He reached up inside her shirt, cupping her breast. Her body burned under his touch. Why had he waited so long? She pressed her pelvis against him, craving skin against skin. If she could take his shirt off one-handed, she would have.

He trailed kisses down her chin to her neck. "You're an amazing woman, LA."

Sliding his fingers under the waist of her pants, he fueled her desire. All the months she'd waited for him came down to this moment. She needed him. He parted her folds and slid a thick finger into her wet heat.

"Oh, God!"

Jake stopped cold. "I'm sorry. I'm rushing this, aren't I? I've wanted you for so long, I couldn't help myself."

She pressed her hand against his. He couldn't end this now. "Please don't stop. I want this, too."

He raised his head staring down at her, his eyes filled with as much lust as she felt. "I…. Shit, I don't have a condom."

"In my brown coat. Right inside pocket." There could be no excuses. She had to be with him.

He raised an eyebrow. "You keep condoms in your barn coat?"

Her cheeks warmed. Why did he think she would bring them to the barn? No one else did chores with her except him and her father. "I kept hoping…."

Jake grinned. "Me, too." He pushed off the couch and dashed for the mud room where her coat hung. While he searched for protection, she stripped down to her panties. The sooner he was inside her, the better.

"Good God, you're beautiful." Jake gazed at her from the archway between the kitchen and living room. He held up a square foil package. "You sure you're ready, because I can wait."

She shook her head. "We've waited long enough. I want you now, Jake. No more interruptions."

In a matter of seconds, he'd flicked off all lamps but one, and removed his clothing. He stood in front of her, pulling her tight against his firm body. Every ripple of muscle in his arms and along his washboard stomach had been earned by hard work. And by her side.

He ran his fingers down her body, sparks leaping across her skin from his touch. After all he'd done for her, she was ready to give him this piece of her. He reached for her thighs then lifted her up to straddle his waist. So close. The tip of his cock pressed against the thin piece of fabric she wore, and she yearned for him to be inside of her.

Leaning down, he swirled his tongue around her nipple, heightening her need. Moisture pooled at her core. How was he so experienced? She'd never known him to have many girlfriends in high school. And none of the guys she'd ever dated had made her body react like this.

He slid a finger under her panties, stroking her clitoris. *Holy fuck!* Lighting shot through her body. She cried out, clinging to him until she could focus again.

And then she remembered her missing limb. She slipped back down to the floor and stepped away from him. "Sorry. Sometimes I forget it's not there."

Jake grabbed her nub. "Don't ever be sorry for who you are." He kissed the inside of her elbow and continued all the way down to where her hand used to be. Every press of his lips set her body on fire. Her heart swelled.

He scooped her up then laid her on the couch. It was time. He knew it, too, and swiped the condom from the coffee table. She took a deep breath, watching him rip open the package then roll it over his erection. God, she couldn't have found a better guy. Why had it taken her accident to see he was the one for her?

With his shaft covered, he lay on top of her, holding her tight against him. She parted her legs, and he pressed against her opening. Her breath hitched as she waited for their relationship to ascend from friends to lovers.

Jake gazed down at her. "Leanne, I love you." Then he plunged into her, before she could respond.

She stifled a cry of ecstasy, gripping his bicep. He rocked in and out, placing sweet kisses all over her face. *Love.* He loved her. And only months ago, she thought no man would ever love her. Now she had Jake, and she wanted to hold onto him forever.

Lifting her legs over his shoulders, he thrust deep inside. She arched against him, meeting him stroke for stroke. The intense pressure of approaching orgasm consumed her entire body. She breathed in short, ragged gasps. His motions became more frantic, and she released in a frenzy of explosions. Jake slammed into her with a groan, shuddering and convulsing above her.

He collapsed on top of her then rolled them both on their sides. She relished being with him, flesh against flesh. Everything had changed between them in a moment of passion and she couldn't have been happier.

Rubbing his thumb along her cheek, he smiled. "You okay?"

She nodded. Tears formed in the corners of her eyes as he brushed the hair from her face. A lump formed in the back of her throat. She loved the man in front of her. Truly loved him. She couldn't imagine him not in her life. If he hadn't been there for her, she would have given up on her dream. Instead, he forced her to keep living.

"Jake, I love you, too. You opened my eyes to so many things these past months, and the best was you. Us."

He kissed her forehead. "I agree."

She lay wrapped in his arms, as content as ever, never wanting to move. But when he began to snore softly, she leaned back and shook him. "Jake, why don't we go up to my bed and sleep? There's more room there."

He groaned and sat up with her. She gathered their clothing then guided him upstairs to her bedroom. The door snapped closed behind her, and she cringed. *Please don't let my parents wake up.*

The noise seemed to liven Jake up and he glanced around. "LA, I don't think this is such a good idea. I love you, I really do, but what's your father going to think when he sees me coming out of your bedroom in the morning?"

She sighed. He was right. "Yeah, I guess that's not the best way for him to find out."

He wrapped his arms around her and drew her in for a long, intoxicating kiss. It pained her to let him go, even though she'd see him in only a few hours.

Pulling on his clothes, he kept glancing at her and smiling. He made her feel special, and she held no regrets about the change between them. Instead, she yearned for more from him. With a final kiss goodbye, he snuck out of her bedroom, taking a piece of her with him.

Leanne crawled onto her bed then snuggled under the covers. She would have enjoyed Jake's warm body next to hers, but she'd have to wait. Eventually, they'd share a bed and so much more. She hoped. She just had to tell her father she was dating the farmhand. He couldn't stop her, but she knew he would have some objections.

She pushed those thoughts away and envisioned Jake staring down at her as he had when he'd made love to her. Everything in her life seemed right as she dozed off.

Leanne groaned as the sound of her parents' voices echoed upstairs. What were they yelling about? Her parents never fought. She rolled over, pulling her pillowcase over her head. Jake had told her to take the morning off and he'd see her at breakfast. He'd said so before the events of the previous night, but how would their lovemaking have changed anything? Had her parents heard?

Her bedroom door burst open. "Leanne, you need to get up and help your father in the barn."

"What?" She raised her head, trying to focus. "What's going on? Where's Jake?"

"I don't know." Her mother threw her arms up in the air. "I can't get a straight answer out of your father. But Brody Jenner is on his way. Your dad just wants you to feed the girls."

She jumped out of bed and wrestled on some clothes, her heart pounding in her chest. What the hell had happened to Jake? Had he been in an accident? *Shit!* She should have insisted he stay the night, even if not in her bed.

She bounded down the stairs and burst outside, gasping from the frigid air. She had to know what had happened to him. Racing toward the barn, she slipped on a patch of ice. Her feet flew up in the air, and she landed hard on her ass, slamming her elbows into the ground. Sharp pain traveled through her body, and she whimpered. With a groan, she rolled to her side and shuffled to get up, pressing her nub and hand to the ground. What a way to start her day. Yet, she still hadn't found out anything about the man she loved.

Her pain was overshadowed by the urgency to find out where Jake was. Cradling her right arm, she treaded carefully the rest of the way to the barn.

Inside, she glanced around until she found her father cleaning Donna's stall.

"Daddy, what happened?" She rushed over, but paused, straining to hear the words he muttered. "Where's Jake?"

He scraped the tongs of the pitchfork across the cement floor. "That good-for-nothing kid up and quit. Didn't even give a reason."

No. She stepped back, her heart shattering. Her life,

everything she knew, crumbled around her. Jake had been there every step of the way, giving up so much to help her. He'd said he loved her. And then he'd abandoned her?

She spun around, running through the barn and out into the pasture. Her footsteps were heavy against the frosty ground, but she kept going until she reached the large maple tree at the edge of the fenced area.

Her tears flowed, freezing against her cheeks as she slid down the trunk. She pulled her knees to her chest and buried her head in her lap. Was everything Jake had said a lie? She'd given herself to him completely, and never truly received his love back? But why? Why would he do such a thing? What had he gained?

She shivered with cold, but there was no way she'd return to the barn. Ever. Everything there would remind her of Jake. She couldn't go anywhere and not recall a quiet moment they'd shared. Now what would she do with her life? When she thought of taking over the farm, she'd always imagined him there with her, at first as her employee, and now as much more.

She slammed her fist on the ground. *No.* She wouldn't let him destroy her life. If he'd taught her anything, it was to never give up. She'd find someone else to work alongside her once she had her prosthetic arm. It would never be the same, but she would take over the farm from her father. As for her heart, she'd pick up the pieces and would never give it to another.

Standing up, she glanced back at the barn. *Shit!* Her mother rushed toward her with a blanket. She wanted to be alone.

"Leanne, oh sweetie, are you okay?" She wrapped the blanket around her and rubbed her arms. "Your father told me what happened."

"I'm fine, Mom. I'm going to get my new hand, and I'm going to take over the farm. Just like I've always said." She refused to stop and dwell on Jake. He could rot in hell for all she cared.

"But, sweetie, there has to be some explanation. I know how he feels about you. Why would he quit so suddenly?"

"Because he's an ass." Like her last boyfriend. But at least Scott hadn't dumped her after the first time they'd fucked.

"There has to be some explanation. Jake's not like that. Have you talked to him?"

"No, and I don't want to. I'm going to help Dad." She started back to the barn.

Her mother rushed along behind her. "Brody's already there. You need to go to the house and get ready."

"Fine." She switched direction, swallowing the lump in her throat. As much as she tried, she couldn't push down the hurt from Jake's betrayal.

"Leanne, I really think you should phone him. Find out what's going on."

She paused and spun around, removing her phone from her pocket. "I know exactly what happened. He asked me out last night, made me think he loved me, and then decided he didn't want to be with a cripple."

Her mother gasped. "No, he wouldn't do such a thing."

"I didn't think so either." She handed the phone to her mother. "So, if you want to call him, go ahead. I don't want to see him again."

Her chest tightened and her eyes burned. She ran back to the house. Jake had fooled everyone in her family.

Leanne stared out the window, watching the many empty fields go past as Tina drove. Empty like her heart. Nothing about the day had made her feel any better. Not even the prospect of having a temporary hand in two weeks.

"C'mon, Leanne," Tina said. "You have to stop dwelling on him. Think of all the good that came out of today. Your appointment went well, and you bought a couple of cute new outfits." She slowed down at the next stop sign "Though you're the most depressing shopping partner I've ever had."

With a sigh, she turned to her friend. "I'm sorry. I didn't expect today to start the way it did." She'd thought her worst days were over, hoped she could put the accident behind her. But her heartache hurt nearly as much as losing her hand.

"I know, but maybe it will end better." Tina accelerated again and pulled into Leanne's driveway within minutes.

She doubted anything could make the day better. She wanted to crawl into bed and sleep, forget about the pain Jake had caused. She glanced in the dining room window and saw the Christmas tree had been set up. *What?* Her mother hadn't waited for her to help? She had participated in decorating the tree for as long as she could remember.

So much for the day getting better.

She shoved the door open, craving her bed even more. Tina was staying for dinner, though, so she had to last a few more hours. Meeting her friend at the trunk of her car, Leanne grabbed her bags then headed for the house.

"So, what are we having?" Tina asked.

She shrugged. Her mom hadn't told her what she'd planned to make, or anything about putting up the tree. "No one tells me anything anymore." No, instead she was fed lies, set up for heartbreak.

Tina gripped her shoulder as she reached to open the door. But it swung open in front of her. Jake stood in the doorway like a mirage in the desert. She wanted to run into his arms, pretend the morning had never happened. Instead, all of her hurt and anger spewed out in her words. "What the fuck are you doing here? I thought you quit."

His smile faded. "I never—"

"Watch your language." Her mother rushed up behind him. "And Jake didn't quit. Your father stuck his nose where it didn't belong."

What the hell? Oh God. And she'd thought the worst of Jake.

Tina snickered behind her. "Sounds like my father. Exactly why I don't live at home anymore."

Jake held out his hand. "Please believe I meant everything I said last night. I love you, Leanne. I wouldn't be here if I didn't."

She caught a glimpse of the pain in his eyes. She wanted to believe him, but getting her hopes up would only lead to more hurt. Until she learned the truth, she would guard her heart from everyone.

With a heavy sigh, she stepped past him into the house. Her mother, Tina, and Jake followed, all quiet as if waiting for her to speak. But the only person she wanted to talk to was her father, to find out what really happened between him and her boyfriend. "Where's Daddy?"

"Still out in the barn. Don't know what he's doing. Brody left a half hour ago."

Leanne went out to the mud room and slipped on her barn boots and coat. Her entire life felt as though on pause. The answers waited for her outside, but what could her father have said to Jake?

"Don't be too hard on him," her mother called.

She hurried to the barn, jaws clenched. Why would her father purposely make her upset? He had to know by now she and Jake were interested in each other. Did he not want them together? Didn't he see what Jake had done for her?

Peeking past the main doors, she saw her father sitting on a wooden stool, talking to Lucy.

"She grew up faster than I ever expected."

Leanne scrubbed her boots then tiptoed inside. "Daddy?"

He didn't answer her, remaining on the stool while he cracked his knuckles.

"Dad, what happened this morning? Why did you tell me Jake had quit?" Her heart thudded as she waited for his answer.

Standing, he brushed off his pants but would not make eye contact with her. He released a heavy breath. "He didn't quit. I fired him after I caught him leaving your bedroom in the middle of the night."

"You what?" Her chest constricted. "Why would you do such a thing? I'm twenty-two, Dad. And besides, Jake's been a part of this farm for years."

"I know, but I was mad, thinking only as your father at the time."

"An overprotective father."

He glanced up at her, his eyes wet. "A father who loves you. One who cares and doesn't want to see you get hurt."

"But Jake would never hurt me. He loves me." At least, she hoped he still did after this morning. "And I love him."

"I know." He glanced down.

"But you hurt me by telling me lies."

Her father spun around and kicked the stool, sending it tumbling down the walkway. "I didn't mean to. I wanted to save you heartache. Instead, I caused it." Facing her, he dug his foot into the floor. "I'm sorry, sweetheart. Can you ever forgive a foolish old man?"

She ran to her father and wrapped her arms around him. She could never stay mad at him. "Of course, Daddy, as long as you stay out of my love life. I can handle that on my own."

"Deal." He gripped her in a tight hug then let her go. "What d'you say we go and get something to eat? I'm starving."

And she was, too, not having had much of an appetite all day. They walked to the house together, his arm across her shoulders. "So, you sure you want to date a farm boy?"

She chuckled. "Better to be with someone who isn't afraid to get his hands dirty than one who avoids dirt completely."

"Very true. How'd your appointment go today?"

"Good. I'll have a trial prosthetic in two weeks, and then if it fits well, my permanent one will be crafted." She couldn't wait to begin using it in the barn and for everyday things.

They stepped up to the door and he held it open for her. "I know I've said it before, but I'm really proud of how you've overcome living without a hand."

She smiled at him then entered the house. She would never have believed in her dream again if it hadn't been for Jake. He gave her strength and hope. She found him in the kitchen with her mom and Tina. The three of them stopped talking and stared.

"Everything okay?" her mother asked.

Leanne nodded. "All is forgiven." Then she glanced at Jake. "I'm sorry for doubting you."

He gave her a half smile. "All is forgiven, right. Now, if you don't mind, there's something I need to ask you." He made eye contact with everyone in the room, including her father. "Would you all join me in front of the Christmas tree?"

The tree that went up without her. She still didn't understand why. "Who put it up?"

Her mother rubbed her back. "I'm sorry for not waiting, sweetie, but Jake asked if he could set it up before you came home."

Without giving her a chance to respond, Jake grasped her hand and guided her to stand before the live spruce. He bent down to reach for something. Then he was on one knee, gazing up at her.

She gasped. What was he doing?

"Leanne, I know we've only been dating for one night." He opened a small black box. "But I've known and loved you for years. Would you do me the honor of becoming my wife?"

What? Her head spun. "But I don't have my hand yet."

Everyone chuckled, but she was still trying to wrap her head around what Jake had asked her.

"The ring goes on the left hand," Tina said.

Leanne glanced at her father.

He shrugged. "You told me to stay out of your love life, but if you want my opinion, you have my blessing. Jake came back here after you'd left to fight for *you*, not his job. I know how much he cares."

A tear trickled down her cheek. She'd begun the day thinking he'd abandoned her, and now he was asking her to marry him.

She gazed into his hopeful eyes, and made her decision. "Yes, Jake, I will be your wife." She smiled amongst her tears as she remembered the old farmer down the road. "If Joe can be happily married to Betsy for fifty years after losing his fingers when his bull stepped on them, why can't I be happy, too?"

She became swarmed in a mass of hugs, her parents and her friend offering their congratulations, but she remained focused on her fiancé. He slid a diamond ring onto her finger and pulled her against him. He brought his lips to hers in a sweet, lingering kiss. She couldn't imagine ever being with anyone else. He'd been there during the worst moments of her life, always encouraging her. And now they would be together for the good times, too.

ACCIDENTAL ROMANCE EPILOGUE

Two years later

Leanne glanced across the tent filled with family and friends. But it was Jake's hand holding hers under the table that made her smile. Their day had been perfect, the warm weather holding on long enough for them to have an outdoor wedding on the farm.

"Excuse me."

She turned her attention to her father who stood at the podium. What was he up to?

"Excuse me, please. Can I have everyone's attention?"

Oh God, he had an envelope. What did he have planned? Embarrassing pictures? A story from her childhood? She peeked under the table, hoping there'd be enough room to hide, but not for her and her huge hoop skirt. It was bad enough they'd had to find a special chair to accommodate the dress. But her father and Jake had insisted she get the gown of her dreams.

"I have an announcement to make." Her father pulled something out of the envelope. A picture.

She hid her face in her hands—the one she was born with, and the prosthesis. She was bound to end up with red cheeks by the time he finished.

"I wanted to show you a picture of my new house."

What? A collective gasp filled the tent. Leanne gripped the table and stared at her father. *What about the farm?*

"You heard me right," he continued. "Marnie and I are moving off the farm."

Murmurs traveled from one side of the tent to the other while Leanne continued to stare in shock. *I thought he was going to keep the farm for me.* Her bottom lip trembled. Why hadn't he told her beforehand? Her wedding wasn't the place. It was supposed to be a happy day. A perfect day.

He raised his arms to quiet the crowd. "Now, before all of you people get your knickers in a bunch, we're not selling the farm."

Leanne held her breath. Then what was going on?

Her father pulled the microphone from the stand and came to stand behind her and Jake. He clasped her shoulder. "We're passing it down to our daughter and new son-in-law."

A lump formed in her throat, and tears welled in her eyes. She stood and gave her father a hug. "Thank you, Daddy."

"It's my pleasure, sweetheart. I know you both will take great care of it."

Jake rubbed her back as she sobbed, wrapped in her father's embrace. She couldn't help herself. A couple years ago, she thought her dreams had been stolen from her. But with the support of her family, friends, and the wonderful man who loved her, she had managed to make her dreams reality again. Perfect.

Home for the summer, RJ heads to the annual fun hair to see if his hot neighbor has also returned from university. When he spots her at the kissing booth, he can't believe his luck. But even though she never spewed racial slurs at him like the rest of the community, will she grant him a kiss?

Missy is tired of the blatant prejudice she's seen all her life. If not for her brother's plea for help, she never would have returned to the small town of Ostrander. When the guy she's had a crush on since grade school asks for a kiss, she knows it will piss of her parents and leave the entire town talking.

After one kiss, RJ wants another, but a sudden zombie outbreak puts him and Missy on the run. To stay alive, they must learn who they can trust. And even if they can trust each other.

IT TOOK A ZOMBIE APOCALYPSE PART ONE: THE KISS

RJ strolled through the booths at the fun fair. Another gathering where people either glared at him or pretended he didn't exist. Growing up in West Vitula, one would think he'd be used to it. But a lifetime of not being welcome in the small town never came easy. Why couldn't his father have secured a position at a hospital in Ostrander, only an hour away?

Women stood behind rows of wooden tables, selling pies, bread, and jams to other women. Some men gathered in various groups, drinking beer from plastic glasses and telling recycled stories from their youth or checking out the college girls who had returned for the summer. Just as RJ had come to do. Yet, he hadn't seen anyone worth his time. If not for the anniversary of his mother's death, he would have stayed away from this town and insisted his father take some time off to visit him.

Kids ran from games to rides to carts selling cotton candy and candy apples, spending their parents' money like it would never run out. But the longest line was for a booth at the very end of the park. Males of all ages, from kindergarteners to seniors who needed a walker to travel ten feet, lined up in front of a hand-painted sign reading *$5 for a kiss*, and beside the words, a pair of bright red lips.

RJ bypassed the line to see who was so in demand with the male population. Sidney Flowers, former captain of the cheerleading squad and all-around bitch. The disgusted look she gave the crowd after she'd kissed various men on the cheek proved she hadn't changed. Yet, no one in line seemed deterred. Only him.

No way did he crave the touch of the girl who'd falsely accused him of killing his own mother and sending his father to the psych ward. All because RJ had caught Sidney helping her boyfriend cheat on a test. Though the rest of the school knew his mother had been killed on the highway by a drunk driver, they seemed to like her version of the story better.

He turned away. He wouldn't pay a penny to receive a kiss from anyone in this town. Well, except one girl, but he hadn't seen her yet this summer, not since two years prior when she'd left for Cremshaw without a backward glance.

"Melissa Ruth Smith, I insist you come back here at once."

Missy rolled her eyes as she stormed away from her father. The man had helped her celebrate her twenty-first birthday yesterday—with a simple birthday cake and a glass of wine—yet still treated her like a child. "It's to help Billy and the band, remember?" she shouted over her shoulder. "That's why I came home." Though she wished she hadn't. Not with only two weeks off between her summer classes and fall term.

"But, the kissing booth?" Her father rushed to keep up with her. "Jesus wouldn't approve."

The religion card. What a surprise. "Jesus wouldn't approve of half the shit that goes on in this town, especially how you treated that family next door." She spun around and faced her father with her hands on her hips. "And you certainly haven't been struck down yet."

"Missy, please don't talk to your father like that." Her mother hooked an arm through hers and paraded her closer to the booth she was scheduled to volunteer at. "It's just, aren't you concerned about the germs? The diseases you could catch?"

"C'mon, Mom. I'm just kissing them on the cheek." She glanced over at Sidney who tapped her watch before kissing Old Man Samson on the small patch of cheek not covered by his fluffy white beard. "Besides, you asked me to come home and help with this fundraiser."

"I know, but there are other things you could—"

"I've gotta go, Mom. Sidney's waiting for me to take over." Jogging over to the booth, Missy took her place beside the bench.

Sidney grabbed her purse and left without a word, no different than when they'd attended high school together. Hence, why Missy had fled West Vitula right after graduating high school. No one who stuck around seemed to change.

The line thinned out with the departure of her former classmate, but there were still plenty of cheeks to kiss and a plethora of greenbacks deposited into the jar, money that would help her brother and the rest of the band get to Nationals. And maybe they would see there was life beyond this backward town.

After numerous kisses, her lips burned. She reached into her pocket for her lip balm and took a break to apply it and let it soak in. When she glanced back at the line, everyone had disappeared. All the males except the one her parents would blow a gasket if she kissed. Which made her want to lay her lips on him even more.

"Fifty dollars for a kiss." RJ held the bill and waved it across the counter. "It goes in the jar if I get a kiss from you."

"I'd do it for five." She pointed to the paper sign on the jar. "But if you're willing to donate more, go ahead."

He walked into the booth and sat on the bench. "You misunderstand me, Missy. I don't want a peck on the cheek. I want a real kiss, your lips on mine."

Her cheeks reddened, making her all the more adorable, and she stepped back. "I, um.... It's not.... I can't."

"It's one kiss." He waved the money around again, enjoying her discomfort. "The same money you'd make kissing ten old guys with beards, or ten creeps who gawk at your cleavage when you bend over to kiss them."

The flush on her face disappeared. Maybe he shouldn't have included that last observation.

"Hey." He needed her attention back on him. "One kiss, and you never know, you just might like it."

"Really?" She placed a hand on his knee then waltzed in front of him with a confidence he'd never seen from her before. "You're that confident of the power of those full brown lips, are you?"

Before he had the chance to think of a response, she snatched the bill from his hand, leaned between his spread legs, and kissed him. He barely had a chance to close his mouth when it was all over.

"Thank you so much for your support." Missy curtsied then stuck the money into the collection bottle.

RJ gripped the bottom of the bench, trying to process the fact the kiss had already happened. He'd hoped for so much more.

"Another." He stood and yanked his wallet from his back pocket. "I'll give you one hundred dollars if I can kiss you." Yanking the bill from inside the leather fold, he held it out in front of him to prove he was good for it.

"Now, that's against the rules."

Her jaw shifted to the side, but when she tilted her head, he hoped she was actually considering his proposition.

RJ hopped off the bench and took a tentative step forward. He'd didn't want her to automatically say no. "You know I've never played by the rules. Why would I start now?"

With a laugh, Missy playfully pushed on his chest. "You're trouble, RJ. And you're looking to get me into trouble with you."

Returning to the stool, he stared into her crystal-blue eyes and smiled. She hadn't said no. "Just a kiss." He nodded to a patch of bushes with a bench set amongst them. "No one will see us over there."

"Is that brown boy bothering you, Missy?"

The twang in the woman's voice bothered RJ more than her reference to the color of his skin.

"No, Shelley." Missy turned her back to him. "He was just leaving."

"Good." Shelley, another of their classmates, sized up the jar of money. "'Cause we don't need his cash. We're doing fine here without it."

The punch to the gut that used to come with such ignorant comments never came. Some people refused to change, especially in this town. But he'd always believed Missy to be different. Maybe he'd been wrong.

"Are you taking over for me, then?" she asked Shelley.

"Yeah, your dad followed me around for the last fifteen minutes to make sure I was here on time. He was really freaking out about your kissing guys on the cheek."

RJ walked away. He'd been dismissed. And if Missy's father was that upset, he was probably waiting with disinfectant or something.

No, there was nothing good about coming back to West Vitula for the summer. His dad still worked the same long hours, so except for the day spent together on the anniversary of his mother's death, RJ was spending his summer alone.

"Wait!"

He turned with the hope Missy was talking to him for some reason.

And she was, standing right in front of him. She grabbed the money he still held in his hand. "You forgot to put this in the jar." Without giving him a chance to question her, she jogged back to the booth and shoved it through the glass bottleneck.

Did that mean he was going to get his kiss?

Missy raced back to RJ, grabbing his hand then pulling him toward the alcove in the bushes he'd pointed out earlier. She only had a couple of minutes before her father would be breathing down her neck again.

No, if she was to have anyone's breath on her neck, she wanted it to be RJ's. After he'd finished kissing her. Or maybe during. But, if her parents caught her lip to lip with him, she'd be dead. At least grounded until she left for Cremshaw again. They still believed her to be a good girl, pure until she married. No way would she confess she'd lost her virginity to a guy she didn't even know. Still didn't, only the smell of his cologne. And she'd said RJ's name in the middle of sex with the stranger. That's when the guy up and left, leaving her in the dorm bathroom to get dressed before someone else walked in.

She'd crushed hard on her neighbor for years but never had the courage to go against her parents' expectations until she'd left home.

Sitting on the bench, she pulled him down beside her. "This is long overdue." She fisted the front of his shirt and leaned into him, closing her eyes. His warm, minty breath met her lips before his soft skin. She nearly melted at the contact, unable to pull away.

What started as a gentle, sweet ballet of a kiss quickly

turned into a frantic lambada. Missy clung to him, desperate for more. She straddled his lap, pushing against him. Why had she waited so long to act on her feelings for him? She'd had plenty of opportunities to be alone with him. Yet, what her parents thought had always seemed to matter. Not anymore.

When he slid his hands under her shirt, she moaned, anxious to feel them all over her body.

"Get your hands off my daughter!"

Missy pushed off RJ and turned to face her mother. "I was just.... We...."

"There is no excuse for that brown boy to have his meaty hands on you." Her mother pursed her lips as if she'd sucked on a lemon. "Get away from him right now."

"No." Missy reached for RJ's hand and intertwined her fingers with his. Her heart beat hard as she stood up to her mother for the first time. "I won't. I'm an adult now, and I can spend my time with whomever I want."

"Melissa Ruth, how dare you talk to me like that." Her mother thumped her hands onto her hips and glared, the woman's signature move when she was angry. "Your father is going to hear about this."

"Good." And maybe they'd let her go back to Cremshaw early, far away from this shithole of a town. She'd definitely outgrown West Vitula, but not her feelings for RJ.

"You wanna get out of here?" RJ jerked his thumb over his shoulder, anxious to be long gone before Missy's father arrived. He'd had enough run-ins with the man over the years, for things like taking the garbage out too early, not cutting the grass often enough, and for parking on the road. Simple things, teaching him to avoid the man at all costs. How would he react when he found out RJ had kissed his daughter?

"Yes." Missy grabbed his hand and pulled him toward the park entrance, their houses only two blocks from there.

They raced across the grass when a roar erupted from the crowd. Missy paused, jerking him to a halt. Had her father reacted that poorly? Then came the screams. People scattered, racing in every direction around them, while others fell to the ground, trampled by those fleeing the park.

RJ focused on their destination and ran faster, not letting go of Missy. His phone vibrated in his pocket, but he refused to stop. Not when he feared the worst. Someone had a gun.

He raced up the steps to his front porch where he finally paused to catch his breath and fish for his key in his shorts. They were probably the only ones who locked their house in the entire town, but previous encounters proved it necessary.

With a shaky hand, he slid the key into the lock. He was already pushing on the door when the lock clicked open. Missy rushed inside without any hesitation. After slamming the door shut again, he locked it then dared a peek outside. No one. They were safe. At least for now.

Missy touched his arm. "What do you think happened?"

He turned from the window and noticed the fear in her eyes. "I don't know. But it's best we stay here until everything is settled."

His phone vibrated again, reminding him he had a message. No one in West Vitula had his number except his father. And all his friends back at Fielding University knew he wasn't around for the summer.

He pulled out his cell and saw the text from his dad. Had those injured in the park arrived at the hospital? Did he know what had triggered the stampede?

RJ pressed on the text and read....

Contagion arrived from Ostrander.

Spread through the hospital.
Stay in bunker.
I'm infected.
Zombies

Zombies? He dropped his phone and stared at it on the floor, expecting it to explode. Zombies didn't exist. He was in some kind of dream. Had to be. Missy actually had come home for the summer. And kissed him. Now, zombies.

"What is it?" Missy bent down to pick up his cell then handed it back to him. "What happened back at the park?"

"Zombies." The word came out before he had a chance to stop it. He didn't know whether to laugh or grab Missy again and run.

A crooked smile formed dimples in her cheeks. "You're joking, right? Trying to help me laugh off what happened."

"I wish." He showed her the message from his father. "My dad doesn't have a sense of humor."

The phone beeped, and she pushed his hand away. "I think it needs to be charged. We should call him just to be sure. Or contact somebody. Maybe he meant something else. You know how stupid autocorrect can be."

RJ rushed to the kitchen, found his charger, and plugged in the cell. But, by then, he'd lost signal. Reception was spotty in West Vitula, but he couldn't get anything. He peeked through the doorway, out to the living room. "Missy, can you get a signal?"

After digging into her purse, she pulled out her phone with a pink, sparkly case. Not at all what he expected from her. Had he missed that girly side, or had someone given it to her, and she didn't want to hurt their feelings? That he could understand.

She held the cell up and moved around the room. "I got nothing. What's going on?"

"I don't know. Maybe we should try outside?" Though

he doubted it would make a difference.

Missy stepped over to window and shoved the curtains aside. "Um, there are people coming. And they don't...look right."

RJ glanced outside. Neighbors walked down the middle of the street, their bodies twitching. And no one stopped to talk to one another. They just kept marching along to some unknown destination. As they came closer, he noticed their tattered clothing, their disheveled hair, and limbs connected at odd angles to the rest of their body, as if they'd been trampled. And now they were up and walking.

"Um, RJ…." Missy squeezed his bicep. "You think we should go? Do what your dad said?"

"Yes." He darted through the living room and kitchen to the mudroom at the back of the house with his neighbor right behind him. Opening the door, he glanced around the backyard for any of the so-called zombies. With the pathway clear, he grasped her hand, and they raced to the underground shelter.

RJ yanked the heavy blast door open then gestured for Missy to enter first.

"Do not go down there with that boy, young lady."

RJ spun around, recognizing the stern tone, one he'd heard most of his childhood. Missy's father.

She looked at the man who'd raised her then at RJ, her eyes wide and face pale. "Dad, you have got to come with us. There is a viral outbreak at the hospital, and it's spreading through town."

No way did he want to be in a confined space with that man. But, if it meant getting Missy to safety, he'd suck up his pride.

"I know." Missy's father lunged forward and grabbed her hand, yanking her away from RJ. "Your mother and brother are sick. We need to get them to the hospital."

RJ heard moaning before two figures appeared around the corner. The rest of Missy's family had been infected all right, their faces gaunt and bodies twitching as they sauntered closer and closer. RJ reached for Missy's other hand. If he took her father by surprise, he could yank her away and lead her into the bunker before the rest of her family came close enough to be a threat. But he underestimated the man's hold on his daughter. There was a pop, and Missy cried out, dropping his hold and slamming her hand against her other shoulder.

"Dad, please. Can't you see what they are? There is no cure, Dad. They're zombies." She pulled from the man's grasp, crying out with every attempt, but to no avail.

"Please, Mr. Smith." RJ darted between the man and his zombie family, pushing him toward the bunker, hoping to budge him or at least to release Missy. "There is nothing you can do for them now. You need to save yourself and your daughter. I can help you."

The man dropped his daughter's hand and shoved RJ in the chest, pushing him toward the approaching zombies. "Don't touch me, you heathen. God will help them get better, not you."

With her father's attention on RJ, Missy had dashed to the bunker and waited on the steps leading inside. RJ spun away from the man and raced to join her. If Mr. Smith wasn't going to come inside, he would get them all killed.

"Can you believe our daughter?" The man raised his hands into the air as he spoke to the zombie who was once his wife. "I thought we raised her better than that."

The zombie who used to be Missy's mom moaned in response, tilting her head to the side and gnashing her teeth.

RJ stood at the top of the stairs in front of Missy, trying to block her view. Zombies ate anything living they could catch. At least they did on any show and movie he'd seen them on. And her mother eating the flesh off her father was not something he wanted to see, let alone have Missy witness.

Focused on Missy's parents, RJ didn't see their son

approach from the side until the kid reached for his arm, the cold fingers across his skin enough to get him moving.

He shoved the kid away then grabbed the door to close it behind him and Missy.

"You're making a big mistake, Melissa." Her father went to help his son up. "That boy's father is the reason everyone is sick. He's a—"

The man's words ended with a scream as his son and wife attacked, biting into his flesh, blood pouring from their mouths.

RJ yanked the door shut then wrenched the locks to set the dead bolts. They were safe inside, but safe did not mean all was well. Missy sobbed on the cot at the bottom of the stairs. She'd just watched her zombie brother and mother attack her father. And he had no idea how to make the situation any better.

IT TOOK A ZOMBIE APOCALYPSE PART TWO: THE ZOMBIES

The first time Missy had wished her parents dead happened on a high school trip to a museum in Ostrander her freshman year. They had decided to chaperone the outing and bring her brother along, believing the cultural exposure would do him good. Though they only meant the exhibits, not the other people at the museum. Being pulled to stand with her parents and brother, so close they moved as a unit, proved embarrassing enough. But their comments about immigrants—as if their own ancestors hadn't immigrated to the country a century before—made her want to die. They had made RJ's life hell, always finding something to complain about and reminding the family they didn't belong. RJ's father had saved countless lives as a surgeon, and RJ saved her and even tried to save her father. Still, her dad refused to see the good in him right to the very end.

Now that her parents were dead, or undead, she wasn't sad she would never see them again, only that they died with so much hate in their hearts. Not at all the way she'd been taught to treat others at Sunday school.

Moving to Cremshaw had been the best decision she'd made. Her parents had wanted her to commute to BDU, but two hours one-way didn't work for her. If not for the stupid band fundraiser, she'd still be there, away from the zombies. Or maybe she'd be in the middle of it, unaware of the contagious disease until she was already infected.

Though the kiss with RJ never would have happened. The beginning of all she'd dreamed of doing with him, yet far better than she'd ever imagined. So why was she sobbing when she finally had what she wanted?

RJ flopped onto the cot beside her, and she screamed, pain like lightning shooting down from her shoulder to the tips of her fingers.

"Shit." He jumped off as quickly as he'd gotten on. "Your arm. I totally forgot."

And so had she, so angry at her parents instead of acknowledging the pain she was in. "What do I do? It hurts so bad." She'd unconsciously held it in front of her, as if she had her elbow in a sling, and used her other hand to support it. Even that hurt now.

"I think the tug-of-war with your father may have pulled your shoulder out of its socket. There are a couple of ways we can do this." His eyes were on her, but not his focus.

"Just tell me. Quick." Bile rose from her stomach, the burning sensation reaching her throat.

"Okay, okay. We'll see if you can do this yourself." His voice rose an octave. Was he more panicked now than he had been escaping the zombies?

"Now."

"Put your sore arm out to the side." He demonstrated the move.

She twisted around, but the agony of the motion made her head spin. "I can't. I'm going to pass out." Her ears rang, and her vision blurred.

"Okay, I'm going to have to put it back into place

then." He patted the cot. "I need you to lie down on your back, with your dislocated arm toward me. I'll help you get into position, but we have to get it fixed soon."

"Yes." She accepted his help, and after a tangled mess of limbs, an awkward flop onto her back, and even more discomfort, she was ready for him to repair the damage done to her.

He grasped her hand, his skin warm and clammy compared her hers. Then he pulled her arm out toward him. She gritted her teeth and breathed through the pain, not any worse, but no better either.

"I'm going to pull now. I promise I'll be gentle, but I've got to do this to get it back into place."

She nodded, almost amused he looked to be in more agony than she was.

When he began to tug, she squeezed her eyes shut, concentrating on breathing through the process rather than screaming at RJ. His father was a doctor, but did RJ know what he was doing?

She gripped the cot with her good hand, but that didn't provide any relief. So she pounded it with her fist instead. RJ's treatment wasn't working. Her fingers slipped from his. He changed his hold on her, clutching her wrist with one hand and her elbow with the other. Then, with his one foot propped on the edge of the cot, he pulled harder.

"Stop," Missy screamed, the torture more than she could handle.

But he didn't, instead giving one last heave. She felt the pop more than heard it, the sharp pain replaced by a dull throbbing.

Though he stopped pulling, RJ still held onto her wrist. "Is it back in place?"

"I think so." She wiggled her fingers, no longer wanting to rip her arm off. "What do I do now?"

He laid her arm across her stomach then began rummaging through a metal box under the cot. "I need to fix a sling for you and get some cold on your shoulder to reduce swelling. Ultimately, I should take you to the hospital, but that's not possible at the moment."

No, it wasn't. She didn't know if she'd ever get to a hospital again. RJ was her only hope. When he set the compress across her shoulder, she relaxed into its coolness. RJ was her only chance to survive.

"Zombies." RJ shimmied onto the cot carefully, rather than flopping onto it as he had before.

Not a word directed at her, yet the same word on her mind. The undead were never part of her fantasies involving RJ. Neither was being holed up in an underground bunker where they would likely starve to death. Instead, she'd dreamed of them living in a condo in the city, letting their children play with others from many different cultures. And never returning to West Vitula.

RJ grazed his fingers across her open palm. "I'm sorry about your family."

She clasped his hand and squeezed his fingers. "No, I'm sorry about them, for everything they did and said to you and your parents over the years, especially after your mom died." They'd been especially cruel to RJ's dad, her mom refusing to get the women's association together to cook meals for them, as they did when anyone else in town lost a member of their family. And her father had called the police on Dr. Dhawan, citing child abandonment when the man had left for work an hour before RJ had to leave for school. "This isn't your fault. None of it ever was."

He brushed his thumb along the back of her hand and leaned back against the wall. "And their behavior is not your fault. You've never treated me the way your parents do, the way the rest of the town does. Or...did."

Missy leaned against his shoulder. The residents of West Vitula as they knew them were gone. All infected and undead. "What do we do now?"

He shrugged, lifting her head. "Stay here until we run

out of food? Then we'll have to go find some more, and kill some zombies along the way."

He said the words so matter-of-factly, as if zombies were just another inconvenience of life, something they'd get through like every other situation he'd encountered in life, instead of the end of the world. "I can't kill."

"No, you *haven't* killed. But you'll learn to." He bent his knee and turned toward her. "We both will have to, if we're going to survive. Besides, they're not really alive anymore."

She drew back from him. "But that's my mom and my brother, people I went to school with. Most of the time I couldn't wait to move away, and there were many times I wished them dead. But I can't bash their heads in." She'd spent her teen years counting down the days until she could move away, ignoring everything that bothered her rather than facing issues head on. She didn't like confrontation, and definitely not violence.

"Okay, don't worry about it." He ran his fingers across her arm. "We'll figure it out as we go. But we're safe down here for now."

She settled against him and hoped he was right. As long as she didn't have to leave the bunker, she'd be fine. She trusted RJ. Her eyes slowly grew heavy until she fought to keep them open. Resting his arm around her, RJ made her feel protected. No harm would come to her with him by her side.

Bang, bang, bang.

Missy bolted upright, unsure if she'd dreamed the sound or if it had woken her. But when RJ grasped her hand and held a finger to his lips, her sense of safety disappeared. Someone or something was outside.

The sound came again, only it wasn't a bang. More like a clawing, hands running over the steel door. Whatever was outside wanted in. It knew they were there.

"Stay here." He put a hand on her lap to enforce his whispered words before he pushed off the cot.

Missy grabbed his shirt. "Don't go up there." No way did she want to be left alone with her arm in a sling.

"I'm not." He pointed to a small television set on one of the shelves. "If they haven't destroyed the camera, I should be able to see what's going on out there."

After RJ pressed the power button, the screen took forever to come on. What started out as a little dot of light grew into live feed of his yard and the zombies in it, all of them wandering aimlessly. All except the one at the door to the bunker. Her father, now one of the undead.

She reeled back at the sight of him, the bone of his right arm exposed through a missing chunk of flesh, muscle, and whatever else used to be there. But, his face was worse. One eyeball hung from its socket while that side of his face drooped past his chin, as if his skin disintegrated and slowly fell off.

And still he banged. He knew they were in there. Instead of wanting her away from RJ, he simply wanted in, to eat their flesh, turn them into zombies as her mother and brother had done to him.

"Turn it off." Her stomach turned. She didn't know how long it had been since she'd last eaten, but she was going to vomit if she had to look at her zombie father any longer.

After flicking off the screen, RJ returned to the cot beside her. He didn't say a word, only held his arms open. And she immediately took refuge in them, hoping the image of her father would disappear if she was enveloped in the warmth of the neighbor who had saved her. Yet, nothing stopped the banging. Didn't zombies tire?

"So, what will your friends at BDU think when you tell them you survived a zombie apocalypse?"

She twisted around and stared at him, unsure if she'd hear him correctly over the noise at the door. "What do you mean? You really think this will all blow over and I'll be back at university in two weeks?"

"You never know." He shrugged. "Let's say it happens.

What will they say?"

She smiled. "I think they'll be more impressed that I finally hooked up with the guy I've had a crush on for most of my life."

RJ's forehead wrinkled. "Who did you hook up with this summer?"

She swatted him. "You, silly."

"Uh, no." He squeezed her knee, making her jump. "Hooking up means a lot more than one shared kiss."

"Well, the summer's not over yet." She gazed at him through her lashes, unsure why she flirted with him. Since their kiss in the park, the entire world had changed. And she had to change. No more flirty college girl. She had to be tough. Or she wouldn't survive.

RJ slipped his arm from behind Missy and gently laid her on the cot. Eventually the banging had stopped, but their conversation hadn't. At least not until Missy had fallen asleep on his shoulder, cutting herself off mid-sentence.

But, before he could sleep, he had a job to do. Opening the cupboard, he eyed the selection of survival weapons his father had collected over the years, specifically the multi-tool axe and a bowie knife. Not ideal gadgets for killing zombies, but they were the best choices to keep the undead away from him for the time being.

After buckling on the utility belt, he loaded up. One chance to do this for Missy because if she woke and found out what he'd done before he convinced her it was for the best, she'd hate him forever.

He clicked on the monitor and flinched at the buzz it emitted. But Missy never stirred. She slept as he hoped she'd continue to do until he returned. On the screen, he noted the position of the zombies in his backyard and Missy's. Five altogether. Missy's mother and brother sauntered in a circle around both yards. The principal of the local high school and the school librarian—always rumored to lock themselves in his office for a quick nooner—stood at RJ's back door, trying to pry their way inside.

Yet, Missy's dad remained outside the bunker entrance, his jaw hanging open while the skin of his face drooped farther down his chest. Maybe he could no longer see. A definite advantage for RJ, since he would be the first zombie eliminated.

After one last glance at his beautiful neighbor, he grabbed the axe from his belt then unlocked the bunker door. He didn't even have the chance to step out before the zombie of Mr. Smith lunged at him. RJ swung hard, not even realizing he'd severed the man's head until it rolled across the grass. He stared at it for a second then shook his own head, the other zombies already alerted to his presence.

Shoving Mr. Smith's body away from the entrance, RJ closed the bunker door then locked it from the outside. He didn't need Missy coming out unarmed, or trying to stop him from eliminating immediate threats.

Her brother attacked next, even more tenacious as an undead than alive. He knocked the axe from RJ's grip then dove for his midsection. He would have made a great defensive tackle if his parents had allowed him to play football. As RJ fell back, he drove his knife into the kid's skull.

With the mother in pursuit, he shoved the boy off him then jumped to his feet. He didn't give her a chance to attack, simply took her out the same way he had her son.

His chest ached, not from exertion but from what he'd just done. As much as he hated the zombies he'd just killed when they were alive, they were still Missy's family. Would she understand? Or had he crossed a line?

Miss Burns and Mr. Gentry had noticed him and ambled in his direction. Retrieving the axe, RJ rushed toward his next two targets. He had no mixed feelings about eliminating them. And neither proved a challenge.

Five zombies dead. But he wasn't finished.

Both yards had fences all around, except between them. Yet another source of conflict between the two families—mostly over who would pay for it. That worked for RJ, except he needed to block the space between the two houses from the front. If he could do that, they'd at least have some room outside of the bunker safe from zombies. And if that worked, they could maybe return to their houses. But would Missy live in her own and not want him around? She might after she learned what he'd done. He didn't have time to dwell on what might happen. He had tasks to complete.

His own car was parked in the driveway, so he only had to block the spaces on either side, between the two houses. Not as big a space if they shared a driveway like some of their neighbors. Though that would have definitely caused more problems.

Leaning against the Smiths' back deck was an old door. He had no idea what they'd planned to do with it, but he would put it to good use. The door wasn't heavy, but awkward to carry, especially trying to fit between his car and the neighbors' house. All while on the lookout for more townsfolk turned zombie.

RJ set the door against his car and the side of his house. Not perfect, but it might slow down the undead or make them change their mind about coming into the backyard.

On his own porch, he tipped the round patio table onto its side, folded up the legs, then rolled it down the stairs and into position on the other side of his car. If he had a spare moment, he'd find something more permanent to block the way, but he had the most time-consuming task yet to complete.

RJ brushed his hands down the front of his shorts, hoping to clear off some of the dirt before he returned to the bunker. He'd considered going into his house to have a shower, but turning on any lights would definitely draw zombies to the area. Plus, the hum of the water heater would be noticed among the eerie silence that had settled over the town.

Grasping the padlock on the bunker, he slid the key inside and turned it. After shoving the lock into his pocket, he pulled open the hatch door and slipped inside. He'd completed everything he'd intended to do, all before Missy woke up.

Or maybe not.

The cot was empty, his neighbor nowhere in sight. *Shit.* Where had she gone? There was no way she could have left.

RJ glanced across the other cot and the two bunks. No one. He searched underneath the cots, pulling out empty totes that were supposed to be stocked with food. Food he'd eaten over the years while pretending the rest of the world didn't exist. A common dream during his early high school years when he was the shortest, skinniest kid in West Vitula. And the only non-white kid. Maybe that situation wasn't such a great reality. But, at least he had Missy with him. If he could find her.

A click came from deeper in the bunker, and a panel swung open.

RJ sucked in a breath. The bathroom. He'd never thought to look there.

"Where have you been?" Missy slammed the panel shut and raced toward him then stopped short. She stared down at his clothes. "What were you doing?"

He looked down at his shirt, noticing the blood and small bits of body parts for the first time. Changing would have been a good idea, even if he didn't have a shower. "I, um...."

Missy turned away from him and flicked on the

monitor. She didn't speak until the screen had cleared and she had examined the feed from each camera. "You killed them, didn't you?"

He sat on the steps. The small space was about to become much more cramped. "I did."

"What's this?"

He stared at her, stunned by her reaction. Instead of screaming at him, telling him how much she hated him for killing her zombie family, she pointed at the screen. The top left-hand corner that showed the back half of her yard.

RJ walked closer. On the screen, she pointed to a mound of dirt, one he'd just finished making. "What is it?"

"It's where I buried them." He couldn't just leave the bodies lying on the ground, visible to Missy when they had to leave the bunker. Especially since he'd made sure they'd starve if they didn't.

"Who? Who did you bury?" She kept her finger on the monitor.

"Your parents and brother. Plus Miss Burns and Mr. Gentry." Digging and refilling the hole had taken less time than it had to move the bodies to their final resting spot.

"And this? Did you really put a cross on their grave?" She finally turned to him, tears in her eyes.

"That's what you do, right? Isn't that what Christians do?" Everyone buried in the local cemetery had a cross engraved into their tombstone, or the stone was the cross.

"Yes, but.... I didn't expect you to do it. I mean, you're not Christian."

"No, but you are. So were they." And every other person in the town. He loved that one hour on Sunday mornings when he could play outside and not have to worry about the glares and snide remarks. Though, as a teen, he usually remained asleep during that time.

"Still, why did you bury them and put a cross on their grave?"

Wait, was she mad at him about the cross? "Because I thought it was the right thing to do. But I guess I was wrong."

"No." Missy touched his arm before taking another quick glance at the screen. "I just don't understand it. They were always so cruel to you, and yet even when they're dead, you still try to do right by them."

"I didn't do it for them." He longed to hold her, kiss her, prove everything he'd done happened because he cared for her. Yet, he resisted the temptation, waited for her to understand.

Missy wrinkled her forehead at him and placed her palm on his chest. "This is about that kiss, isn't it? The one at the park before the zombies arrived?"

"It's about more than that." Did he have to spell it out for her? He'd thought the kiss meant something more, especially the way she reacted to him. But maybe she'd just been rebelling against her parents, wanted to get caught to piss them off. Like every other girl in town he'd believed had any interest in him. He slumped back on the cot. "Forget it. It doesn't matter."

"It does." She joined him, sitting cross-legged and taking his hand in hers. "It does matter, or you wouldn't have done it. I want to know why."

"I killed them for you, so you could remember them alive rather than dead." RJ shifted on the mattress. "I buried them so you wouldn't have to see their bodies. And I added the cross because I thought that's what you would do."

She squeezed his hand. "All while risking your own life." Leaning closer, she kissed his cheek. "Thank you."

He yearned to tell her so much more, how he'd crushed on her since the third grade, had a collection of love poems he'd written for her in his desk drawer, and even how she was the only person he'd ever fantasized about spending the rest of his life with. All to get her clothes off and fuck until they died of starvation or were eaten by zombies. But he didn't because they had to survive. This couldn't be the end.

Missy woke in RJ's arms, her shoulder aching but still much better than it had felt after her father had wrenched it from its socket. How she had ended up in the middle of a zombie apocalypse with the one man she'd longed for still baffled her, but she didn't want to be anywhere else.

She snuggled a little closer. Then her stomach rumbled. A cavernous space that hadn't been filled since the ketchup and mustard-covered footlong she'd managed to gobble down out of sight of her parents at the fun fair.

Did RJ have any food stashed in the bunker? She hoped so. Otherwise, they'd have to venture out and face the undead again. And she looked forward to that as much as spending a year with her parents rather than returning to BDU. That was, before they turned into zombies.

Slipping from the cot, she adjusted her arm in the sling RJ had constructed for her. After a quick trip to the bathroom cubby she'd found last night, she searched the shelves at the back of the bunker. A couple of empty water bottles and a half eaten box of crackers. Her stomach wasn't picky, so she popped one of the crackers into her mouth. Stale. No, not just stale; it had a weird taste to it, almost like mold had considered growing on it but hadn't quite gotten around to it yet. She tossed the box back onto the shelf with the empty bottles.

Shit. Unless RJ had some secret stash, they had no choice. She'd have to channel her inner warrior and learn how to kill a zombie. Otherwise, she might as well let them maul her now. She couldn't depend on RJ all the time.

"You figured it out, huh?" He rolled off the edge of the cot and stretched his arms into the air, giving her a peek at his glorious abs. Her friends always said they wanted a guy who had a six-pack. Yet none of them ever gave him a second glance. Hardly even a first one. And the only six-pack their boyfriends had was one of beer.

"That we have no food? Yeah." She slipped on her

sandals, not exactly zombie-killing footwear, but if she made it to her house, she'd find more appropriate attire. And lots of food. Her mother had kept the cold cellar well stocked, always canning something on the weekends when she wasn't at a women's association event. She'd tried to get Missy involved in making the preserves, but she'd rather have stabbed a pen in her eye than spend the day with her mom. Any time they were together, Missy always received a lecture about something she had done wrong, something that didn't please the community and the church. Now, she wished she had paid attention, just to learn the process. And she was glad her mother had spent all that time canning. She and RJ would be set for months. "So, let's go get some."

"Not so fast. I'll go get something, and then I'll be back." He stood at the bottom of the stairs, as if he could block her way.

She grabbed the knife he'd placed on the table in the front corner of the bunker. It scared her even to hold the heavy blade, but she refused to be left behind again. Besides, even if she did tell him about the food in the cold cellar, there were other things she needed to grab from her house. "I'm going with you, whether you like it or not."

"Not like that, you're not." Before she even realized he'd moved, he took the knife away from her. But, he gave it back after turning the serrated side to the bottom. "Are you sure you can use this? I mean, your arm likely hasn't healed yet."

No, but she'd give it her all. Not even twenty-four hours in the bunker, and she was ready to go mad. She'd do whatever it took to get out—and find food—even if only for an hour or two. "I have no choice. And I'm not leaving everything up to you."

"Fine." He brushed past her to the other side of the space. "But, we're not going anywhere until we survey the property. I want to know what to expect when we go out."

She didn't expect to, either. Guns-ablazing wasn't her

style, but she knew where to find those, too. Better weapons than the knife and small axe RJ had. And she actually knew how to use them. Her father had insisted she and her brother learn to shoot a gun and to disarm a person holding one. The school shootings on the news had brought about a new round of distrust toward their neighbors and prompted the weapons lessons. Little did her father know, it was every other guy at her high school who had a gun, usually kept in their truck.

"Shit." RJ slammed his fist against the shelf.

"What is it?" She glanced at the screen showing their properties. Five zombies. The same number he'd taken out by himself the night before. "We can handle them."

"Maybe." He pointed to a portion of the screen showing the space between their houses. "I blocked this area last night, and nothing's moved. That means they're climbing. Probably stronger now."

"Then we need to get to my house." She pointed toward the door, a shot of residual pain shooting from her shoulder to her finger. But she wouldn't let RJ know it hurt. She had to go, too. "I can get food and weapons. We'll be set."

"Fine, but you're behind me." His face became stern, a look she'd never seen on him before. "I saw that wince. Until your arm is better, you're going to have to let me clear the way."

She nodded. As long as she wasn't stuck in the bunker, she would do whatever he said.

"There's only one zombie right now between here and your back door." He looked from the screen to her. "I'll take it down and then get you inside. As soon as I eliminate the rest, I'll join you."

"Are you sure? Can't you just leave them for now?" She'd need his help to load everything.

"No. We're likely going to have our hands full on the way back. A clear path is the best option." He tapped the screen, pointing to the back of her yard. "I'll grab this wagon, too. I'm sure it will help."

"Great idea." The same wagon she used to pull her brother around in when he was just a toddler. When he got bigger, he'd wanted to pull her around. He'd dumped her into a fire hydrant trying to take her around the corner, resulting in the scar across her right knee. She remembered seeing RJ peeking out his window as she passed in front of his house after the accident, tears streaming down her cheeks and blood covering her leg.

Without bothering to turn off the screen, RJ headed for the bunker door. "Lock up behind us." He handed her a padlock before cranking open the inner locks. Like an exploding water balloon, he burst out the door, axe held in front of him. He took the first zombie down with one swing to the head before Missy had a chance to close the door. The others closed in on them. Missy still had a clear path to her house, but she couldn't leave RJ to kill them all by himself. Not if they were stronger than before. And these undead moved faster than the ones she'd seen wandering down the street before they'd hidden in the bunker.

Veering to the left, she chose the lone zombie. The undead body of a guy she'd attended high school with. A few years older than her, he'd been captain of the football team and still wore his letterman jacket. With no scholarship, he didn't succeed any farther than the local convenience store where he worked as a gas jockey. The same guy who'd offered to take her into the back room and show her a good time. Remembering the way he'd leered down her top, she had no problem plunging the knife into the side of his head. He dropped with a thud, flesh flying off him at the impact and landing on her bare legs. She shuddered, trying not to freak out. The sooner she got inside, the sooner she could wash off the zombie bits.

"Missy, get going!" RJ kicked the head of another schoolmate aside and rushed toward his blockade where two more zombies tried to climb their way into the backyards. He'd already downed four to her one. But give her a gun, and she'd take them all down.

She dashed to the back porch and twisted the door handle. Could zombies do that action? Would she find some inside? Examining the main floor of the house she grew up in, she found no one, and nothing out of place. She was safe for now.

Heading down the basement, she nearly tripped on the stairs in her rush to gather supplies. She'd wanted nothing more to leave the bunker. Now, she only wanted to grab what they needed and hurry back.

Her mom had kept plenty of rugged cardboard boxes that had been used to transport the fruit and vegetables she'd bought home from the market. They'd work to carry the jars to the bunker. She'd already loaded three when she heard footsteps coming down the stairs.

"Missy? You down here?" RJ peeked below the stairwell.

"Almost done." She squeezed some small jars of blueberry jam amongst the vegetables then grabbed the convenient box handles. She couldn't budge it, the pain shooting down her arm, blinding. Breathing away the agony, she was ready to admit defeat. "But I'm going to need your help getting them up the stairs."

"Not a problem." He joined her in the small, cold space. "Go get anything else you need. If I have a chance today, I want to grab a few things from my house, too."

"Okay." Though she wasn't sure if she wanted to go with him there or preferred to stay in the bunker. Being out in the open of her once too-safe town felt like walking down Lincoln Street on Ostrander in the middle of the night. Not something she wanted to dare even with the best protection.

After grabbing basics like soap, her toothbrush, and toilet paper from the bathroom, she headed to her room, shoving the bathroom supplies into the smaller of her two travel cases. She would have had both suitcases almost completely packed already, anxious to leave again for BDU, except her parents had insisted she put everything back in its old place rather than "living like a hobo." Her clothes were easy enough to grab, two piles already washed, dried, folded, and waiting on her bed for her to put away. The one thing her mother didn't do for her. What else did she need? Tampons and pads. Yes, that would be a problem soon enough, and she didn't want to have to run slalom around zombies when the time came.

Confident she had everything she needed, she zipped up the cases. A rustling behind her stopped her cold. Something was there, and something big. The door was right in front of her, and RJ wasn't anywhere to be seen. Behind her was the wall. And her window.

She bit her bottom lip. Did she dare look? With her heart ready to jump out of her chest, she placed her palm on her bed and slowly turned around. She screamed.

Her other neighbor, Mrs. Caldecott—who'd worn nothing but her housecoat and curlers after the death of her husband—had her hands propped on the windowsill and was trying to get inside. She'd climbed the tree! A zombie had actually climbed the tree outside her window and wanted in her room.

"What is it?"

Missy turned to RJ, still in shock. The woman gnashed her false teeth at them, leaning closer until her head was inside. "She.... I...."

RJ didn't wait for her to finish. He raced over to the window and slammed it shut, knocking the woman's head clean off. Curlers and all, the head stared up at them, no longer ready to eat them, but far from the smiles that used to greet Missy whenever she passed the woman's house.

"Let's get out of here." She no longer wanted to set foot in her room. There was no way she was touching that head to get it out, and her stomach churned at the sight.

RJ nodded. "I have everything by the back door. But,

before we go, you said you have weapons?"

"Yes." She grabbed the handles of her luggage and headed out the door. At one time, she'd thought having RJ in her room would be a dream come true, but not anymore. Not with pieces of zombie lying around.

At the back door sat multiple boxes of food and cases of water. More than she had loaded up. She glanced over at RJ, amused he felt so comfortable in her home. "I see you found the pantry."

He pursed his lips together and nodded. "We needed more than just that stuff in the jars."

"Well, you should have kept looking." She headed to the large, shelved closet just off the kitchen. "My dad has a stash of weapons in behind."

Reaching along the trim of the front portion of the side wall—the only space in the closet that didn't have any shelving—she found the indent and wiggled her fingers inside. Giving it a pull, she removed the panel to expose an arsenal. Or not. The rack that had once contained a variety of automatic weapons sat empty. A rusted old .22 bolt-action rifle remained, the gun having belonged to her great-grandfather. Plus two compound bows, the crossbows also missing from where they'd once hung.

"Shit, someone's been here." Missy rubbed her hands over her face, ignoring the lump in her throat. While her father had kept his weapons hidden, he must have told someone about them. Maybe one of his buddies at their late night poker games. And that meant there were others not yet undead. Were they still around, or had they simply taken the weapons and left town?

RJ's face fell, his eyes wide. "Not good. We've got to get back. Now!"

"I know." She grabbed the remaining bows and the quiver filled with target and field tipped arrows. Her father had ensured she knew how to shoot them all, stressing it took more skill to find her target with a compound bow than anything else he owned. If that's what she was left with, she wouldn't dare leave it behind.

RJ leaned out the small space he'd left open between the door and the frame. From the numerous kitchen windows, he and Missy had searched the yards for zombies that may have come in while they stocked up. The only ones they'd spotted had been those killed on the way inside. No new bodies, either. Were they safe?

Grabbing a box of preserves, he headed outside. His heart thumped. He was sure someone else watched him from nearby. Maybe not one of the undead, but a survivor, the person or group who had taken the rest of the guns. After loading the first box on the wagon, he stacked the others around it. If they could get the load back to the bunker without any run-ins, they'd be set. He'd wanted to grab some of his own things from home, but that wasn't an option now. Not with other threats that may be all around them. Instead, Missy had grabbed some of her father's clothes for him. As much as he'd rather go naked, he was grateful the clothes would actually fit, that her father didn't have the beer gut many of the man's friends did.

Ready to go, RJ nodded back to Missy. She bolted out the door, weighed down by a pack of clothes for him and their new bows, dragging two suitcases behind her. They weren't prepared for an attack, but he'd told her to drop everything and run if they had to.

The bushes rattled at the back of the yard. Both of them froze. They'd just reached the troweled divider line Missy's father had used to show how far he had to cut the lawn. The halfway mark.

"What is it?" Missy whispered.

Slowly turning his head, he peered into the shrubbery. "Not sure. I can't see anything." He started moving again, pulling the wagon behind him. If they stayed there and waited to find out, they'd never make it the last twenty feet.

Missy jolted ahead of him, reaching the bunker door first. Her face was as white as a sheet of printer paper. "Open it. Open it, now."

He fumbled with the lock, his hands shaking. When he finally yanked the door open, Missy threw the bag and cases down the stairs, no concern about breaking anything inside. If only he could do the same with his load.

She wrenched one of the bows from her shoulder, positioned an arrow on the string, and drew back. Aiming the arrow at the bushes, she tilted her head toward him. "Hurry up and get that stuff down there. I'll cover you."

Quite the change in roles. Though he didn't doubt she knew how to defend herself, he'd worried about Missy when they'd first headed down into the bunker. She'd been traumatized and injured by her father, not willing to kill anything. Now she was guarding him, ready to take out any threat with an arrow.

"Hurry!"

RJ snapped out of his thoughts and grabbed the top box. He rushed down the stairs and set the food on the cot. He'd put it away once they were safely back inside. Just as he reached for the last box, snarling came from the area they'd heard the bushes rustle. A cat lunged out and raced toward them. Not just any cat, but a giant white house cat with its fur knotted with blood and half of its face missing.

He sucked in a breath, stunned by the sight. Animals had been affected by the virus as well. Yet the cat didn't reach them. It thumped to the ground five feet away, an arrow embedded in its skull.

Missy stepped over to the animal, planted a foot on its body, and pulled the arrow out. Definitely not her first time using that weapon.

She waved the arrow at him. "Get going."

Why did he pause to watch her every time she did

something he didn't expect? He had to stop, or his habit would get them killed. He carried the last box down then rushed back up to get her. She'd downed another creature in that short time, retrieving an arrow from what looked to be a raccoon. They were ferocious enough without being undead.

"I'm done. Let's go."

She glanced around the property once more then headed down the stairs. Finally inside, he heaved the door closed behind them and activated the locks. They had food, water, a few changes of clothes, more weapons, and whatever else Missy had grabbed from her room. Set for a while, and safe from all threats.

"I need something now." Missy rubbed some sanitizer she'd grabbed from somewhere into her hands then tore into the plastic covering the water to retrieve a bottle. With her empty hand, she grasped a bag of cheese-covered nacho chips and sat on the smaller cot across the aisle. She ripped the bag open, releasing the smell of artificial flavoring, enough to make his stomach growl. Not an ideal meal, but he wasn't picky at that moment. After cleaning up and grabbing his own bottle of water, he flopped down beside her.

"You know...?" She pointed a chip at him, her mouth half-full. "We make a great team. I wouldn't want to go through a zombie apocalypse with anyone else."

"I feel the same way." He popped a couple of the chips in his mouth and chewed. She was so easy to be around. There was no way to deny his attraction to her, but he saw more in her than that. She cared. If only they'd spent more time together when they were younger.

She bumped his shoulder. "Did you really sleep with Charity Louis in the girls' locker room?"

He nearly choked on the chip in his mouth. What had prompted her to ask that question? He raised his eyebrows? "Do you really want to know?"

She shifted to face him. "Yes. I mean, I know you're

not a virgin, but that rumor always made me curious."

He shook his head. "Not a rumor. She wanted to piss her dad off. You know, Mr. Louis, the boys' phys ed teacher? I had sex with Charity on the bench closest to his office. He caught us just as we were putting our clothes back on."

"Really?" She wrinkled her nose, her mouth in a weird grin. "Why?"

"Teenage boy." He shrugged. How else was he supposed to explain why? "I knew it wouldn't happen again, but I wasn't going to say no."

After rolling her eyes at him, she wrinkled her nose. "Have you ever...done it...down here?"

He couldn't help but smile. "No. This was where I went to be alone. I never brought anyone down here. Well, not until now."

"Did you ever...." Tucking her hair behind her ear, she no longer met his gaze, only the occasional quick glance. "Did you, um, you know, fantasize down here, think about someone, sexually?"

If she knew the truth, she'd probably burn the sheets she sat on, and then her clothes. Maybe him. He touched her knee. "What do you really want to know? What is this about? You've been through a great deal lately. Just say what you want to say."

"I...." She set the bag of chips aside and gulped, her bottom lip quivering. "I just want to forget. Help me forget for a little bit."

Leaning forward, she slowly closed her eyes until her lips met his. Her touch was tentative, but he wanted it just as much. With gentle plying, he deepened the kiss, ready to give her whatever she wanted. He clasped her hips then tugged her toward his lap. The less distance between them, the better. Without breaking contact, she straddled his waist and set her hands on his shoulders. His recurring fantasy was playing out exactly as he'd imagined.

He had no hesitation about sliding his hands under the

hem of her shirt and along her sides. Gasping, she leaned back and thrust her hips toward him. He tensed underneath her, anxious for more, for their clothes to be off and him deep inside her. Pulling her back to him, he ran his tongue up her long, exposed neck. When he reached her ear, he kissed his way back down, all the way to the neckline of her shirt. Not enough; he wanted more.

Bunching the bottom of her shirt, he lifted it. She raised her arms until he had it all the way off. No objections. RJ continued where he'd left off, tasting her precious porcelain skin. Running his thumbs under the edge of her bra, he kissed her exposed cleavage, his hardness straining in his shorts. As much as he wanted to rush through the foreplay, plunge into her, and fuck her until he couldn't see straight, he refused. Missy was so much more than a one-time lay. She mattered, and he would take his time to ensure she enjoyed this moment as much as he did, that this happened again. And again.

She thrust another time, her thighs tightening around him as she moaned. "I want you, RJ. I always have." Before he had a chance to help, she yanked off his blood-covered shirt then pressed her groin even tighter to him.

He didn't hesitate to snap open her bra. If she wanted him to have her, he would do so obligingly. After tossing the black lace into the air, he couldn't do anything but stare. She was beautiful. And he wanted to feel, to taste, every part of her.

Cupping one of her breasts, he ran his tongue across the peak. The skin around it reacted, pushing the nipple farther out, giving him better access. He licked the tip again then ran his teeth along the darker skin. A move she obviously enjoyed, digging her fingers into his back, her breathing suddenly ragged.

RJ slid his hands to her back and kissed across to the other side. Lining his teeth along the erect flesh, he held her. She leaned back, thrusting her chest closer to his face. She rolled her hips over him, making his hard on almost unbearable.

"Oh, Arjun," she sighed.

He froze. No one called him by his real name. Not even his father. He didn't know anyone at school even knew it, let alone how to pronounce it. The school teachers couldn't. That's why his parents told him to use RJ instead. He hadn't heard the name since his mother had dropped him off at school the day she'd died. And now....

He held Missy close, resting his chin on her shoulder so she couldn't see his face, couldn't see the tears threatening to spill.

Hips thrusting, she kissed his neck, making the memory fade. He held her hips and matched her motions, his desire ramped up as high as it could go. At this rate, he'd be done before he took his clothes off.

"I want you, Arjun. I'm ready." She fumbled in the front pocket of her jean shorts and pulled out a condom. "Do you want this? Do you want me?"

"More than you can ever imagine." He helped her shuffle off his lap then moved the boxes of food off the big cot as quick as he could. He wouldn't make her wait.

Missy hurried to remove her shorts and panties. Trying to kick them off, she nearly tripped, in too much of a rush to be careful. RJ held a hand out to her and pulled her into him, his kiss sweeter than anything she'd ever tasted. The more slow and delicate he was with her, the more she wanted him, craved to know what he would feel like inside her. Not just in her heart and her dreams. His erection pressed into her stomach, and she considered jumping onto him, bringing her opening closer to him so she didn't have to wait any longer to find out.

Every girl he'd been with in high school had told their friends he wasn't any good but for some reason thought they needed to secretly tell her he was a great fuck, even if it was quick. Why did he make her wait? Was it because she'd called him by his real name? It's what she'd called him in her fantasies, and the name she'd called out during her first sexual experience.

Reaching between them, she cupped his balls, massaging them, hoping to move the action along.

"Oh, my heart, I want you so bad." He leaned down and plucked the condom from the cot. After tearing open the package, he rolled it on.

His heart? No other guy who showed any interest in her thought with his heart. But RJ had never been the "other guy."

Back in his arms, her desire spiked. When he ran his palms across her butt, she jumped and wrapped her legs around his waist. She. Was. Ready. But the tip of his cock only grazed the edge of her folds. He held her up. He wouldn't let her sink onto him, feel the connection she wanted. "Please!"

With a sly grin, he shook his head. He turned her around and laid her on the cot. Was he old-fashioned and wanted to do it missionary position? Well, fine, as long as it happened soon.

Kneeling between her legs, he stared down at her. No contact except for his gaze. But, it penetrated her more than she'd ever expected. She could see the same lust in his eyes that coursed through her own veins. What was he waiting for?

Planting the soles of her feet on the mattress, she lifted her hips. What would it take for him to get the message?

"Missy, my heart. Are you sure this is what you want?"

That word again. "Yes. I've never wanted anything more. Never wanted anyone the way I want you."

"You killed today. I don't want this to be something you'll regret." He placed his palms on her knees and ran his hands slowly up her thighs.

She'd regret it if this didn't happen, if they went out tomorrow, or another day, and he died. Or she did without having sex with him. "No regrets. Only you and me finally getting together."

"Okay." He trailed his hand lower, between her legs.

She shivered with anticipation.

His touch was gentle yet confident. Two fingers between her slick folds. Then two fingers inside, filling space where she yearned for more.

"Yes, Arjun." So many years of wondering what it would be like, and now she had the chance. It was happening but not fast enough.

He thrust his digits deeper, his palm pressed to her clitoris. "Why do you call me that?"

She whimpered. He wouldn't stop, would he? "Because that's your name. It's what your parents called you and the name on the kindergarten class picture."

He flicked his wrist, and she thought her head would explode with the fiery sensation. "It's weird to hear you say it, but...I like it."

From the automatic O of her lips, she attempted a smile. She wasn't searching for his approval at that moment, just his cock inside her.

Grasping his arms, she tried to pull him toward her. He chuckled at her, a deep throaty laugh that almost made her mad. Why was he amused by her desperation?

But, he obliged, crawling his way up her body, showering her with kisses all the way. When his lips met hers, she held him tight, sharing her passion, her desire, her desperate want. And then he pulled away, gasping for breath.

"Oh, my heart, you were so worth the wait." He raised his hips, and she opened her legs, ready to take him in.

The tip of his cock rested at her entrance. She rolled her hips, trying to coax him inside, but still, he waited. His eyes were open, hard, intently focused on her. If not for her overwhelming need, she might have been afraid.

"My heart," he whispered. Then he plunged inside.

No pain. No regrets. Just a fullness she'd never felt before, not just between her legs but in her heart and her soul. Her entire world had shifted that much more.

IT TOOK A ZOMBIE APOCALYPSE PART THREE: THE OTHERS

Missy grabbed Arjun, the zombie coming right at him. Why wasn't he moving? She yanked on his arm, trying to get out of the way, but when he turned to look at her, his eyeballs bulged from his head, and his sallow skin hung lazily across his cheekbones. He'd already been turned. She spun around to run, but he clutched her wrist, his grip too strong to escape. She reached for her bow, but it was too far away. He gnashed his teeth at her, intent on eating her. The man she'd made love to, gone. She screamed as loud as she could, her only option, hoping someone would come to her rescue.

"Stop!" He pinned her to the ground, holding her arms above her head. "Stop, you're okay."

Zombies talked? Since when? Maybe he hadn't fully turned. Maybe there was some human left in him? "Arjun, let me go. Don't hurt me, please."

"I'm not going to hurt you, Missy." He relaxed his grip on her. "You're dreaming. You woke me up when you tried to pull my arm off."

She flung her eyes open and stared up at Arjun.

"Sorry."

But her apology was interrupted by another scream. Not from either of them, it came from outside the bunker. She glanced up at the door then at Arjun, his wide eyes reflecting her own fear and confusion.

"Someone's alive out there." Who knew how many were holed up somewhere like they were? Living in tornado alley, most of the town had backyard bunkers or safe rooms in their homes. Those who didn't had a neighbor who did. Her family had always dashed across the road to the Walkolm's, not willing to be enclosed in a small space with Arjun and his father.

He chewed on his thumbnail, a habit he'd always had when writing a test at school. "I know, but for how long?"

A lump formed in her throat. They couldn't just leave the person out there. "We have to help. Do something."

"No." Arjun put his hand on her stomach. "If it's zombies, there's nothing we can do but kill them all. And if it's the person who stole the guns, we're the ones who will be dead."

Another scream. Missy jumped from the bed and threw on her clothes and the boots she'd grabbed from her house. If she was going to take out more zombies, it didn't matter that her T-shirt and shorts had blood on them. "I'm going. I can't pretend I don't hear what's going on out there."

She tossed the quiver over her shoulder and grabbed her bow.

"Wait." Arjun started to dress, but with less urgency than she had. "I'll go with you, but you let me check it out."

"No. I'm a better shot than you." He needed to hurry, or they'd be too late to help.

"Exactly." He grabbed his weapons, leaving the other bow behind. "You stay back and be my lookout. If it's just a zombie we're dealing with, I can handle it. But, it's the living threat that worries me."

"Fine." She unlocked the door and plunged into the humid air. At least they didn't have to worry about the heat down in their prison. She braced for any undead lurking in the yards, but the way was clear. No one, not even the person in distress, stood in their way.

With her bow at the ready, she waltzed through the yard as she'd seen the actors do on cop dramas. Even if she wasn't safe, the process definitely provided the confidence she needed.

At Arjun's car, he stopped her. "Stay here. I will signal if the way is clear. Otherwise, I want you to cover my back."

She nodded. That she could do, and had no issues with remaining hidden to protect Arjun. If his suspicions proved accurate, she might have to kill someone still living.

The shriek of terror came again. Arjun kissed her then climbed over his car to get out to the front yards. He didn't even give her a chance to react before he was gone. She covered him, following his path through her bow sight. Had he already located the person in distress?

The streets were strangely quiet. She'd expected all the zombies to be drawn to the screams, the guarantee of flesh and brain. But they must have congregated elsewhere, none to be found.

Except one. Missy sucked in a breath, having located the person who'd been screaming. Delilah Hammond, a young widow who'd given birth to a daughter within days of learning her husband had been killed overseas in combat. She'd moved back home to live with her parents the same day Missy had arrived. And she stood in her driveway, screaming as the zombie of Old Man Samson tried to claw his way into her car.

Arjun held his axe high and raced for the former oldest living person in West Vitula. The zombie fell quickly after getting his head knocked off, but Arjun missed seeing the zombie approach from the other side. So did Delilah. Missy drew back, aimed, then released the arrow. A direct hit to the temple, but not before the zombie had sunk its teeth into the young mother's shoulder. The arrow pierced them both.

She'd killed someone alive. Missy turned and threw up the little contents of her stomach all over the side of her house. Maybe the woman would have turned undead soon, but she was not a zombie when the arrow shot through her skull.

Missy was a murderer. More of her stomach emptied, the muscles pulsing over and over until there was nothing left. Bile burned her throat, and tears poured down her cheeks. She'd insisted on coming out to help, but she'd done the opposite. Instead of saving someone, she'd ended their life.

RJ leaped out of the way as two bodies fell toward him. Missy had killed them together with one arrow. She definitely did have great aim. Two zombies to his one. Though he suspected Delilah had just turned. She had the telltale gaunt face, no fat under her skin to give her face the fullness it once had. But her earlier screams had been deafening. Not a zombie sound, but one of a mother concerned for her child. The baby sat in the back of her mother's car, strapped into her seat and wailing for attention. Old Man Samson must have heard the baby after attacking her mother, deciding the young one a better meal and leaving Delilah to slowly become undead.

Well, Missy wanted to rescue someone. Now they had a baby to take care of. RJ left it in the car. It was safe there for now. He darted around the nearby yards, searching for any other zombies that might attack when he had the little one in his arms. There were none. Strange. He and Missy hadn't taken out even a tenth of the population. Had that many people survived? Where were they now?

Opening the back door of the car, he unbuckled the

chubby little girl. Her body convulsed with sobs, her face blotchy from tears. And, of course, snot bubbles formed and popped out her nostrils as she breathed. When he grabbed her to pull her out, she scrunched up her face as if ready to start bawling all over again.

"Not so fast."

RJ froze at the male voice. Had Delilah's father survived? If so, he'd gladly give him the baby to take care of. Keeping his hands out to the side, he cautiously ducked out of the car then turned to face the man. Nope, not Mr. Hammond. Shutting the car door with his foot, RJ raised his arms into the air, the best option when someone had a gun pointed at your head.

"Mr. Steckly. What can I do for you?" A friend of Missy's father, the man spent many Saturday and Sunday afternoons in the Smiths' backyard, drinking beer and calling out racial slurs.

"Get on your knees and beg for mercy." He nodded toward the ground. "Or I'm going to blow your head off, as I've always dreamed of doing."

RJ knelt on the driveway, but he wasn't going to beg. If the man wanted to shoot him, he'd do it regardless of what he said. "I was just trying to help the baby. That's all."

"Baby?" He released a loud snort. "No one here would want you to touch their baby. You're dirty, unclean, probably a pedophile."

RJ released a heavy breath and bit his tongue. It was no secret that Mr. Steckly toured the high school after last period, offering girls rides home. And RJ had seen the way the man drooled over Missy when she'd lived at home. Mr. Smith never noticed, believing his friends to be godly, never straying from their blind faith.

The man touched the barrel of the gun to RJ's forehead. "I'm going to take the car with the baby inside. Then I'm going to be back and take your car. You don't have a problem with that, do you?"

"No, the keys are in the dish just inside the front

door." The car was the least of his concerns. Even getting shot didn't matter. But Missy was back there. He hoped she didn't see what was going on, didn't try to interfere.

"Good boy." The man's finger began to twitch on the trigger.

RJ's heart raced, and he closed his eyes. If there was such thing as reincarnation, he wanted to return to the physical realm where his parents now existed, be reunited with them. But would he ever find Missy again?

The baby suddenly began to wail. A shot rang out. RJ expected to be pulled from his body, from this world. But he remained on his knees, listening to the baby cry. Opening his eyes, he saw Mr. Steckly still standing above him, the gun he held now pointing to the ground. A hole in the man's head dripped blood, and his chin hung down, as if off its hinges. Then, in slow motion, he fell backward, his head hitting the pavement with a loud crack.

RJ was afraid to move. Someone else had a gun. Obviously not a friend of Mr. Steckly's, but no one in town who owned a gun was a friend of his.

"Oh my God. Are you okay?" Missy rounded the corner of the car and fell to her knees. "Did he hurt you?"

"No, but"—he peeked over the hood—"someone has a gun. They shot him."

"I did." Her eyes hardened as she stared at the prone body.

"Where did you get the gun?" The last he remembered, they didn't have any.

"I found the shithead's car and my father's guns." She rubbed the barrel of a camo rifle. "This one is mine."

"And now the shithead is dead." A loss he wouldn't regret.

"He deserved to die. But she didn't." A tear trailed down Missy's cheek, and she shook her head. "I made her baby an orphan."

"No." RJ wrapped his arms around her and held her. "No, she had already turned. She was a zombie that last time she screamed."

"Really?" Her chest heaved as the baby's had after it stopped crying. "I didn't kill her?"

"No, and you saved her baby." RJ wiped away her tear then stood and offered her a hand up. "We've got to get her to safety before she alerts anyone else to her presence."

Opening the door, RJ reached inside for the little girl, but grabbed the diaper bag instead, passing it to Missy. She could sling it over her shoulder with her cache of weapons. He took hold of the baby and pulled her tight against his chest. "Let's go."

A baby? What was RJ supposed to do with a baby? He'd never been around any. Sure, his cousins back in India had kids, but the moment they started a family, they no longer had time to face chat with him. Even the texts slowed down until they downright stopped. So he'd never had the chance to learn anything from them. Didn't care to at the time. Now he wished he had. At least he might know some way to get the squirmy little thing to stop crying.

"Do you know what's wrong with her?" He held her out to Missy. "How to make her stop?"

Missy—after stashing away her weapons and sanitizing her hands—plucked the child from his outstretched arms. "Well, if she's anything like the kids I've babysat, she could need her diaper changed, she could be hungry, or maybe she's really tired. We'll try them in that order."

Changing a diaper? Could it really be that simple? He located the bag he'd grabbed from the car and snatched out one of the disposable nappies. "Here you go."

"Ha ha. Typical." She laid the baby down on the cot and took the diaper from him. "Are there any wipes in there?"

"What do you mean, typical?" he asked, searching through the bag.

"Any guy I've ever met will do anything to avoid changing a diaper." In a matter of seconds, she had the old one off, the baby cleaned up and covered again. "I've had fathers call me at home and offer me ten dollars to change their kid's diaper while their wife was away. Some of them still texted me when I went to university."

"Oh." Next time he'd have to pay attention to what she did so he wasn't one of those guys. "Maybe I can feed her?" While looking for the wipes, he'd found a bottle and a can of formula. And the baby hadn't stopped crying though she didn't fight Missy nearly as much as she had him.

"Sure." Missy rocked the baby in her arms while he poured the off-white liquid into the plastic container. "We don't have anything to warm the bottle, so hopefully she'll take it like that."

RJ sat on the cot, a bead of sweat dripping down his forehead. If they didn't get the baby quiet soon, they'd have zombies pounding at the door to add to his growing headache. "Okay, ready."

"Yeah, sure." She laughed as she handed him the little girl. "Now, let her head rest against your bicep, and hold her close to you."

The little girl wiggled and whined, but as soon as he stuck the bottle in her mouth, she relaxed, making little cooing sounds as she fed. No cares that it wasn't warmed. RJ sighed with relief. Finally, she was quiet. Maybe he could get used to having her around. Though, they really had no choice. At some point, they'd have to go back out for diapers and formula, first to the Hammond's house then the grocery store. A farther journey each time. And more dangerous. They still had no idea how far the zombie virus had spread, if there was a chance to stop it, or if they were just biding their time.

He looked over to Missy, glad to have her company

and her help. Yet, they hadn't had a chance to talk about what happened between them. Did she regret having sex with him?

She smiled at him as if she knew he was thinking of her. "You know, that's a really good look on you."

"What, relief that we finally managed to calm her down?" His headache had lulled as a result.

"No, your feeding her as if she were your own child. It looks so natural." She stroked the baby's forehead.

"Sure." Except the child didn't have his skin color, and he'd never imagined starting a family at his age. "What's her name, anyway?"

Missy scrunched her forehead. "Um, Yvette, Yvonne, or something like that. I know her grandmother called her 'Little Evie.'"

"Evie, I like it." He held her a little closer, watching her eyelids grow heavy as she continued to drink. "I think she's tired, too." And so was he, fighting his own urge to close his eyes and sleep.

"Okay, sit her up and burp her before she's completely out. Otherwise, she'll wake up screaming because of a gas bubble."

"Burp her?" He really knew nothing about babies.

"Yeah, like this." Missy slid Evie onto her knee and held her chest with one hand while rubbing and patting the baby's back with the other.

Out of nowhere came a giant belch, bigger than any of the beer burps he'd shared with his friends after a night of drinking. "Wow, that was impressive."

"What's more impressive is that nothing came back up with the burp." Missy handed the baby back. "See if she'll drink any more. I'm going to find us something to eat while she's napping."

A strange sense of vertigo washed over RJ. In two days, he'd gone from a guy ready to enter his junior year at college and trying to finally land the girl of his dreams to a family man with a wife and baby. Well, she wasn't his wife, but he wouldn't object to the notion.

"How about beef jerky and some...." She held a jar in front of him. "Whatever this is? Pears, I think."

"Whatever you pick works for me." The foods they'd salvaged weren't part of his usual diet, but, stuck in a bunker, he wouldn't dare complain. He had to make do.

She set the jar down and leaned toward him. "You know, I wouldn't want to be down here with anyone else but you." She kissed him hard and quick, enough to ease his mind about whether she held any regrets.

Evie refused to take any more formula, instead falling asleep in his arms. She was so still, so quiet compared to when he'd first held her. Keeping her that way would be hard, but he planned to let her rest and get some sleep himself before leaving the bunker again. He moved some blankets and pillows around with his free hand then laid her into what resembled a nest. She didn't wake up, just lay there with her little hands clenched in fists.

"Here." Missy handed him a bottle of water and a fork before she sat beside him with the food.

RJ glanced at the baby, but she didn't stir, not bothered by the motion. He shook his head, unsure if he cared about keeping the baby quiet more for his own sake or for that of little Evie.

Missy put the food between them, and they shared a sweet-and-salty meal. Not something he ever wanted to eat again, but enough to satisfy his hunger, and increase his drowsiness. After cleaning up from the meal, Missy returned to the cot and leaned on his shoulder. She was asleep, snoring softly, before he had a chance to say anything to her. But, he wasn't far behind, catching his head falling toward his chest a few times until he finally dozed off.

This time, though, they weren't woken by screaming but a knock on the door.

Missy nudged him. "Wake up. Someone's here."

"Huh?" He wiped his eyes, trying to get them to focus.

"What do you mean?"

"Someone's knocking on the door. They want in." Her eyes were wide.

"Well, go check the monitor. See how many zombies are out there." Of course they had to wait until everyone was sleeping to show up.

"No, it's not coming from that door." She pointed toward the back of the bunker. "It's coming from over there."

RJ's blood chilled. There was nothing on the other side of the bunker except dirt. It was underground. "Maybe you heard it wrong. You were sleeping, after all."

"No." Missy shook her head. "I thought that, too. Then I heard it again."

Bang, bang.

Yes, definite knocking from the back of the bunker. Had one of the undead managed to dig a hole to the other side? He stood up and pointed to the sleeping baby. "Stay with her."

Missy looked like she wasn't about to move anyway, her body frozen in place.

As RJ grabbed his axe and headed to the rear, an area he didn't spend time in because there was nothing but empty closets and a toilet, the lights dimmed. Another bang, and dust flew into his face. He spat and brushed his arm over his eyes. When he looked again, he stuck his hand out to the wall. Faintly, he could see the outline of another door. A narrow one, but a definite second exit.

He glanced back at Missy. "There's a door. Should I open it?"

"Wait." She moved the baby out of sight then grabbed her rifle and stood beside him. "Open but stand back. If I need to, I'll shoot."

He couldn't let her kill again. Not after what had happened when she thought she'd killed Evie's mother. But he had no choice. She knew how to use it. He didn't. "Okay, on the count of three."

She nodded. "One, two, three."

He stuck two fingers through the recessed ring and pulled. The difference in air pressure made the attempt difficult, but he finally managed to budge it, and waited for Missy to fire.

Only, she didn't.

"Hello, Melissa. It's good to see you"

RJ knew that voice, believed the person to be dead. But he wasn't. RJ darted around the door. "Dad?"

Missy felt lightheaded. Was she dreaming? Dr. Dhawan was supposed to be dead. Or, undead. She'd read the text he'd sent to Arjun that said he'd been infected. Why was he standing in front of her? Had someone found a cure? Her parents. No. Could they have been saved?

"Dad?" Arjun appeared beside her. "You said you were infected, told me to head down here."

"Yes." Dr. Dhawan folded his hands behind his back. "I did tell you to come down here. But I was never infected. I wanted you to believe I was so you wouldn't come to the hospital."

Missy put a hand on the wall. What was he saying?

"A colleague of mine from West Vitula Community Hospital was trying to find a cure for the RFG-8 virus. There have been squirrels up in Canada with it, and it's slowly spread farther south." He rocked back on his heels. "At first, he thought it was rabies, but none of the vaccines worked. He was working in the lab when he noticed the original vials of the virus were missing."

"Missing? How can things like that go missing in a hospital? Especially something so dangerous?" It had already turned most of the town into zombies, and her into a killer.

"No one knows. We didn't have time to find out. Whoever stole them didn't take them far. They dumped the virus into the ventilation system, infecting the entire south wing of the hospital." The regret on the doctor's face had to mean a lot of people became zombies.

"But not you." Arjun held her hand while waiting for more of his father's explanation.

"No." Dr. Dhawan shook his head. "I was in the north wing, seeing patients in emerg. I managed to get some patients and staff down here, but far more were attacked by the infected patients, and the virus kept on spreading."

"Wait." Missy leaned forward, unsure if she'd heard him correctly. "What do you mean by down here?"

The doctor gestured behind him. "This is one of a few paths to a large underground community. I used one from the hospital to get there."

"What do you mean? There's no underground community." If there were, her family would have known about it. Her parents made a point of knowing everything that happened in the community.

"Yes, there is." Mr. Dhawan looked from his son to Missy. "It was a well-guarded secret, only the land owners whose property we crossed told about it. Although, if we could go under without their knowledge, we did. Those who knew were paid well to keep quiet, and guaranteed a living space down there should a nuclear attack happen. The corporation sponsoring our research played on that fear."

"But, why was it really built? Where was it built?" Arjun asked the exact questions she wanted answers to.

"The where is easy. The stench of the dump kept residents from sticking around for too long. And no one questioned the extra equipment." Dr. Dhawan rubbed his hands together. "The why is a little more complicated. You see, we work with a lot of viruses that are sent to Ostrander General. The backlog there is immense, and we are qualified to help them. But, sometimes, we receive projects that aren't logged into the system. All research is supposed to be completed outside of the hospital. In a space that could be contained if any of the viruses got into the air. Where nothing would spread."

He took in a deep breath. "That didn't happen yesterday. Dr. Manford had some time in between surgeries and managed to sneak the virus past security and up to the lab in the south wing, trying to get some research done in his spare time. During his next surgery, someone broke in and stole the samples. By the time he realized the virus had been removed from the lab and exposed to the ventilation system, it was too late."

"So, in this underground community, is the same thing going to happen that happened above ground? Is everyone living there now going to be exposed to some new virus?" She didn't want to leave their bunker for a place more dangerous. If so, they might as well live out on the streets and wait for the zombies to attack them.

"No." Arjun's dad shook his head. "The research facility is deep underground and extremely secure. Only myself and another doctor now have access. No one else can get down there. If Dr. Manford hadn't removed the virus from there, none of this would have happened."

"How far has it spread?" She hoped there was a chance to fight it, stop the spread before it affected the entire world.

"To the next counties. Those who do not have the virus have been evacuated across the state. The army and state police have set up boundaries with a shoot to kill order. If all goes well, it won't spread any farther."

"So, we won't be stuck down here forever?" She hadn't spent much more than a full day underground, and already she was ready to break lose.

"No, not if everything goes as planned." Dr. Dhawan rocked forward on his toes.

"Thank God." Missy quickly pursed her lips together, trying to pretend she hadn't said those words. She knew no god had anything to do with the spread of the virus or the containment of it. "Thank goodness for everyone's quick action to contain this. So, what do we do now?"

He gestured for them to follow him down the dimly lit hallway. "Come with me. I'll get you both settled in to wait it out until we receive the all clear."

And leave everything they'd gathered behind? "But, wait! We have weapons, food, and—"

Arjun squeezed her hand. "And a baby."

Dr. Dhawan spun around and glared back and forth between the two of them. "I know you couldn't have had your own that quickly. Where did you find a baby?"

"It's Delilah Hammond's daughter. She was attacked, but we saved her baby." She refused to tell the entire story, would keep the secret until she died. So long as Arjun did the same.

"Oh, I must tell Marjorie at once." He motioned them again to follow. "Bring Yvette, but leave the rest here. We'll come back later for it."

The trek seemed to take forever. Over two miles of tunnel, twisting and turning steel that dripped condensation and reeked of earth and rust. Little Evie rested on her shoulder, and Missy fought the onset of tears. Being responsible for raising a baby scared her, but the idea of giving her up, never seeing her again, crushed her heart a little. So did the idea of returning to BDU, going back to her life before the virus. Some things would never be the same. She was an orphan, had no family left. At least none in the same state. She'd complete her education on the scholarships and money she'd earned. But that didn't matter. Her thoughts concentrated on Arjun, what would happen between them when life returned to normal. Would their relationship continue? Or was she a one-time thing? Just a last-person-on-Earth relationship that no longer mattered because it wasn't the end of the world.

The light ahead brightened, and Missy saw a group of people waiting for them. Mrs. Hammond met them first, her arms outstretched.

Arjun stood between them. He kissed the little girl on the forehead before taking her from Missy's arms and handing her over to her grandmother. "We are sorry we couldn't save your daughter. But, she managed to keep Yvette in the car, and that's how we were able to get her to safety."

"Thank you." Mrs. Hammond nodded to both of them. "First, your father saves my husband's life. Then he saves both of us by bringing us down here. And you two saved my Little Evie. I can't thank you enough."

Missy handed over the diaper bag. "She might be hungry now. And need her diaper changed. We did that before she went to sleep but didn't have a chance before coming here."

"That's not a problem." Dr. Dhawan ushered Mrs. Hammond down the closest corridor. "I will bring you any necessary supplies after I get my son and Miss Smith settled."

The woman nodded and disappeared around a corner.

Arjun's father took them farther into the underground community, the walls more pristine than the tunnel there. "RJ, I have a room for you downstairs in my apartment. Melissa, your room is down this hallway."

"Um, Dad?" Arjun hung back, taking hold of her hand. "I want to stay with Missy."

Dr. Dhawan stopped and slowly turned around, giving the slightest hint of a smile. "Oh, really?"

"Yes." Arjun nodded. "We've become close, and since she lost her entire family, I don't think she should be alone."

"And what do you think of that, Melissa?" He cocked his head to the side. "Do you want my son, RJ, staying with you while you are down here? Don't be afraid to say no. There are many others down here who you know."

Missy nearly laughed at the scowl Arjun gave his father. "If it is okay with you, Dr. Dhawan, I would love for Arjun to stay with me." She pulled him closer and leaned on his shoulder.

"I see." He took a few steps then unlocked the door in front of him. "This is your first apartment together." He chuckled as he handed her a key. "Only one key, so you two must stick together. In the morning, we will go back for your things."

Arjun hugged his father before entering the room. Missy hugged him, too. "Thank you for raising such a wonderful son."

He smiled at her before he turned and left them.

After walking into the room, Missy closed the door. "Well, we have a bigger bed."

"And a chance to sleep without being interrupted." He stripped down to his boxers and tank top then lay across the bed. "Come join me."

Glad to be rid of the blood-covered shirt and shorts, she tossed them in the corner of the room and slipped onto the bed. Plenty of room for both of them, though she couldn't help but cuddle next to him, his touch keeping her from remembering everything but what they'd shared. And when he kissed her lips, drew his hand down her body, the idea of sleep vanished.

Two weeks later...

RJ handed Missy her books while leaning in for a kiss. "I'll meet you in the food court for lunch."

She nodded, her eyes twinkling, finally losing the dullness that had haunted them since she'd saved his life. "Have a good class. I love you, Arjun."

"I love you, too, my heart." He kissed her again before rushing off to his first class at BDU. Fielding had been destroyed during the outbreak, and after some last minute negotiations, his father had secured a spot for him at the same university as Missy. Her roommate hadn't minded either, so long as he paid an equal share of the rent, and didn't steal her food.

Outside of the business building, he met his friend, Sahil, another transfer from Fielding.

"So, things are looking up for you."

He wrapped an arm around his friend. "Yes, they are. I couldn't be happier."

"And Missy's roommate?" Sahil paused and turned to look at him, suddenly serious. "Are you sure she wants to meet me?"

"Yes." RJ slapped him on the back. "I showed her a picture, so she knows how ugly you are. But, that didn't scare her away. She's joining us at lunch."

"Okay." Sahil gulped then nodded. "Maybe this happened for a reason."

RJ clenched his shoulder. "It's karma. Hate can never win." It had taken a long time to see the resulting effects of his actions, but it had all been worth it. He and Missy were beginning a life together, one that wouldn't be scrutinized by the community they lived in. West Vitula had suffered immeasurable damage, with everyone being relocated, and the town itself put under quarantine. His father had accepted a job at Ostrander General, and he had Missy. It took a kiss followed by a zombie apocalypse, or maybe just a viral outbreak, to make it happen.

She doesn't want a lot for Christmas…

Claire Otton dreads spending another holiday alone. When her best friend convinces her to approach the sexy mall Santa, she takes the chance and asks him out, hoping for so much more.

He's waiting under the mistletoe…

Although Andreas Castellanos blends in on Earth, he knows he will never belong. But when the gorgeous woman he'd been staring at invites him to dinner, he has a hard time saying no.

All they're asking for…

Can these two lonely souls find magic together or will their secrets steal their chance of a happy Christmas?

HEY, SANTA
CHAPTER ONE

"You can't be serious." Claire mustered the dirtiest look possible for her best friend.

Tiffany held out her hands and air-squeezed the man's firm rear end from a distance. "C'mon. Look at that ass."

"Yes, but a Santa Claus? How do I know what he looks like under that suit and beard?" Imagining removing the white hair to find a wrinkled old man, she shuddered.

"Only one way to find out." Smacking Claire's butt, Tiffany urged her forward. "Go ask him."

She planted her feet. Thank goodness she hadn't worn heels for their marathon shopping trip two days before Christmas. "If you're so interested, why don't you?"

Tiffany rolled her eyes, sighing. "Because I'm engaged to be married to the love of my life. You're the Grinch who needs to get laid."

"I'm not a Grinch," she snapped. Breathing deeply, she counted backwards from ten. "I'm sorry. This is a very stressful time of year for me."

"I know." Tiffany cupped her elbow. "I just want to

see you happy at Christmas again. It doesn't have to be a miserable holiday anymore. That's part of the reason I dragged you with me today."

She swallowed the lump in her throat, tears welling already. *Please don't let me turn into a blubbering mess in the middle of the mall.* While she appreciated her friend's concern, she coped better on her own. "I…I should go home. I can't pretend it didn't happen."

"No, but you can't stop living, either." Wiping the tears with one of the many tissues she kept stuffed in her purse, Tiffany gave her a brief smile. "You don't need to be alone anymore. Give someone a chance for goodness' sake. Your parents and brother would want you to be happy. *I* want you to be happy."

But happiness no longer existed in her world. Hadn't since she'd arrived home for the Christmas holidays four years ago. No one came to pick her up at the airport. Instead, she'd taken a cab and been dropped off at a smoldering pile of rubble that used to be her family home. Her parents and younger brother had been asleep when an arsonist set fire to the attached garage. All dead. Her family never made it out. The young punk had been caught and sentenced to serve the rest of his life in prison, but she'd lost everything.

She bit her bottom lip to avoid crying again. Without them, she had very little support. The only person remaining in her life who gave two shits about her was Tiffany, and she'd be married in a few months. Moving on with her life.

Maybe that is *what I need to do.* But who wanted a damaged woman who'd dropped out of university? Surely, no one worth spending her life with.

"Please, Claire." Tiffany rubbed her arm. "Will you ask him already? I saw him before he changed into the suit. He's hot. And he has to be patient since he works with kids. If this doesn't work, I'll never get on your case again."

"Fine," she grumbled. *A bad date has to be better than sitting at home by myself.* "This is the last time. No more double dates or trying to set me up with a guy in any way."

Tiffany held out her baby finger. "Pinky swear."

After sealing the promise, Claire patted the puffy skin under her eyes. "Is my makeup running?"

"No, you look beautiful, as always." Grabbing her shoulders, her friend spun her around. "Now, go get him before he's swarmed by a bunch of kids. And hopefully, soon he'll fill your stocking with all kinds of Christmas cheer."

Her cheeks warmed. She wanted more than a night of fucking, though that wouldn't hurt, either. But Santa? Really? What was she supposed to say? *Hey, Santa, I saw you bending over, and I think you have a nice ass. Want to go out sometime?*

Andreas blinked, trying to wrap his head around what the sexy woman in front of him had just asked. He'd stared at her miles of long legs showed off by black tights, and her full, glossy lips, but he never expected her to leave her friend and come over, let alone ask him on a date. The only women who ever approached him were already married and concerned about the results of their child's picture with Santa Claus. Or, the single moms who thought he'd make a great baby daddy. *Um, no.*

"You want to go out on a date? With me?" he asked.

She nodded, her eyes glassy, as if about to cry if he said no. He would hate himself if that happened. But, her expression changed in an instant, her stare hard. "Forget I said anything." She stepped back. "You're looking a little green anyway."

Green? Shit. He thought he'd perfected his appearance. *Guess not.* Yet, he refused to let the woman leave before he agreed to see her again.

"Wait! You haven't gotten your candy cane yet. And to

get one, you have to sit on my knee and tell me what you want for Christmas." Anything to get her closer.

She grinned, his cock twitching from her wicked stare. And when she sat on his lap, her soft hair brushing against his cheek, he groaned. No other female specimen compared to her in sex appeal. He stared at her lusty curves, wanting to touch and lick, imagining her pouty lips around his cock. So much time had passed since his last sexual encounter. He yearned to taste her, fuck her until she screamed his name. But so many reasons left him treading carefully around women, least of all to get caught groping someone while on the job.

He feared the authorities looking into his background. One he didn't have. At least not until five years ago.

"So, you really want to go out with me, not knowing what I look like? This isn't some dare, is it?" He'd been through that, too, from a bunch of giggling young women. Thankfully, he hadn't fallen into their trap. He wanted the woman in front of him to be serious.

"Well, you're the most muscular Santa I've ever seen. And your suit is tight in all the right places." She shifted on his knee. "As long as you're not old enough to be my father, then yes, I really would like to go on a date with you."

"Not even close, I hope. I'm twenty-eight." He tried to ignore his desire to find a quiet corner for a quickie. Frickin' libido rejected the idea of letting the woman out of his sight.

"Works for me." Her hip rubbed against his cock. "So, how about dinner?"

"Yes," he hissed, changing his focus to imagine something fugly as a distraction, like the governor in drag maybe. In his bed. He had to get rid of his hard-on before some mother brought her kid over. With a shudder, he returned his attention to the woman on his lap. "When were you thinking?"

She faced the sign listing Santa's hours. "You're done

at seven? How about nine? I'll make reservations at Barnaby's and meet you there."

Barnaby's? Not too chic, yet not a restaurant where he would run into more of the kids who sat on his knee all day. A much better place to get to know the woman in front of him. And maybe he'd have her for dessert.

A family lined up to see him, two screaming kids among them.

The woman on his knee rose. "I should go."

"Wait." He grabbed her wrist, but let go at the collective gasp from his elves.

Everyone in line stared. He cringed, waiting for her to slap him.

Shit. He had to save himself. "I don't even know your name, how to get ahold of you if I'm going to be late."

Sitting back down, she reached into her purse. *Mace?* He squeezed his eyes shut. Instead of spraying him, she rolled up his sleeve, pressing something against his skin. He dared to look, opening one eye at a time.

Claire Otton followed by her phone number. "If you get caught up, give me a call." She stood again, facing him, her cheeks glowing. "Otherwise, I'll see you at nine. And don't make any plans for the rest of the evening, either."

He swallowed the urge to follow her, take her into the closest storage closet or washroom. "Claire, you didn't tell me what you want for Christmas."

Leaning in close, she gave him a breathtaking view of her cleavage. "Stick around," she whispered. "And you'll find out."

Shivers ran down his spine. *Fuck, she knows how to send my dick into overdrive.* But in an instant, she disappeared and one of his helpers placed a wailing kid on his lap.

Is it nine o'clock yet? Sneaking a look at the kiddie-pool-sized clock on the wall, he groaned. *Fuck, only four.*

HEY, SANTA
CHAPTER TWO

Claire smoothed her dress across her lap. The short hemline didn't come close to reaching her knees, or barely her butt for that matter. Though a festive red color, the dress's plunging neckline revealed even more skin. She shivered in her chair, ready to ask for her coat back. Why did she have to buy the shortest dress possible?

Like she needed it anyway, with her date already ten minutes late. She doubted he would show. Who wanted a socially inept woman? Heck, what man wanted to start dating someone two days before Christmas? She sighed, resting an elbow on the table. *Why did I ask out Santa?* She didn't even know his name, what he looked like. Yet, she'd given him enough personal information to stalk her. *Way to go, numbskull.* She might as well have given him her house key. And since Tiffany had driven her to the restaurant, she'd have to take a cab back home.

"Hi, Claire. Sorry, I'm late."

She jerked her head toward the deep, husky voice. Her Santa had arrived. But instead of the white-haired, bearded man with the fuzzy red suit, she stared at a Greek god.

Broad shoulders. Muscles constricted by the sleeves of his dress shirt. His wavy brown hair looked wet, as if he'd recently stepped out of the shower. Or maybe snow had started to fall since she'd arrived. Pulse racing, she dared to gaze into his crystal blue eyes, the part of him she remembered from their meeting in the mall. Yet, even with his tanned complexion, something seemed not quite right with the color of his skin.

Was he as nervous as her? Her last non-double date occurred so long ago, she didn't know how to act.

Not wanting to be rude, she stood to greet him. He had, after all, arrived rather than standing her up. And the sooner he touched her, the better.

Resting his hand on her hip, he moved closer, kissing her cheek, his lips soft and gentle. His breath smelled of fresh mint, a far cry from the last guy Tiffany had tried to set her up with.

"It's good to see you again, Santa." She tried not to swoon, her legs like jelly.

He chuckled, still holding onto her. "It's Andreas. Andreas Castellanos. Andy, if you want."

Wow, my very own Adonis.

"Has anyone ever told you how gorgeous you are?" She covered her mouth. *As if I said that.*

When he let her go, her cheeks burned with embarrassment at the foolish comment. He probably heard that all the time. And she'd likely behaved like every other female he'd ever been out with. *Way to start the date!*

He pulled out her chair. "I do hear it every once in a while, usually followed by, *but you're not what we're looking for.*"

Parking her butt, she glanced up. "You're a model?" Her pussy clenched as she pictured him modeling *Calvin Kleins*. Then taking them off. But why date her, or better yet, work as a shopping mall Santa during the day?

After sitting across from her, he leaned back in his chair. "No, I'm an actor. Though the only gigs I've gotten lately are as the dead guy in police dramas. I have to take other jobs to pay the bills."

"An actor?" *What if he becomes famous someday? All of the events, the paparazzi following them around, my story splashed all over the tabloids?*

Whoa! Slow down. Tonight is about dinner and sex.

Any time spent together afterward came as a bonus, not guaranteed.

"Those people obviously don't know what they're doing. I think you'd make a great witness, maybe even the killer."

He smiled, reaching across the table. "Why, thank you. I'll be sure to suggest those roles during my next audition."

The instant she joined hands with him, a spark ignited her desire. *Please let tonight be the end of the loneliness.* Every glimpse she caught of his mesmerizing eyes left her speechless, a staring idiot. She imagined riding him like a cowgirl, him thrusting deep inside her, fucking her in every position imaginable. What she'd dreamed of for so long. And now she'd found the right guy. Searing heat flared from her pussy up to her cheeks.

"So, what do you do?"

She pushed the naughty thoughts aside for later. "Pardon?"

"What's your job? What do you do for a living?"

"I'm a sales rep for a pet food company." Though, most people didn't know what that entailed, not unless they worked in the industry.

"So, you have a lot of pets then?"

"Sadly, no. I don't have any." *Never again.* Her childhood cat had passed away in the fire along with her family. The one time she broke down and bought a Siamese fighting fish, it died while she attended a weekend trade show. She refused to take that chance again. No one or no *thing* could depend on her.

He furrowed his brows. "Yet, you work for a pet food company?"

She shrugged, having had to explain the same thing many times. "I travel a lot for work. I don't have anyone nearby to take care of a pet while I'm away." Which led to some very lonely nights.

Though, I hope tonight will be different.

While conversation flowed freely between them, she never mentioned her family. Just as he never mentioned his. Like he needed someone finding out he'd crash-landed on Earth from another planet. *What's her story?* Why did she keep her relatives a secret?

He stared into her whiskey-colored eyes, trying to figure her out. Perhaps she didn't get along with her parents. Or maybe she'd arrived from another planet, too. No, not possible. She fit in too well.

Everything about Claire mesmerized him. He knew what the night would lead to, understood her expectations, but unlike the other women who asked him out, Claire kept him intrigued. He refused to say no. She didn't lay her life's story on the table, and kept her flirtations subtle. A sexy smile. The light touch of her foot along his leg. As a result, he craved her even more.

Then dessert came. She slid around the table, moving closer. Heavy drums thudded in his chest. His palms grew sweaty. Why did she affect him like no other woman?

He scooped a spoonful of the fried ice cream, dipping it in the chocolate sauce, and held it out to her. She wrapped her full lips around the spoon, her gaze locked on him. She moaned gently, and he shifted in his seat, his cock ready to burst from his pants. He pulled the spoon out with much hesitation, imagining his cock in its place. "Come back to my place after dinner."

She licked her lips, her face full of lust. "I hoped you would ask."

One spoonful after the next, he fed Claire the entire

dessert, his hunger for her primal. And he thanked the heavens for the similarities between his people and those on Earth.

He'd never make it past the front doors if they didn't leave right then. Arm in the air, he gestured for the waitress. "Can we get the check, please?"

The woman nodded, and delivered the bill shortly after. Tossing enough cash on the table to cover their tab and a tip, he stood, offering his hand.

Claire gazed up at him, then away, as if suddenly afraid.

He squeezed her fingers. "Having doubts? Because, if you are, I can drive you home. We can end the date and go out again another time." He didn't understand his strange attraction to the *Terran*, but he forbade himself from ignoring it. There had to be a reason she stood out amongst all the others he had met since arriving on the planet.

Chewing her bottom lip, she stepped forward. "I'm ready to get out of here. I don't want to go home, or be alone."

To my house then. Reaching his car, he supported her arm while she climbed inside. Bringing her home guaranteed nothing, not without her taking the lead. If anything happened at all. Because his secret remained his top priority. Always.

Yet, he understood her loneliness, experienced the same thing himself. Not one of his crew members had followed him to Earth as he'd been told, and at first he assumed it to be a joke—*make the new recruit think we abandoned him.* After five star cycles on Earth, he gave up on them ever arriving to rescue him. He had carved out an identity and lived as a *Terran*, a being of his new planet, never sharing his secret with anyone. He refused. Popular Earth culture proved what would happen to him if anyone found out. For once, he longed to find someone he trusted enough to know the truth.

Never going to happen.

Terrans were just as likely to stab him in the back as any of his own people. Hence, he kept to himself, forever stuck on Earth.

Starting the ignition, he shuddered as doubts crept in. *Can I satisfy her, make her want to be with an alien?* On his own planet, he'd only dated a few women. Claire had depth and an air of mystery he wanted to explore, but he had to remain in control before his curiosity landed him in trouble.

HEY, SANTA
CHAPTER THREE

A quaint little red brick house on a quiet side street. That's what Claire walked into, clinging to Andy. Not at all like the house she expected her date to live in. Didn't all actors live in apartments and condos? At least until they made their first million.

After a quick glance around the simply furnished living room, she pivoted to face him. All of his passion seemed to have disappeared. He hadn't uttered a word the entire drive, hadn't touched her since leaving the restaurant. Had he changed his mind? Had she done something wrong? *And what's with his green pallor?*

"Are you sure you're feeling okay? I can leave if you want, take a cab home."

"No!" He cleared his throat and rubbed his palms down his pants. "Sorry, I guess I'm a little nervous. It's been a while since I've done this dating thing."

She chuckled, a wave of relief easing some of her anxiousness. Even the Greek hottie had a vulnerable side, and she found it refreshing. "Me, too."

Fumbling with the zipper behind her back, she

unfastened her dress. She slid the straps over her shoulders and the material slithered down her body, to the floor.

Andy's jaw dropped. Exactly the reaction she'd hoped for.

"I…I don't know what to say."

"Say you want me. Say that tonight I'm yours." She cringed. *Am I going too fast for him?*

He rushed forward and claimed her lips in a hard, demanding kiss. Her mind stopped functioning, filled with undeniable need. *Andy.* She'd never wanted anything more in her life. Her own Greek god. As if Eros had seen her nighttime fantasies and plucked him away from Mount Olympus to meet her.

Fitting his firm body to hers, he guided her blindly until her back hit a hard surface. *Oh, God.* She moaned into his mouth, brushing her leg along the outside of his thigh. She craved him inside her, fucking her until they came.

He gripped her legs, lifting her up the wall. Straddling his waist, she sucked in a quick breath. She didn't care where he took her, so long as he didn't stop. At least he hadn't shoved her out the door after seeing her nearly naked. He actually wanted her. *For now.*

Propping her higher, he slid his hands over her ass to reach between her legs. Her shoes clattered to the floor. *Yes, please.* He slipped her thin panties aside and she gasped. Her head spun.

With easy caresses and the occasional quick pinch, he teased her clit, desire rushing straight to her core. He kissed her, plunging a finger into her heat at the same time. *Breathe, dammit!* Every nerve ending lit up with maddening pleasure. She clung to him in desperation. How had she gone so long without?

Another digit. Then a third. She writhed in delight. With his thumb, he stroked her clit, tearing away any last bit of resistance. *So close.*

Claire gripped his muscular arms, panting. "Oh, God!"

Not slowing down, Andy continued his tormenting

ministrations.

Her muscles tensed and she burst like a Fourth of July fireworks display, the spasms rocketing through every limb. Tremors continued for several seconds, leaving her numb and struggling to hang on. "Holy fuck!"

He carried her across the room, lowering her onto a plush couch, his fingers still dancing inside her pussy, continuing their magic. Lifting her hips, she ached for more.

"Andy, I want you in me. Now." She craved the complete experience, a night full of satisfying, do-it-till-you-can't-move sex.

He pulled a square package from his pocket and unzipped his fly, then rolled a bright blue condom over his thick cock. Pulling off her panties, he tossed them across the room.

Why isn't he removing all of his clothes? But he drove deep inside her, and she didn't care. Finding her G-spot on the first plunge, he sent her over the edge again, and again.

"Let's have a shower together." Claire rubbed his arms, glancing up at him, her eyes still filled with lust. "We can wash each other. Or just get dirty again."

Andy's cock sprang to life, ready for another round. But he had to stop, unable to allow things to go any further. "I can't." He zipped his fly and buckled his belt, regret torturing his soul.

"Why not? We have all night, right?"

He wished for that and more. But he knew his limitations. "The thing is—"

She stepped back, her gaze guarded. "I get it. A one-time thing." Gathering her clothes, she dressed before he had the chance to stop her.

Standing in front of him, she pressed a finger to his chest. "I understand the one-night stand deal, but I expected you to want more. I was willing to suck your cock, try new things. But you're going to miss out because you're in a rush to get me out of your life."

Suck my cock? Something he'd never experienced before. And what other things did she want to try? His dick throbbed, ready to burst.

She stormed over to the foyer. "Now, if you would phone a cab to take me home, I'll go wait outside."

Shit! "No."

"No, what?" She glared at him, her nostrils flaring. "No, you don't want me to leave, or no, you don't even have the decency to call me a cab?"

He swallowed his pride. "I want you to stay." What power did this woman have over him? Even angry, she still piqued his curiosity. Not just when it came to sex, but he longed to hold her. And never let go. "But no shower. How about some coffee?"

Tilting her head to the side, she dug the toe of her shoe into the floor. "Doing things a little backward, aren't we?"

He grimaced, shifting from one foot to the other. "Whatever works, right?"

The animosity seemed to leave the room, as he'd hoped. She gave him a half-smile, rocking on the tips of her toes. "You really want me to stay?"

Self-preservation twisted his gut, but he still nodded. "Yes. Come in, sit down, and I'll brew a pot of coffee." He rushed to the kitchen. *Did I make the right decision?* If she left in the next few minutes, he refused to stop her. But if she stayed, he had to keep his mouth shut, never letting his secret slip.

HEY, SANTA
CHAPTER FOUR

Claire sighed, snuggling against Andy's chest as they lay on the couch. Even through his shirt, his steady breathing brought her peace. The sexy Santa had more in common with her than she'd ever imagined. They'd both lost their parents, had no family nearby, and had few friends. He was someone she could relate to. Someone who understood the loneliness of life on your own.

He stroked her face, filling her with contented warmth, yet she missed the fullness of him inside her already.

"It's late. Why don't you come to bed with me?" His muscles tensed under her. "That is, if you want to stay."

Her heart raced. He actually wanted her to spend the night? After the rough start at his place, she hadn't even expected to be invited to stick around after sex. Yet, she remained there, hoping for more. As much as he offered.

Her throat constricted. *What's going to happen in the morning? Will he send me on my way and never call?* Staying a few more hours wouldn't change the outcome. But, at least she wouldn't be alone.

"Yes, I'd like to stay." And she wanted to get his shirt off. Even if they didn't have sex for the rest of their time together, she craved the skin-on-skin contact.

Fingering the top of his shirt, she began to unbutton it.

He grabbed her wrist. "Don't."

Adrenaline rushed through her veins and she gasped. *What did I do wrong?* She didn't dare move for fear of his next reaction. She didn't want to leave yet. But, if he asked her to go, she'd flee faster than a stock car on a racetrack. Even with the heartache, she didn't want him to see her cry. And she refused to beg.

His grip loosened. "I'm sorry. I…I have scars. I'm very self-conscious of them."

That's it? She kissed his nose, hoping to lighten the mood. Many people had scars. He had nothing to be ashamed of. "I won't judge. I won't even ask you how you got them. It's just…I need to touch you."

He stood, shuffling away from her and running his fingers through his gorgeous hair.

How does he look so good at this hour, after hot sex?

He faced her, his gaze devoid of any emotion. "This is exactly why I don't date, why I don't get close to anyone."

Her stomach lurched. She'd scared him away, wanting too much, too soon. Commitment issues plagued her, too. Certain if she got too close to someone, she would lose them as she did her family. *This was a bad idea. I never should have listened to Tiffany.*

Grabbing her purse, Claire headed for the door. "Thanks for dinner. Merry Christmas." Unable to look at him, she clutched the doorknob. *So much for this holiday season being any different from the years before.*

"Wait."

No. She craved the euphoria of a connection, not the piercing pain of rejection. Yet, her feet refused to move, leaving her standing at the door like a fool.

"You want me to take my shirt off? Fine, I will. But promise me you won't scream. And if you want to leave after, I understand."

She paused. What kind of scars could be so bad she'd scream and run away?

"Okay, turn around."

Circling slowly, she snuck a peek to see the scars he hid. But not a single mark marred his body.

Instead of scars, she stared at his green body, the same color as new spring grass.

What the hell?

Her mouth fell open and Andy braced for her screech. It never came.

Claire took a hesitant step forward. "What *are* you?"

That was better than the reaction he expected. "Would you believe an extraterrestrial?"

She crossed her arms then quickly dropped them back to her sides. "No. I don't believe you."

"Well, I don't have any other explanation for you." Many times he'd wished to explain away the color of his skin, but nothing plausible ever came to mind.

He waited for her to turn tail and run. But she stayed rooted to the floor, blinking rapidly before finally glancing away. The silence bothered him more than anything. He needed a reaction, longed to read her thoughts. "Well, what do you think?"

She met his gaze. "I know you're not crazy."

"But, you're scared." Who wouldn't be the first time they met someone from another planet? He'd jumped like a solar flare the first time he met a *Terran.* Thank goodness the woman had assumed him sick and pointed him in the direction of the antacids.

"I am, a little. Though I'm more curious than anything." She reached out to him, as if letting a dog sniff her.

"I'm still the same guy you were cuddling with minutes ago, the same guy who made you come." Telling her was a mistake. A huge mistake.

How am I going to clean up this mess?

Her cheeks flushed. "I'm sorry. I just never expected to date an alien." She inched forward, maintaining eye contact. "I mean, except for the color of your skin, you look human. Scientists have said that there is no way an extraterrestrial would look like us."

Glancing away, he shook his head. "With the millions of habitable planets in the universe, one cannot assume that evolution only happens the same way once. I've learned of several other intelligent species that are *very* different from us, but Earth is not the only planet with humanoids."

She flattened a palm on his chest, her eyes growing wider. "I have so many questions."

He released a heavy sigh. "I do, too, like why you're taking the news so well. But, I'm really tired. And I need to get some sleep." Even though he wanted to be with her again now that she knew the truth, see if she really accepted him as an alien. "If I'm going to spend one more day with kids telling me what they want for Christmas, that they know I'm not the real Santa Claus, or simply screaming, I need to be well rested to keep my cool."

She smiled, no hint of fear. "You still want me to stay?"

"Only if you want to." The first test as to whether she really wanted to be with him now that she knew the truth.

"I do."

"Okay." Stepping around her, he locked the front door, his heart beating faster than the speed of light. *Will telling her come back to bite me in the ass? Will she tell the world of my origins?*

His instincts told him no. But, if she did, he would move across the country, become someone else. It hadn't been so hard to create his current identity when he'd arrived on the planet.

He wrapped his arm around her and guided her to his room, taking the biggest chance of his life. For some mysterious reason, he wanted her around.

HEY, SANTA
CHAPTER FIVE

Alien. Christmas Eve and she lay in bed with a guy from another planet, cuddled up against his warm green body. When Claire first noticed his green tinge, she never expected extraterrestrial ancestry to be the reason. But the tan color on Andy's face and arms had washed away; the green hadn't.

Filled with the buzz and comfort of being in his arms, she snuggled closer. One night she didn't have to spend alone. Others might have run away with the knowledge she had, but she never wanted to leave his side. If he had plans to hurt her, he'd have done so by then.

Shifting onto her back, she grasped the firm cock that rested between the cheeks of her ass. Andy moaned, but his eyes remained closed, mouth gaping open.

She giggled. *Just like any other male on Earth. I wonder if he tastes the same.*

Anxious to find out, she slid under the covers. Licking the tip like a frozen treat, she tasted the same briny flavor of any other guy she'd been with in the past. She took his whole cock into her mouth, rolling her tongue around the base. He woke up and groaned, fisting a clump of her hair.

"This is a far better way to wake up than by a damn alarm clock."

With a grin, she kept pace with his gentle thrusts.

He stopped, pulling her back up. "Lie on top of me and swing yourself around. I want to taste you, too."

Holy shit! Sixty-nining with an extraterrestrial. Poking her tongue into her cheek, she mentally slapped herself. *You can't keep thinking about him like that. Or, you're going to let his secret slip.* Especially if she were to have a serious relationship with him. If he wanted that. If a relationship was even possible for his kind.

God, why couldn't she shut off that part of her brain, live in the now?

Twisting around, knees on either side of his head, she lay across his well-toned body. No matter where he came from, he exuded perfection. And with the truth out in the open, she craved his full attention.

Returning her concentration to his cock, she swallowed him to the back of her throat. Then she let off, repeating the motions over and over. Each grunt from Andy encouraged her to continue, to make him come.

He grabbed her thighs, perhaps because he was close to release, but instead he spread her legs open until her pussy stuck in his face. With one lap of his tongue, she lost control, electric tension shooting from her clitoris to the tips of her fingers, toes, and her brain.

Lifting away to catch her breath, she feared choking or biting him, not a memory she wanted to have of their time together.

He licked again, the thrill even greater. With each pass of his tongue, she struggled to hang on to her sanity, gripping the sheets, desperate to cling to something. For a guy who had limited experience with women, he certainly knew what buttons to press.

No longer able to support herself, she let her weight fall on Andy. Then he tongued her ass. Unexpected.

Explosive.

She burst, fire rushing through her veins. Every synapse fired simultaneously. If spontaneous combustion existed, she'd just experienced it.

"Holy, fuck, Andreas!"

He gripped her hips. "You like?"

"Yes." She'd never had such an intense orgasm and wanted to give the same to him. She couldn't be selfish.

Orgasm somewhat subsided, she settled between his legs and focused once more his cock. He pulled her off again. *Doesn't he like oral sex? Is it some kind of alien thing? His weakness?*

"Are you still up for having a shower together? Washing each other?"

"Of course, but don't you like getting head?" Were there guys who *didn't* enjoy oral sex?

He groaned. "I love it. Your mouth is pure magic. I just have to relieve myself before you continue."

She giggled, glad her assumption had been incorrect. She didn't want to be labeled as a bad lover.

Following him into the bathroom, a sudden rush of hope and courage filled her. She waited until he'd flushed then pressed her body to his. "Hey, Andy, since we're both not doing anything for the holidays, why don't we spend it together? You could come over to my house when you're done working. I'll make a special dinner, and you can stay the night if you want… maybe spend Christmas together?"

Cringing, she glanced at the floor. She hadn't meant to say all of that, but once she started talking, it all spilled out. *Now comes the rejection.* Because no guy spent Christmas with a woman he'd just met. Her expectations were way too high. She'd done it again, set herself up for disappointment.

He slowly rubbed her back, giving her some hope. He had, after all, revealed his secret to her. That had to count for something, right?

"Claire, based on my few years here, I understand how

lonely the holidays can be. I'd love to spend some more time with you."

Her heart swelled. She didn't have to be alone for Christmas. And maybe, just maybe, she actually had a chance with this guy.

Andy slumped onto the ornate Santa chair, observing the lineup of restless kids. One more day and the job ended. He no longer had to wear the hot, confining suit. *Time to leave the city.*

He had no choice but to leave after revealing his secret to Claire. Lust and loneliness had driven him to keep her at his house. He'd opened his mouth, making the biggest mistake of his life, telling her information no one on Earth should ever know. Not if he planned to stay out of a government laboratory.

Sure, he wanted to trust her, but he'd just met Claire. When she finally stopped to think about what he'd told her, she would freak. People on Earth didn't accept an extraterrestrial so easily. Some rejected those in their own culture, from their own neighborhood. They ostracized individuals simply because of a different skin color, believed in another god, or fell in love with someone of the same sex. He refused to take the chance letting anyone else learn of his place of origin.

Even if Claire did accept his differences, what would happen if the relationship didn't work out? He refused to wait and find out. After his shift, he needed to pack up his few belongings and drive across the country, make a new name for himself, and never tell anyone where he came from again.

The first child in line, a chubby eight-year-old, rushed over and plopped down on Andy's knee. A repeat visitor. "Listen, as I said before, I know you're just one of Santa's helpers, but I wanted to make sure you got my message to the big guy." The boy paused and smiled while the camera flashed.

"Yes, I told him you wanted the newly released version of *Xbox*, not the one you said in your letter." The kids came as a welcome distraction. He couldn't second-guess himself. He had to leave.

"I always send my letters early to make sure Santa has plenty of time to get my gifts. It's not my fault *Microsoft* released a new version right before Christmas." The boy hugged him then slipped from his knee. "Thank you. Merry Christmas."

"And a Merry Christmas to you, too." A little greedy, though far less difficult than most of the kids who had visited him over the past two weeks.

Next came the screamers, two babies who clung to their mothers while he tried to hold them for a quick picture. Why did parents do that to their kids? Why did they do that to *him*? And his day had only begun. Children kicked him, removed his hat and tossed it away, and snapped his beard. One kid with a wet diaper sat on him, the contents squeezing out onto his lap. He had to take a break to change after that, causing even more upset children.

The line kept going and going, with no end in sight. Didn't parents know Christmas had already started on the other side of the world? Santa had to return to the North Pole. Andy had to pack.

He waited for the next child to come. Instead, a woman walked up to the platform, carrying multiple bags filled with wrapped presents. His heart pounded in his chest. *Why is she here?*

Andy had been so sure of his decision to leave, ready to move on. Seeing Claire in front of him brought doubts he didn't need. He yearned for the temporary sense of peace he'd felt with her that morning, to reach out and hold her. Forever.

No. It can't happen.

She sat on his knee, resting her arm across his shoulders. “Hello, my sexy Santa.”

He longed to kiss her, reenact everything they did the night before. But he had to keep his distance. They’d spent one night together, and he’d already made mistakes. Any more time together and leaving became that much more difficult.

“Hi, Claire. It’s great that you stopped by, but I can’t chat. I’m kind of busy.” The sooner he finished, the sooner he left this city.

“I know.”

She kissed his nose, sending a rush of desire through him. His nose of all places. Why did that affect him? He needed her gone, needed a clean break.

“I have to get home to start dinner. But I wanted to ask you to wear the Santa costume home. I have a special surprise for you.”

A surprise? *Oh, shit, I’m going to become a lab rat.* She’d called the authorities.

Although, what if she hadn’t? She’d stayed long after he’d told her of his origins. Had sex with him again. Even helped him apply the cover-up make-up to his arms and face that morning. Did he really have a chance at a future with her? Could she truly accept him as an alien?

“I’ll see you later.” She squeezed his hand before departing.

Could he do that? Could he walk away and leave behind a chance at happiness, at never being alone again?

Andy swallowed the lump in his throat, glancing back to the kids in line. He had no choice.

HEY, SANTA
CHAPTER SIX

Claire stared out the front window, glancing up and down the street. No traffic at all. By then, kids were likely tucked into bed, their parents shoving mountains of presents under the tree.

Even with the meal finished cooking long ago, she hadn't eaten. The scent of turkey hung in the air, reminding her of Andy's rejection. He'd never showed. Another Christmas Eve alone.

Two texts, a phone call, and hours of waiting hadn't gotten her any response. He wasn't coming for dinner. Or ever. She'd expected too much from an obvious one-night stand. Although, after he'd told her of his ancestry, she believed he trusted her, wanted something more. Obviously not.

Must have been an act in order to get sex from an Earth girl.

And she'd proven how easy she was.

With no one to seduce, she plucked off the Santa hat from her head and tossed it across the room. Along with the sexy Mrs. Santa outfit that lifted her boobs nearly to her chin and the presents under the tree, she'd spent too much money that day. For nothing. God, why had she been so stupid to believe he'd wanted more than one night?

Stripping out of the rest of the costume, she left the fabric in the middle of the floor and headed to her bedroom. Clean-up could wait until morning. By then, she hoped the hurt had eased, though likely replaced by anger—at the alien who'd lied to her, and at herself for believing him.

She flopped onto her bed. *Fuck!* Her eyes burned. Tears threatened to fall. But she held in the ache, instead thickening the wall around her heart. Never again would she let a man, *or whatever he was*, get so close, so fast.

❧ ☙

Andy pulled into the driveway. He'd turned around several times on his way, regretting his decision. But he refused to change directions again. Finally, he reached the place he needed to be.

Climbing out of his car, he shut the door behind him and headed up to the house. All dark. No lights on inside, or in the entire neighborhood, only street lamps to light the way. He breathed deeply and walked up the stairs. As he pressed the doorbell, his hand shook. *No going back now.* For the first time since arriving on the planet, he knew where he belonged.

But would anyone be there to open the door for him? Did he still have a chance at the life he wanted? Or had he ruined all chances of happiness on Earth?

❧ ☙

Ding-dong.

Claire rubbed her face, cheeks itching from all of the tears she'd shed. Sleep hadn't come easily for her after being stood up. *God, I'm pathetic. One night and I'm ready to tie the guy to the mattress and keep him forever.*

The doorbell rang again. Groaning, she rolled out of bed. Had Andreas finally arrived? But what had kept him so long? She slipped on her robe and slippers then plodded down the stairs.

Seizing her cell phone from the coffee table, she peeked out the front window. Just in case a stranger stood there rather than her very tardy Santa. *You're lonely, not stupid, Claire.*

On her doorway stood the man of the evening, a jolly old Saint Nick, in full costume. *Like I'm going to fall for that trick.*

She glanced across the yard, looking for Santa's ride. And then she saw it. Stepping back, she gasped. He didn't have reindeer and a sleigh, but the same sports car she'd ridden in the night before. *Andy.*

Her stomach lurched. *Why is he so late?* She'd invited him for dinner, not a middle-of-the-night rendezvous.

Before good sense had a chance to stop her, she unlocked the door and opened it. "What do you want?"

The screen door stood between them, her last shred of proper judgment.

"I'm sorry I'm so late. I got scared."

He presented a bouquet of flowers—roses, asters, and mini carnations, all in the colors of Christmas. Where he'd found them at such a late hour, she had no idea. But flowers didn't buy her forgiveness.

"I never asked for a relationship, just someone to spend the holidays with." Though, she'd hoped for so much more.

"I know, but that's not it. I worried about what I'd told you. No one else knows, and I can't risk the wrong people finding out."

With a sigh, she gripped the door handle. "I'm honored you trusted me enough to tell me. And I understand you don't know me that well, but I will never tell anyone. Not even my best friend." Nothing mattered to her more than someone keeping their word. Which he hadn't. Yet, putting herself in his shoes, she understood his actions.

"I can only give you my sincere apology. I'm so sorry for any hurt I may have caused."

Through the screen, she stared into his crystal blue eyes, uncomfortable with the silence. But she didn't know what to say. Was she ready to forgive him?

"Will you let me in, Claire, or will I forever be on your naughty list?"

Did she want to let him in, open herself up to getting hurt again? He had trusted her, but did she have the same confidence in him?

Pushing the door open, she swallowed her hesitation. "You missed a great dinner. I went all out, only to let everything go to waste."

Andy stepped inside, pulling her into his arms. "If you'll let me, I'll make it up to you, tonight, tomorrow, and forever, if all goes well."

He offered everything she wanted. But too soon. She didn't know him well enough. And she had so many questions about his planet of origin, how his otherworldly lineage affected the possibility of a relationship with him. Would he ever return home?

"How about we make it through the holidays first?"

Kissing her forehead, he gently rocking her, filling her with a sense of peace. "Deal."

She longed to stay in his arms forever, forget about the loneliness of the last few years. But she had a hard time staying focused. She craved sleep, and in Andy's arms, she'd lost her resolve. "Now that my Santa has finished delivering his presents, why doesn't he join me upstairs for some much needed rest?"

"So long as in the morning, he can cook breakfast to make up for tonight."

With a contented heart, she smiled, willing to give him a chance. For the first time in years, she had company for the holidays.

This Christmas, Santa granted Claire her wish. She wouldn't be alone.

BONUS STORY

After a family emergency that wasn't her fault, Dena Volger yearns to sleep through New Year's Eve and forget it all, wake up to the new year with a new outlook, and maybe even a new family. Minutes from home, she hits a creature with her car. But instead of the deer she expects, she finds a sexy, naked man on the side of the road. With green skin! Now, she must decide what to do with him.

ALIEN KISSES AT MIDNIGHT

Dena slumped into the driver's seat and slammed the door shut. She gripped the wheel and breathed in deep, attempting to control the anger surging through her. She yearned to stick around the hospital, ensure her niece's convulsions stopped but her blood pressure would skyrocket if she spent one more second in the presence of her brother and sister-in-law. They blamed her for ruining their plans for New Year's Eve. If not for the doctor stating Emily should have been brought to the hospital earlier in the day when her fever had spiked, Dena's parents would have likely blamed her, too.

Resisting the urge to bang her head against the steering wheel, Dena started her car. She put it in drive and headed for home. Definitely a night she wouldn't soon forget. No matter how much she wanted to.

Turning right at the next set of lights, she drove out of the city, her home on a small plot of land in the country with a dairy farm on one side and woods on the other. She yearned to crawl into her warm bed. Screw staying up for the countdown to the new year. She had no one to spend it with anyway.

Snow started to fall. Big, fat flakes stuck to the windshield. Dena flicked on her wipers before turning left onto a gravel road, her house at the end of the mile and a quarter. A dark figure leaped in front of her—a deer. She slammed on the brakes, gripping the wheel to keep from swerving into the ditch. The animal thumped against the hood. Too late. She hadn't slowed enough. When her car finally halted, Dena jerked the car into park and rushed out. She was lucky the deer hadn't hit her windshield. Her last vehicle ended up in the scrap yard that way.

Spotting nothing but a slight dent in the hood she glanced in front of her car. Instead of the brown-furred creature she expected, a naked man kneeled on the ground.

Holy shit! What was he doing out on her road, naked? Was he drunk? Had she hit him hard enough to knock his clothes off? He didn't seem injured in any way, no blood, scratches, or limbs sticking out in awkward directions.

Lifting his knee, he grabbed her bumper, attempting to stand. He stared up at her, as if just noticing she stood there. Tilting his head to the side, he furrowed his brows.

"I'm so sorry. I didn't see you until the last minute."

He didn't respond, simply kept his attention on her.

"Get in the car. I'll take you to the hospital." If her vehicle still worked after the collision. He still needed to be checked out, even with no indication of any injury.

"No hospital." He backed away from her. "I'm fine."

"Then let me take you back to my place. You can warm up and I'll find you some clothes." A stupid move, but she couldn't leave him on the side of the road. Especially after she'd hit him.

"I...." He glanced up, though nothing was visible to Dena in the sky beyond the falling snow. "Sure." He wiped the flakes from his face on the way to the passenger side of her car.

Closing the door behind her, Dena cranked up the heat for the two minute drive to her house. She tried to avoid gazing at his groin when they'd been on the side of the road, but once she'd parked in her driveway and turned off the ignition, she couldn't help a quick peek. Not near as small and shriveled as she'd expected with the temperature outside.

Pervert. God, why was she even thinking about that? He was a drunken stranger. He shouldn't even know where she lived.

"I can call someone for you. You can come inside and warm up while you wait." While her brain told her inviting a stranger inside was a bad idea, her gut indicated otherwise.

"No, there's no one." His eyes grew wide, but his pupils weren't dilated. Not drunk. More scared. But, why? Was he afraid of her?

"Is there anywhere I can drive you?" She wouldn't drop him off naked, but refused to force him inside her home.

"Not any place nearby. I come from far away." After he unbuckled his seat belt, he opened the door and left her car.

Dena followed him out, surprised to find him staring up at the sky, all the stars visible in the darkness. Weird since it had snowed only a few minutes ago. She spotted Cassiopeia then spun around to find Vega. "Do you normally stare up at the stars?" She did, but most of her friends considered watching the stars to be standing on the sidelines of a red carpet event.

"Yes, but not from this vantage point." He quickly glanced at her before returning his attention to the sky. "I can't believe I'm actually here."

Here? As in at her house? "What's that supposed to mean?"

"Alive." He turned to face her, his nakedness catching her off guard.

"I'm so sorry I ran into you." She stared down at the driveway and dug her toe into the gravel. "I didn't think I hit you that hard."

"No, no. Not you." He touched the arm of her coat, the warmth of his palm evident through her sleeve. Was that why he didn't seem affected by the cold? His body generated enough heat to keep him warm? If she didn't get inside soon, she'd yank him closer to heat up more than her arm. "Why don't we go in now? We can figure out what to do next from inside." And get some clothes on him before she jumped a complete stranger. But who could blame her? He had radiant blue eyes, shaggy yet short brown hair, a broad chest, and he was toned all over. Not the dehydrated, muscle-bound freak look, but he definitely took care of himself. The model she would have pinned on her bedroom wall in her younger years and left up because he was so hot.

Squeezing her legs together, she swallowed her lust for him. She was helping a stranger, nothing else. Hoping he'd follow her, Dena walked to the back entrance to her house then unlocked the door. She turned around to find him directly behind her, not even a foot of separation, and jumped.

He clasped her arms, steadying her on her feet. "Sorry. I would like to get inside now. I'm starting to feel the cold."

After quickly guiding him into her home, she locked up behind her. Sure, she lived in the country, but anyone could drive by. And more than once she'd woke to a stranger sleeping off a night of partying in the ditch in front of her house.

Dena spotted the guy already sitting on her couch. She stared at the back of his head, thankful for a break from his sexy body. "So, my name is Dena. What's yours?" Figuring out what to call him was her first priority. Then getting some clothes on him.

"Haul." He shifted to face her. "My name is Haul."

Interesting. Not a name she'd heard before. "Okay, Haul...." She pointed a thumb over her shoulder. "I'm going to find you some clothes."

Anxious to get his hot body covered, remove some of the temptation, she took the stairs up to her room two at a time. She dug to the back of her closet for a pair of sweat pants and cotton shirt an old boyfriend had left behind and never returned for. They didn't even smell like the guy anymore, but she wouldn't mind if they took on Haul's scent of woods and spices. Rushing back down the stairs, she gasped. She couldn't see him where she'd left him. Had he slipped out, vanished back into the cold?

Glancing over the top of the couch, she spotted him on the floor, hands wrapped around himself, his body shaking uncontrollably, as her niece had been earlier that night. She tossed the clothes aside and grabbed the heavy quilt draped over her rocking chair. The gift from her nana would provide more heat. Shoving the coffee table aside, she laid beside him on the floor and spread the blanket over them both. She pulled him in close, hoping her body heat would help, too. Especially since touching his bare skin sent a rush of desire through her veins.

But she couldn't dwell on her lust. She had to warm him up before his organs shut down. "Haul, I need to call 9-1-1, get you to the hospital." She had little to no medical experience. He needed a doctor.

"No, no hospital." His words came out slurred, not a good sign.

Dena reached for his arm, pressed on his wrist to feel for a pulse. There, but weak. Shit. "I can't have you die. You need medical attention."

"No! If you take me to a hospital, I'll die." He pulled her arm around his body and settled against her until she spooned him. "I need you."

With his words coming out clearer, she lost some of her panic, but wasn't sure she alone could help him.

His chill began to creep into her, the vibrations of his never-ending shaking. She pulled the blanket tighter around them, snuggling in as close as she could. "Haul, please don't die on me."

She'd already dealt with one medical emergency that night. Every instinct told her to call for help. And she would if the man in her arms went unconscious, but as long as he responded, she'd follow his wishes.

"I won't. I'm better now." He tossed off the blanket and stood as if not plagued by a medical emergency.

His thick cock stood erect, but only distracted her for a second before her attention diverted to the rest of Haul, especially the color of his skin. She scooted back, but halted when the coffee table hit her back. Her heart pounded beneath her ribs and she ran her palms across her eyes to ensure she saw him accurately. His skin had turned a light green, the color of mint gum. And she was sure he hadn't looked like that when she'd welcomed him into her home. "You're, you're... What the hell are you?"

He looked down at himself then back at her with a sexy, wry smile. If she wasn't so scared, she'd be a puddle of lust at his feet.

"Well, I guess you now know why I couldn't let you take me to the hospital. You see, I'm not exactly from around here."

Dena pulled her knees into her chest. "Not here, but where?"

Holding a hand out, he stepped toward her. "Please don't be afraid. I mean you no harm."

She swallowed the lump of fear in her throat, barely able to catch her breath. "What—are—you?"

Stopping, he lowered his arm. His confident expression washed away into one of sadness, eyes dark and hollow. "I am humanoid, like you, but I am not from this planet."

Not from this planet? What was that supposed to mean? He was an alien? No way, had to be a dream. She pinched her arm then winced. Shit. Nope, all real. A hot, naked alien stood in front of her. "What do you want?"

He sat on her couch, elbows on his knees and head resting in his hands. "I don't know. I would say to go back home, but I don't think that's possible."

"Why not?" The question came out before she had the chance to stop herself.

"Because this is my punishment for not following an order."

"What order?" Her muscles tightened. Were his people planning to attack Earth? Invade?

"To push a button."

Huh? "And you're being punished for that?"

He ran his hands across his lap. "We were supposed to start terra forming a new planet, make it suitable for a colony to survive."

"Not Earth, I hope."

"No, no, another solar system. And while the planet didn't have a large population, I could still sense life forms on it. I refused to start the transformation before we investigated."

"So, you were punished for having a conscience?" Feeling less worry, Dena rose from the floor and sat in the rocking chair.

"Yes. The planet had already been scouted for life, and none was found. But, I couldn't deny the readings on my com unit."

She would have refused, too. "So, they send you here? Why?"

"Punishment, torture, disposal."

Gripping the arms of the chair, she leaned forward. "They sent you here to die?"

"If you were sent here from another planet, do you think you'd survive?"

"No." She shook her head. "If anyone ever found out—"

"Hence, why I can't go to your hospital."

"But, I know."

He pursed his lips and nodded. "Yes, you do."

The information she now knew weighed like an anvil on her chest. She could keep his secret, or phone the police, tell the world an alien had landed on Earth. If anyone believed her enough to check out her claim. "And what do you want me to do now?"

He stared at the floor for a moment before focusing on her. "Whatever you want. My life's in your hands."

It definitely was. A responsibility she didn't crave. Rising from the chair, she scooped the clothes from the floor and tossed them at Haul. "What I want is for you to put some clothes on." He was hot no matter the color of his skin or what part of the universe he came from.

Heading into the kitchen, she grabbed two wine glasses from the cupboard and set them on the counter. She needed a drink after an evening of craziness. And Crémant d'Alsace would do the trick. After pouring the pink bubbling liquid into the glasses, she headed back to the living room, where Haul sat on the couch, no longer naked, and his skin tone more suitable for blending in on Earth. She handed him some wine. "How do you do that, change the color of your skin?"

"It takes a lot of concentration." He sniffed the glass then quickly held it away. "And this definitely won't help."

"Okay, then." Dena downed her glass then set the empty flute on the coffee table and took Haul's. "So, how do I know you're not going to kill me?"

His eyebrows raised as he laughed, a deep sound that made her feel foolish for asking the question.

"You found me naked, with nothing. How would I hurt you?"

She put her free hand on her hip. "You're probably stronger than me, and I don't know, maybe you have some superpowers or something."

Shaking his head, he patted the cushion beside him. "I assure you, I do not. Besides, why would I harm you after you welcomed me into your home and saved my life?"

Dena shrugged. "You could be lying, waiting to kill me and then take over my body."

"Read me." Standing, he coaxed the wine from her hand and set it on the end table. "Put the tips of your fingers against my scalp and read me."

"I'm afraid I don't know how." His kind had to have some telekinetic powers.

Haul clasped her wrists and raised her hands to the sides of his head. "Clear your mind and let me show you."

Lights flashed in her head like a fluorescent light turning on for the first time. The image cleared and she saw the bridge of a spacecraft, reminding her of the sci-fi shows she sometimes watched as a kid. Only everyone had green skin like Haul. Different shades, but all the same color. And then the scene he'd described played out in her head. He was condemned to Earth, a fate worse than death in the opinion of his people. She felt the twist of his gut at the sentence, the panic at being left on a foreign planet where he was expected to die, and the jarring pain when she hit him with her car. Then she saw herself through him, saw her own wide eyes when she'd realized she'd hit a person, not an animal. The next few moments were blurred, but when the vision cleared, they were at her house, on the floor. She filled with warmth, a sense of hope. Maybe Earth wouldn't be so bad.

A new image filled her mind. Of her and Haul together, writhing against one another. He worshiped her, did everything to her she'd imagined when she'd looked at his perfect, naked body. She drew in a ragged breath, his lust overpowering her own.

Haul yanked her hands away and let go. His face lost all color. "I'm sorry. You weren't meant to see that. If you want me to leave, I understand."

"No!" She shoved his chest, must have caught him off guard. He landed on the couch with a thud. "No, don't go. I liked what I saw. Just, you're still new, and I...." Crap, what did she want to say? She only knew she didn't want him to leave.

He held his hands up. "Okay, if that's what you want."

Oh no, had she scared him? She flopped on the couch to his left. "What do we do now?"

"I guess, whatever you would normally do if I wasn't here."

After the incident with her niece, she'd planned to sleep as soon as she arrived home. Now, she didn't think that was possible. "It is New Year's Eve. We could watch the countdown. I'm sure we still have a few minutes."

He leaned back on the couch. "Okay, whatever that means. Sounds good."

"New Year's? You don't have that?"

"I'm not sure what it is."

Tilting her head to the side, she tried to figure out how to explain it. "Earth takes one year to rotate around the sun. And we mark every complete rotation with a party."

"Interesting. But why would you pick such a cold night?"

Dena flicked on the television. "I know, right? The decision was made long before I was born. Probably by someone who didn't live where they got snow."

"You mean there are places on Earth where they don't get snow? And I got stuck here?"

Grabbing her throw pillow, she smacked him with it. "Hey, you're lucky you're still alive. I can call the hospital if you're worried about a little snow."

He placed his palm on her lap. "You won't, right?"

Intertwining her fingers with his, she shook her head. "No." The simple connection left her head spinning with lust. Why did she want to get it on so bad with a complete stranger, one who arrived from another planet?

"So, what exactly happens at a New Year's party?"

Dean leaned against him, resting her head on his shoulder. She had to trust him and might as well be comfortable in her own house. "Well, we set resolutions, goals we want to accomplish over the next year. And we count down the minutes and seconds until midnight. When the new year is officially here, we drink champagne, and, um, kiss."

Haul cocked an eyebrow. "I like that idea."

Heat balled low in her belly. Squeezing her legs together, she remembered being in his mind, all the things he wanted to do to her. Much more than kissing, but they had to start somewhere.

"The time has come, folks...."

Dena faced the television, paying attention to the program for the first time since she'd turned it on.

"Let this new year be the one...."

The one what? Where she had sex with an alien? A tornado of butterflies swept through her gut. Could she go there without any regrets?

"Where all your dreams come true..."

She squeezed Haul's hand. Dreams? Fantasies? Did it matter?

"Make a final wish...."

Someone on her side to make her family gatherings more bearable. Could the sexy stranger from space be that person?

"Get ready. The countdown begins. 10, 9, 8, 7, 6, 5, 4, 3, 2, 1. Happy New Year!"

Taking a deep breath, Dena closed her eyes and leaned into Haul. "Happy New Year."

Her words were swallowed by his kiss, soft lips plying against hers, pulling her into his world. Leaning back on the couch, she pulled him over her. She was either making the biggest mistake or best decision of her life. But, she wouldn't know if she didn't have him, experience the alien she found on the side of the road.

He trailed his fingers along her side, his touch leaving her head spinning. She'd never been so desperate to have sex with anyone. With his hand on her ass, she lifted her leg over him, enjoying his weight between her legs. Why had she told him to put clothes on? They only created a barrier for her now.

She grasped the hem of this sweatshirt and lifted it up, running her palms across his toned back. But, it wasn't enough. She needed a deeper connection.

Sitting up, Haul straddled her waist and tossed the sweatshirt across the room. He tucked his fingers between the front of her blouse and tore it open, sending buttons flying. Obviously just as anxious as her. When he reached for her bra, she slammed her hand on his.

"No." The piece of lingerie was her favorite. It fit her on her best and worst days of the month. No way did she want it destroyed regardless how much she wanted the alien to fuck her. She set her thumb and forefinger on the front clasp and slipped it open, letting her girls free.

Haul wasted no time. Hands under her shoulder blades, he licked and sucked her nipples, sending her lust into overdrive. She thrust toward him, still craving more. Everything.

Reaching to her waist, she unbuckled her belt and jeans. Whatever it took to get him inside her. Through his jogging pants, the length of his hardness rubbed across her thigh. She slipped her hand under the elastic waistband and grasped his cock.

He stilled and stared down at her. "Do you really want to do this?"

"Yes." She had no doubts, yet she needed something first. If not for his pause, she might have forgotten. Made a horrible mistake. "But we need protection."

He furrowed his brows as if confused and stood. "Protection from what?"

"Pregnancy. Sexually transmitted diseases...." Grabbing his hand, she pulled him up the stairs toward her bedroom. "I'm not ready to have your child, and I have no idea who you've been with before me."

She released his hand then raced to her bed, shedding her clothes on the way. By the time Haul reached her and had removed his pants, she'd found a condom in her nightstand drawer. He stood at the foot of the bed and she scooted over to him, encircling his cock in her hand. With a gentle squeeze, she licked the tip.

Haul jerked. "Cosmos! What did you do to me?"

The alien hadn't had oral sex? She smiled to herself. Reaching around, she clutched his ass cheeks and took his cock into her mouth. Bobbing on and off, she swirled her tongue across the head, enjoying the tightening of the muscles in Haul's legs.

Hands on her shoulders, he pushed her back. "You need to stop. I can't handle anymore."

Maybe not now, but if he stuck around, she'd do it again. And she yearned to know what he could do with his tongue between her legs after the pleasure he'd inflicted on her nipples.

She swiped the condom and tore open the package. Pinching the tip, she rolled the latex over his shaft. "We're good to go."

As he kneeled on the bed, she shuffled back to give him more room. She didn't need him falling off the bed when she orgasmed. If he was as good as she hoped. Only one way to find out.

She grasped his sides and yanked him on top of her. With the weight of his cock between her legs, she tensed. Would she be able to satisfy him? It had been far too long since she'd gone to bed with a man, the few guys she'd dated in the past year not worth inviting back to her place.

"Ash laheda valensia." He kissed the side of her face, working up to her mouth where he stole her worry away. She had no idea what he'd said, but it sounded beautiful and made her want him more. Wrapping her arms around him, she held him close and deepened their kiss. In an instant, he slipped inside her, as if their bodies were meant to be joined. For a guy from another planet, he had no compatibility issues with her.

He rocked in and out, holding her tight.

Every synapse in her body fired, making her aware of nothing but Haul, his closeness, the softness of his lips as he worshiped her body, the way his cock flared, hitting her G-spot. Her muscles tightened, the familiar heat pooling low in her belly and ready to explode. She clasped his arms, the pressure becoming unbearable. Then she released, her head ready to pop off with the force of rapture rocketing to every extremity.

Haul wailed, jerking above her, his movements far from steady. As he gasped for air, she lost her sudden rush of endorphins, her concern for only him. Was he going to die on her? Did sex kill his kind?

His eyes closed. When they opened again, his irises glowed a bright yellow. Dena gasped. Was this the real Haul? She'd had sex with him and now he planned to abduct her? Maybe kill her?

"Ash laheda valensia." His lips didn't move, but she'd heard his voice in her mind. *You are the one I need.*

Needed for what? Experiments?

He chuckled softly. "I will never bring you harm. And I feel confident you will not harm me."

Crap, he did have superpowers, could read her thoughts and project his own into her mind.

"Only those you project loudly. And so far, it's only been your fear of what I might do to you."

Releasing the breath she'd held in, she brushed a hand along his cheek. "I'm sorry. I just have to get used to this. Dating someone from another planet is new to me."

"Me, too." Haul sat up and rolled the condom off, tying up the end. "Got another one of these? I'd like to do that again."

Wow, willing to go another round without a nap? That never happened with her previous lovers from Earth. She reached behind her and pulled open the nightstand drawer. "There's a package full of them in there. I think we'll be good for a couple of days." Or one night, depending on his libido. She couldn't wait to find out.

Dena woke to her phone buzzing across the night stand. Reaching for the blasted object, she tried not to disturb Haul, his arm draped over her waist. What a night they'd had. And not a dream, the real thing. Far better than any fantasy she could have imagined.

She glanced at the caller id. Her mother. Great! Stifling a groan, she accepted the call and put the phone to her ear. "Hi, Mom."

"Hi Dennie. Where are you?"

She rolled her eyes. It was eight o'clock in the morning. Where did her mother expect her to be? "I'm at my house. In bed."

"Why aren't you on your way here? We have so much to get ready."

The shrill in her mother's voice made her cringe. "We're not eating until four. Why do you need me over before noon?" If she didn't dread the woman's wrath, she'd stay in bed all day, see what other positions she and Haul could get into. Far better than spending the day listening to her sister-in-law told the same stories she told at every family gathering.

Haul lifted his head from the pillow. "What's going on?"

"Nothing," she whispered, covering the mouthpiece. She ran her finger tips over his stomach, so tempted to reach for his glorious cock, hop on for another satisfying ride.

"Dena, who's there with you? I heard a man's voice."

Crap, how was she supposed to get out of this? Her mother would want to meet Haul if she told her she was sleeping with him. Not an option if his skin remained green. But, it would be nice to bring him along, have a distraction from the stress of her family gatherings. "I'm in bed with my boyfriend."

"Dena Agatha Volger, how dare you not tell me you had a boyfriend. Why haven't I met him yet?"

Because she'd met him less than twenty-four hours earlier. Yet, she didn't dare tell her mother. Sex lectures from the woman proved more tortuous than placing her palm on a hot stove. "We've only been dating for a month, and because our relationship is still fairly new, we felt we needed to spend time with our own families over the holidays, see if we would last before we met each other's family." A perfectly reasonable explanation.

"And yet, you're sleeping with him."

"It's not as if we only just met." She would burn for all the lies she told her mother. "I met him through work. We started having dinner with a group of friends, and ended up dating."

Haul ran his palm across her stomach before he reached between her legs, brushed his finger across her clit. Body tense, she held back a moan. "Mom, I gotta go. See you around noon." She and Haul could have all kinds of fun before then.

"Okay, but be sure to bring that boyfriend of yours along. If he's having sex with my daughter, he needs to meet the family."

She ran her hand across her forehead, trying to ignore the rush of lust from Haul swirling his tongue around her nipples. "If he's not busy, sure." Ending the call, she set the phone on her nightstand then rolled over onto Haul, straddling his waist. His cock brushed along her ass, but she ignored it for the moment. "How long can you make your skin look like mine?" Somehow, she had to introduce him to her family so her mother didn't show up another day when she didn't expect her.

"Forever." His skin tone flickered to match hers then changed back to green. "Unless I'm sick or craving intercourse with you."

"That works." She'd get her fill in before driving to her parents' place, draw the green out of him. "You're going to meet my family later today. As long as you don't go green in front of them, you'll be fine. And don't worry about them asking questions. My sister-in-law will interrupt to talk about herself, and draw the attention away from you."

Color drained from his face, not the way she wanted.

"You're turning me in?"

"No." She reached in her drawer, grabbed a condom and slipped the covering over Haul's cock. "I'm introducing you as my boyfriend, someone from Earth." Lifting her hips, she slid onto him and slowly rocked until his cheeks returned to their natural tone.

"Okay." Clasping her waist, he guided her back and forth. She reveled in the completeness of having him inside her. A missing piece she'd finally found in the most unexpected place. So what if he'd only arrived on the planet the day before. He certainly knew how to bring her pleasure, and she had little doubt he'd fit right in on Earth.

"Dena, this feels so good."

She couldn't agree more. Palms on his chest, she doubled her speed. Rapture invaded her body and mind until she reached her tipping point and screamed with ecstasy.

Last year had been dull and boring for Dena, but her new year had already started on a high note, and she didn't ever want to come down.

BIBLIOGRAPHY

1Night Stand
Beneath the Starry Sky
Celestial Seduction
Unknown Futures
Satin Sheets in Space
Sudden Breakaway
Another Night, Another Planet
His Alien Virgin
Her Alien Hero
Intergalactic Heat ~ ebook and print anthology

Alien Next Door
Alien Adoration
Alien Admirer
Alien Attraction
Alien Next Door: The Complete Series ~ ebook and print anthology

Galactic Defenders
Bryce
Jager
Jace (coming soon)

The Underground
Never Gonna Let You Go
Never Gonna Desert You
Never Gonna Say Goodbye

Single Titles
Accidental Romance
Alien Lover
Beyond Reach
Cosmic Sutra
Crash Landing

Hey, Santa
It Took A Zombie Apocalypse
Made For Her
Taken by the Billionaire Alien Next Door
The Power of Three
The Star Princess
Love in a New World ~ ebook and print anthology
Cosmic Desires ~ ebook and print anthology

writing as Paisley Brown (erotica)
Sexy Suitors from Space
Sex Boot Camp

ABOUT THE AUTHOR

Jessica E. Subject is the author of science fiction romance, mostly alien romances, ranging from sweet to super hot. Sometimes she dabbles in paranormal and contemporary as well, bringing to life a wide variety of characters. In her stories, you could not only meet a sexy alien or two, but also clones and androids. You may be transported to a dystopian world where rebels are fighting to live and love, or to another planet for a romantic rendezvous.

When Jessica is not reading, writing, or doing dreaded housework, she likes to go to fitness class and walk her Great Pyrenees/Retriever her family adopted from the local animal shelter.

Jessica lives in Ontario, Canada with her husband and two energetic children. And she loves to hear from her readers.

http://jessicasubject.com

Also find Jessica on Twitter, Facebook, and Instagram.

www.ingramcontent.com/pod-product-compliance
Lightning Source LLC
Chambersburg PA
CBHW070855250626
47159CB00003B/1069
* 9 7 8 1 9 8 8 4 2 8 0 6 2 *